THE M...
BABY ...

BY
PAULA ROE

Published in Great Britain 2010
Harlequin Mills & Boon Limited,
Eton House, 18-24 Paradise Road, Richmond, Surrey TW9 1SR

© Paula Roe 2009

ISBN: 978 0 263 88183 7

51-1010

Harlequin Mills & Boon policy is to use papers that are natural, renewable
and recyclable products and made from wood grown in sustainable forests.
The logging and manufacturing processes conform to the legal environmental
regulations of the country of origin.

Printed and bound in Spain
by Litografia Rosés S.A., Barcelona

Despite wanting to be a vet, choreographer, hairdresser, card shark and an interior designer (though not all at once!), **Paula Roe** ended up as a personal assistant, office manager, aerobics instructor and software trainer for thirteen years (which also funded her extensive travel through the US and Europe). Today she still retains a deep love of filing systems, stationery and travelling, although the latter is only in her dreams these days. Paula lives near western Sydney's glorious Blue Mountains with her family, an ancient black cat and a garden full of rainbow lorikeets, magpies and willy wagtails. You can visit her at www.paularoe.com.

Grateful thanks to my wonderful writing group,
The Coven, for the hours of brainstorming,
encouragement and Saturday morning brunches.
Oh, and for letting me immortalize your names in print.
I owe you all a large decaf soy caramel latte!

Dear Reader,

Just like my navigation skills, sometimes my stories begin in one place then end up somewhere completely different. This one was no exception. I did know a few things—secret pregnancy, forced marriage, Outback business in trouble—but that's where the similarities ended. Cal and Ava started with different names and occupations, different pasts and conflict, and even though I loved that story, it just wasn't the right one for them. And because I never throw my ideas away, the original version is sitting in my filing cabinet, waiting for its time to shine.

It's exciting to see my first "Outback" story come to fruition. Even though Gum Tree Falls and Jindalee are purely fictional, I did do some research in and around far western NSW where Ava grew up (no hardship—it's gorgeous country). Creative license is a beautiful thing, so I renovated "The Toaster"—the controversial but expensive apartment block at Sydney's Circular Quay—into a very tall, very elegant building where Cal lives. I don't know about you, but I'd love to have the Quay, Opera House and Royal Botanical Gardens as my daily room with a view!

Come and visit me at www.paularoe.com, where there's more behind-the-scenes info about *The Magnate's Baby Promise*.

With love,

Paula

One

It's my company. Mine.

The mantra throbbed in Cal Prescott's brain until, with a growl of frustration, he slammed his palms on the desk and shot to his feet.

Victor had really done it this time—not only pitting his sons against each other for the ultimate prize of VP Tech but demanding an heir in the bargain. With a sharp breath Cal whirled to study the panoramic view of Sydney's Circular Quay and Botany Bay below, the gun-metal arch of Sydney Harbour Bridge nestled comfortably in the foreground. The unusually sunny June morning did nothing to smooth his anger; Victor's trademark directness still smouldered away in his gut.

You must both marry and produce an heir. The first one to do so gets the company.

Zac, his stepbrother, didn't deserve VP Tech. He was Victor's real flesh and blood, yes, but the younger man had turned his back on them years ago. It was Cal who'd stuck with family, who had put in the long hours, steadily growing the business until his One-Click office software package had finally cracked the biggest seller spot in Australia last year.

Cal Prescott didn't walk away. Ever. He'd put every waking hour, every drop of sweat into his stepfather's company. Damned if he'd let it slip through his fingers now.

With long-legged strides he stalked over to a discreet wall panel and jabbed a button to reveal a well-stocked bar. He smoothly poured himself a glass of whiskey, neat.

Making money, proving himself, had been an all-consuming desire for so long he barely remembered a time he hadn't lived and breathed it. And with every million he'd made, every deal he'd brokered, he could've sworn he'd seen pride on Victor's craggy face, felt the rush of approval when the gruff, emotionally spare man imparted brief praise. Obviously he was good enough to bring in millions but not good enough to be a Prescott, to be automatically entrusted with the legacy of VP Tech.

Unfamiliar bitterness knotted his insides, curled his lip. Victor hadn't even given him the courtesy of an explanation; he'd simply issued the ultimatum then left on some business trip, leaving Cal to sort through the bombshell's wreckage.

The phone rang then and Cal sat, grabbing the receiver.

"There's a woman I'd like you to meet," Victor said by way of greeting.

Speak of the devil. "You're back."

"Yes. You remember Miles Jasper, the Melbourne heart surgeon?"

The sour taste of futility burnt the back of his throat. "No."

Victor ignored him and continued. "He has a daughter. She's twenty-seven, blond, attractive and—"

"I don't give a damn if she's Miss Universe," Cal ground out. "I'm not some prize stallion at auction. I may have agreed to this ludicrous arrangement, but I *will* pick my own wife." He slammed the phone down with a satisfying crack.

After a long, drawn-out moment he dragged in a controlled breath, slid a sealed envelope from his desk drawer and slowly centred it on the desk with meticulous care.

Thanks to a local investigator and a helpful cabbie, his obsession with the elusive Ava Reilly could now be put to rest.

For the past nine weeks he'd refused to think about *her,* about that one amazing night, shoving it from his mind with the decisive efficiency he was renowned for. But now, as he let his thoughts wander back to their chance encounter, the walls began to crack.

Long limbs, soft black hair and a pair of bright blue

eyes teased his memory. *Ava.* A movie-star name, one that evoked a woman with poise, elegance. Presence.

She'd gotten under his skin and stayed there, disrupting his thoughts at awkward times—in meetings, with clients. The worst were the early mornings, before the sun rose. Time and again he'd hauled himself from the depths of a hot erotic dream where her mouth had been on his, her lips trailing over his chest, her skin hot and silky beneath his hands. It had left him frustrated and aching with need way too many times.

He'd been determined to forget her, forget what had just been a one-night stand. Ironically, he'd gotten his wish three days ago. Three days since his stepfather had issued his ultimatum, seventy-two hours in which VP Tech had dominated his thoughts and he'd seesawed between dull, throbbing rage and aggravated tension.

With a flick of his wrist, he ripped open the envelope and scanned the report.

After too many broken nights and unfocused days, he'd taken action. Now he steeled himself for reality to shatter the fantasy. She could be married, or engaged. His thoughts darkened. He could've been her last fling before she'd settled down to marry her childhood sweetheart—

As his eyes flipped over the paragraphs, his brows took a dive. Ava Reilly owned a bed-and-breakfast in rural western New South Wales.

He reached for his computer mouse, clicked on the Internet connection and typed "Jindalee retreat" in the search engine. Seconds later he was looking at Jindalee's basic Web page. No wonder she was up to her eyeballs in debt with the bank about to foreclose next month. The place was under-promoted and unremarkable for a simple outback town with less than five hundred people.

He went back to the report, skimming over her financials until he got to the summary of her weekly errands. Cal snorted. That PI was thorough, he'd give him that.

Approximately eight weeks pregnant.

"What the hell?"

Office walls suddenly closed in on him, tight and airless, forcing Cal to take a deep gulp.

In one sharp movement, he crushed the offending paper and hurled it across his office, where it hit the wall with a soft thud. *No. No way. Not again.*

A shuddering breath wracked through him as shock stiffened every muscle. He'd had that, once. A baby. *His baby.* A child to follow in his footsteps, to nurture and love. To shower with his wealth and experience and to ensure the past was never repeated. He'd been ecstatic when Melissa had told him. Vulnerable.

Stupid.

She'd faked everything and he'd vowed never to repeat that failure again.

But this…*this* changed everything.

He tightened his jaw, teeth grinding together. After making mad, passionate love, Ava had run like a thief in the night. If not for those black bikini knickers he'd found tangled in the sheets, it could have all been just a delicious, erotic dream.

His thoughts spun out of control, fed by heated memories. And as he recalled every sigh, every touch, his shock morphed into something more sinister. Swiftly his mind clicked through options. Chance encounter or deliberate? Perhaps part of a calculated blackmail plan?

His harsh laugh exploded in the quiet office. If the child *was* his, it provided a neat solution to all his problems.

He slammed down his glass then picked up the phone. "Jenny—arrange for a car and inform the airstrip I'll be flying within the hour."

Replacing the receiver with deliberate slowness he stood, a low curse softly rumbling across his lips.

His baby.

Shards of intense possessiveness stabbed, threatening to choke off his air. If Ava thought he'd pay up and stay out of her life, she was very much mistaken. Every single day, in the midst of everything he'd attained, who he was and where he'd come from were never far from his mind. And no long-legged, dark-haired seductress with wide blue eyes would compromise his beliefs.

With gnawing apprehension, Ava realized she had to face facts—Jindalee was spiralling into a money pit and she had no way of stopping it.

She sighed, eyeing the final notices spread before her on the kitchen table. Absently she ran a frustrated hand over the tangle of hair that had slipped from its ponytail. She'd been certain people would jump at the chance to spend time at a real get-away-from-it-all rural retreat, so certain she'd sunk all her parents' insurance money into the venture. She'd converted the homestead into a reception and dining area, built a five-cabin extension and refurbished the kitchen.

All to emphasise her spectacular downfall.

Her rooms were empty most weekends and she didn't have the money or experience to keep on advertising. Despite her fierce determination to ignore the town gossips, she knew they'd feed on this until her belly started to grow, and then the Gum Tree Falls grapevine would be buzzing anew with "have you heard the latest on Ava Reilly?"

With burning cheeks she stood, eased out the kink in her back and took a deep breath. Tentatively, she placed a hand on her still-flat stomach.

A baby. Hers.

Wonder and shock tripped her breath, adding a shaky edge to the inhale. She tried to swallow but tears welled in her eyes. Quickly, she dashed them away. She hadn't gone looking for a one-night stand, yet the stranger had commanded her eyes the instant he'd settled on the barstool next to hers at Blu Horizon, an exclusive cocktail lounge at Sydney's Shangri-La Hotel. He'd radiated confidence and wealth as if powered by some inner sun, from every thread of his sharply tailored black suit to the closely cropped, almost military haircut. Yet there was something more, something a little vulnerable beneath that chiselled face, all angles and shadow.

It was only after she'd snuck back to her girlfriend's

place at 2:00 a.m. that she'd discovered the real identity of the man who'd rocked her world. Mr. One-Click, heir apparent to the great Victor Prescott's vast technology empire. Cal Prescott's computer software had recently become number one in national sales. Hell, she'd just upgraded her office computer with the latest version.

She snorted at the irony. Cal Prescott was one of the richest men under thirty-five, a man who regularly dated supermodels and socialites. He was a man who avoided emotional entanglements, who revelled in his bachelor lifestyle. If working long hours and staying single was an Olympic event, he'd have a cupboard full of gold medals.

It was a good thing you left. A smart choice. The *right* choice. Still, a tiny doubt niggled. How could she single-handedly bring a baby into her life, a debt-ridden life to which she could add the grim possibility of being homeless, too?

She'd wavered between absolute joy and utter despair a million times this past week. And every time she always returned to one realization: fate. Karma. Destiny. Whatever it was called, the universe was telling her that despite everything, this baby was meant to be.

Ava Rose, life never throws anything your way you're not capable of handling. Her mother's favourite phrase teased her mouth into a too-brief smile before the familiar throb of loss hit. She let it sit there for a second before shoving it aside. Death and tragedy hadn't defeated her before. A new life wouldn't now.

She dropped her hands to the table and gathered up the

papers. The pity party's over. It was time to take action and get her life back on track. Somehow.

"Doing your paperwork, I see."

Ava whirled, her brain tingling at the sound of that oh-so-delicious voice. A millisecond later, her stomach fell to the floor.

Cal Prescott stood in the doorway, broad and immaculately dressed in a dark grey suit, a chilly gleam in his eyes. Those eyes, once so intensely passionate, now so cold and distant that she wondered if she'd just imagined that night in Sydney two months ago. Those same eyes had creased with serious concentration as they'd shared hot, wet kisses in the privacy of his Shangri-La Hotel penthouse suite. Flared with hunger as he'd slipped her dress from her shoulders—

She slammed the door on those memories, barely managing a croak. "Cal."

"Ava." Cal's voice, a slow-burning rasp that had turned her on so quickly, so completely, was the same, but little else was. His face was a study in frozen control, eyes reflecting only an impersonal, razor-sharp study as he remained still, somehow dwarfing her kitchen even from the relative safety of the doorway.

She was alone with Cal Prescott. Again.

The air thickened, heavy with expectation. A warm throb started up between her legs as she swallowed a single desperate groan.

"What…" She croaked then cleared her throat. "What are you doing here?"

His lip curled but he said nothing, a broad, tense statue intent on letting the moment swirl and grow. She steeled herself as his eyes flickered over her in thorough scrutiny, gathering up her dignity with a smoothing of her wayward hair. Yet his eyes followed those fluttery movements until she firmly jammed her hands in her back pockets.

He snorted, a sound so full of contempt that Ava took a cautious step backwards.

"Are you pregnant with my child?"

Ava grabbed the edge of the kitchen counter, reeling from the blow. How could he know? She'd barely had time to get used to it herself. She'd driven into Parkes for an over-the-counter test, then followed up at a free clinic. She'd told no one, not even Aunt Jillian.

She opened her mouth but nothing came out. Like an idiot she just stood there, blinking in shock.

"Who…how..?" She finally managed.

"Do not play the innocent, Ava." His eyes narrowed, his jaw tightening imperceptibly. "Now answer me."

The subtle threat behind his silky words, the fury reflected in every tightened muscle, was all too clear. Ava felt her cheeks flush and just like that, she snapped.

"Do you think I *planned* this? I didn't even know who you were until after I—" she paused.

"Ran away?" He finished, his eyes way too perceptive.

She crossed her arms, refusing to let him see he'd struck a nerve. Yet her mind raced a million miles an hour until something finally clicked. "That's why you're here. You think I want money from you." Bile rose in her throat, acrid and burning. "Get out of my kitchen," she ground out.

"I'm not going anywhere. Is the baby mine?"

For one heartbeat, she seriously considered lying, but just as quickly rejected it. Apart from the fact she was a terrible liar, she *wouldn't*. Not about something this important. So with fear of the unknown fluttering in her belly, she slowly nodded. "Yes, Cal. It's yours."

He paused. "A paternity test will prove it."

"Yes," she said firmly. "It will."

His cold mask cracked, morphing into an expression so raw that she had to take a step back from the intensity.

He strode to her, the distance between them evaporating into an excruciating invasion of her comfort zone. He was Cal Prescott, and he was there, *right there* and amazingly, the urge to touch him, to smell him, thundered through her senses. She wanted to melt right into his very bones until she couldn't tell where she finished and he started.

Anger poured off him, slamming into her, breaking through her thoughts. Then with a soft curse he abruptly whirled, shoving a hand through his hair, leaving short, tufted peaks in its wake. Hair that emphasised his ruthlessly angular face and framed those rich brown eyes to perfection. It was a face so achingly distant, one that screamed control and power in every muscle, every line.

"What do you want?" He demanded now, pinning her with sharp intensity.

Instinctively she placed a hand over her belly,

which only succeeded in drawing his attention. Abruptly she shoved her hands back in her jean pockets. "From you? Nothing."

His gaze narrowed. "Don't lie to me. Not now."

"I'm not lying! I didn't even know I was pregnant until a week ago."

"So that's the way you're going to play it." When he crossed his arms, utterly convinced of her guilt, her frustration ratcheted up.

"I don't care what you think," she hissed back. "It's none of your business!"

He stilled, staring at her, while all around them there was silence, as if the earth itself was awaiting his comeback with bated breath.

Then he smiled. The sheer triumph in that one simple action sent a chilling wave over her skin. It was the smile of a man used to getting his own way, a man who made thousands of million-dollar deals and steamrolled over his detractors. It was a smile that told her he'd won.

Won what?

"You being pregnant with my child is none of my business?" he said now, arching one derisive brow up. "On the contrary. I've given this a lot of thought. That child needs a father. We'll get married."

Deep below the surface, the bombshell exploded, sending shock waves through Ava's insides. Oblivious to the aftermath, Cal flipped open a sleek black mobile phone and dialled. "I've already applied for a wedding licence and my solicitor will finalise the prenup. I dislike large engagement parties so we'll skip that, of course. But I have booked dinner at Tetsuya's with my parents tomorrow night, so—"

Ava finally found her voice. "What are you doing?"

"Hmm?"

"Are you crazy?"

"What?" When he put his hand over the mouthpiece and glared at her like she was some sort of annoying irritation, Ava saw red.

"You can't *force* me to marry you!" She jammed her hands on her hips and shouted the last word, anger surging up to scorch her throat.

Slowly, Cal hung up, forcing restraint into every muscle of his body. Her hands fisted on her hips, hips that curved into the worn denim and came this close to being indecent. His eyes travelled upwards, past the ratty shirt that skimmed her waist, the rolled-up sleeves over tanned forearms, to the low neckline that revealed a smooth expanse of throat.

He finally fixed on her face, a face he'd seen in his dreams, deep in the throes of passion. Her silken black hair was half up, half down, the remnants of a ponytail feathering her jaw. A stubborn jaw that was now rigid with fury.

It was the offer of a lifetime, marrying into the Prescott wealth. He may have preempted her blackmail attempt but she'd still be well compensated. What the hell was she ticked off about? Thrown, he glanced at her mouth.

It did him in, seeing that lush mouth again. Gentle

creases around her lips denoted a lifetime in the sun, but all he could think about was the softness of that flesh when it had teased and tempted him. How she'd placed hot, searing kisses across his chest, trailed her tongue over his belly before—

With a silent curse, he scowled, which only seemed to anger her.

"I am *not* marrying you." She enunciated the words as if he was missing a few brain cells.

He scowled. "Why not?"

Her eyes rounded in incredulity. "Because for one, you don't tell someone you're marrying them, you ask them. Second, we don't even know each other. And third, I don't *want* to marry you."

"I know you need money to save this place. I'm making you an offer." When she remained silent, he turned the screw a little more. "You get your money and I get a wife."

Her breath sucked in. "I don't need your money."

"Because you've got so many other offers, right? Your neighbor…Sawyer?" He lifted his eyebrows mockingly. "He's mortgaged to the hilt." As he watched her face drain of color he said flatly, "What, you didn't know?"

She said nothing, just stared at him with those bright blue eyes full of recrimination.

"The way I see it, you don't have a choice," he said now. "I'll give you until tomorrow to think it through, but we both know your answer."

Ava was speechless, floored by the depth of his arrogance. "If you care so much, then why not just sue for custody?" she finally whispered. "Why marriage?"

"Because I do not ignore my responsibilities." His voice tightened in the spacious kitchen. "Did you intend to tell me about this baby at all?"

She quickly drew a hand over her stomach as the blood rushed from her face. She couldn't think, couldn't even breathe with his ever-watchful eyes, the lingering scent of his warm skin, the aftermath of his luscious voice in the air all around her. "I…didn't think you'd want to know. You're Cal Prescott and—"

"You don't know what I want." Fury flickered, working his jaw. "You walked into my life, spent the night, then walked right out again."

"So this is your way of getting back at me?"

"This is not about you. It's about a child." His eyes dropped to her belly, then up again, his expression unreadable. "My child."

He effectively ended their conversation with a flick of his hand, a white business card between his two fingers. When she didn't take it he slammed it down on the counter. "I'll see you tomorrow."

Almost as if he couldn't stand to remain in her presence a second longer, he turned and stalked out the door.

Two

Ava was still standing in the kitchen, Cal's card clutched in her cold fingers, when her Aunt Jillian walked in with a handful of grocery bags, a warm smile on her weathered face. "Ava, darling, I thought we could have chicken for—"

"Cal Prescott was just here."

Jillian put the bags on the table. "The man you met in Sydney?"

"The same."

Jillian opened the fridge and shoved a block of cheese inside. "Really? Is he interested in staying at Jindalee?"

Ava swallowed. Even though she'd given Jillian the sanitised version, her aunt was a perceptive woman.

"Not exactly. Apparently he thinks I'm trying to black-mail him—and with this place teetering on the verge, I can't say I blame him."

Jillian whirled, her lined face a mask of shock. "Oh, my. That's not good."

Ava sank into a kitchen chair and put her face in her hands. "I don't believe this. And now he…" She sighed. "Jillian, I have to tell you something. Sit down."

Jillian kept right on putting away the groceries. "If it's about you being pregnant, I already guessed."

Lord, did the whole world know? Ava's jaw sagged until she snapped it shut with a click. "How? When?"

"You can't hide a sudden craving for cheese-and-pickle sandwiches. Plus," she gently reached out and smoothed Ava's hair, "your hair went curly. Your grandma and I were exactly the same. It's a Reilly thing." Jillian quickly enveloped her in a hug. "Darling, are you okay with this?"

"Yes." With a relieved sigh, Ava let herself sink into the embrace even as her head spun with the last hour's events. "You're not upset I'm not married?"

"It's not the Middle Ages, darling. And I'm not your father," she added pointedly.

Ava just squeezed Jillian harder. "Cal thinks I did it on purpose," she muffled against the woman's soft shoulder. When Jillian pulled back, Ava avoided her aunt's eyes, unable to face the questions there. "And now he's demanding we get married."

Jillian went back to unpacking. "That's very chival-rous of him, especially in this day and age."

"No, it's not! I can't even begin to list the things wrong with this—we're complete strangers, we live separate lives, have careers, not to mention what the town would say—"

"Oh, my giddy aunt!" Jillian slammed a can of tomatoes down on the counter. "Your business is about to go under, you're pregnant by a rich, attractive, single man—a man who wants to do the right thing and *marry* you—and you're worried about what a bunch of old busybodies would say?"

Ava stared at her, stunned. Her Aunt Jillian was the most easygoing person she'd ever known. She'd never raised her voice in anger, never blown her top.

"You're saying I should marry him?" Ava said slowly.

"I'm saying a child has a right to know his father. From what I've read, Cal Prescott never knew his."

"His mother remarried. He *has* a father."

"But his birth father ran out. 'To know the man, at first know the child.'"

"What?"

"Cal Prescott is a man with obvious trust issues, dear, which can make people do extreme things," Jillian explained as she started unpacking the apples. "I do wish you'd pay attention a bit better." Her face suddenly softened. "Or are those hormones kicking in already?"

Ava sighed. "It is *not* hormones. And don't change the subject." She leaned back in her chair, her mind tossing and turning. "I just don't know what to do."

Jillian rolled her eyes. "You both have something each other wants. So you make a deal."

"Have you not been listening about the whole black-mail thing? The only thing he wants is the baby." She laid a protective hand over her belly. "And he's not getting that."

"Darling, do you think he'd actually try to take away your child?" Jillian asked with a shake of her head. "Sounds to me the man just wants to be a father. And he can save Jindalee into the bargain. Unless…" she hesitated. "You don't want Jindalee."

Ava flushed. Jillian knew her better than anyone, even her own parents. Jindalee land had been in her family for over a hundred years. The sheep station had been her father's dream, a culmination of hard work and town status. Ava had known from a very early age she was a distant fourth in his affections, streets behind the land, her mother, then her younger sister, Grace. The uncompromising man had often accused her of being too wild, too selfish, too carefree. And she'd proved it in spades at twenty when she'd single-handedly destroyed everything.

Not selfish anymore. She closed her eyes, picturing his silvery head held proud, a dark frown set in a face lined with age and the elements. She'd put her own share of worry lines on that face.

Her eyes shot open when Jillian placed a gentle hand on her shoulder. "You don't have to prove anything anymore, Ava," the older woman said softly. "He's gone. He loved this land, but—"

"So do I." It was the simple truth. She loved the gently sloping hills, the craggy gum trees that housed the native corellas and lorikeets. The kangaroos that grazed in the morning mist and the stunning sunsets that spread across the big navy sky. It made her heart expand with joy every day at the sheer beauty of the land. Her land.

"Ava," Jillian said now, her eyes sympathetic. "It doesn't have to be so hard. No one will think less of you if you sell."

"But *I* would." Ava stood, walked over to the counter and began washing the apples. She'd not sunk everything into this property just to see it fail. And if Cal was on the level, then she didn't even have her neighbour's buyout offer as backup.

Hope bloomed, a tiny thread of light bobbing along a sea of uncertainty. She let it sit there for a couple of seconds until caution doused it. Before she charged into any decision, she had to pin down the details. Cal was offering her a chance to save Jindalee. She might be guilty of many things, but looking a gift horse in the mouth was not one of them. It'd be a cakewalk compared to what she'd already been through.

A cakewalk.

On Saturday at 10:00 a.m., after her two paying customers had checked out, Ava knew she couldn't stall any longer. She'd called and offered to drive the twenty minutes to Parkes, but Cal had preempted her. Now as she watched from her porch, a brand-new red Calais slowly made its way down the dirt road. It finally stopped in the small designated parking area, directly below the huge gum tree.

Ava took a breath, then another, dragging in the comforting kitchen smells to give her strength—vanilla, coffee and fresh-baked apple pie, aromas that said "welcome, come on in!"—or so she'd read in a decorating magazine.

When Cal finally unfolded himself from the car, she did a double take. She'd expected expensive casual: a polo shirt, sharply pressed pants, imported Italian shoes. But he surprised her in a pair of faded Levi's, work boots, a brown leather jacket and white cotton T-shirt, the latter hugging like cling wrap, outlining every muscular dip and curve of his chest. Natural command and raw sexuality oozed from his every bone and Ava couldn't help but stare.

He stalked purposefully up her steps with a long-legged stride that indicated he'd no place else to be, his dark eyes shuttered and focused squarely on her. She threaded her fingers once then released them and suddenly the air was filled with his warm, spicy scent.

"Ava," he said, making her name sound sexier than the promise of a hot, wet kiss. Lord, he undid her. Did he remember how in the dark of night, she'd confessed her name on his lips made her want to melt in a puddle at his feet? How he'd sensuously turned that confession against her and sent her body into a whimpering frenzy with every word, every whisper?

She quickly turned and walked in the kitchen door, but not before she caught his mouth twitch for one brief second. She groaned inwardly. He remembered.

Thankful that the warm kitchen disguised her flushed cheeks, she said over her shoulder, "We'll go into the lounge room."

As she led him down the hall, the tide of impending doom tugged at her legs. Her lounge room was welcoming and expansive, with cream walls and pine colonial-style furniture, but she couldn't help but think Cal could buy a place like this a thousand times over. He was decisive, powerful and obscenely rich. If Jillian thought to sell her on all those attributes, she was sorely mistaken. It only proved to her that Cal was unfamiliar with the word "no."

His closed expression pitched her stomach into queasy unrest. This man, with his brooding thoughtfulness and silent staring, who'd stormed back into her life and accused her of blackmail, was a complete stranger to her.

What on earth was she thinking?

She sat on the chaise longue and folded her legs under her, watching as he remained standing.

"I apologize," he began stiffly, "for yesterday. I believe I could have come off a little…"

"Pushy?" she offered, surprised.

"Determined," he amended firmly. "I'm not used to making deals based on…" He ran his eyes over her and for one second, something flared in the dark depths before he shut it down. "…personal matters."

Ava could only stare. When he unflinchingly met her eyes, something clicked. He was actually *embarrassed* at admitting that—a man worth billions, a business genius who was a dead ringer for Russell Crowe and attracted women by the boatload. Yet his expression said he'd rather eat glass than reveal any emotional vulnerability.

Despite herself, despite his demands, she felt a tiny thread of sympathy unfurl. Yet before she could say anything, he crossed his arms and swiftly changed the subject.

"What I'm offering is a business proposition. You need money. In return, the baby—and you—will have the Prescott name and all that entails."

The smooth conciseness of his proposal took her aback for one heartbeat. In the next, she realized exactly what was happening: Sheer brute force hadn't worked, so he was playing his next hand. Calm reasoning. She wondered what he'd try next if she refused. Seduction, perhaps? To her annoyance, a gentle anticipatory buzz tripped over her skin.

"Won't a wife put a downer on your lifestyle?" she said now, shoving those distracting thoughts aside.

His eyes bored into her. "Let me make this clear—you are having my baby. Which means I want *you*."

Hot excitement fired through her veins, steamrolling every other thought into oblivion. She tried to will it away but it kept on coming, a constant pounding wave that alternately thrilled yet alarmed her.

With a deep breath she finally managed to gain some

modicum of control. Cal was simply claiming his child, that was all. He just wanted what she could give him.

So why was she acting like a jittery fool in love?

She dragged her eyes away, her mind spinning. Why couldn't he be the man who'd stormed in her door and accused her of blackmail? At least that way she could refuse his demands with a clear conscience.

Bottom line—losing Jindalee was not an option. And her other choices included bankruptcy and poverty. She also had Jillian to think about; she'd convinced her aunt to sell her little café and come live with her. And Cal was offering more than financial security, a chance to keep the land and ensure the Reilly legacy stayed in the family. He was willing—no, demanding—to be a presence in her child's life. A man who wanted all the responsibilities that being a father entailed.

That was more than a lot of children got these days, herself included.

She finally glanced up, only to catch Cal studying her with an intensity that made her itch to smooth her hair and check her teeth.

"What kind of arrangement did you have in mind?" she said now.

"A legally binding contract. You marry me and in return I'll pay off all your debts, plus give you any assistance necessary to see this place turn a profit."

"I'm not handing this place over to some manager. The land and property remain in my name."

"Naturally. But I do expect you to be in Sydney

whenever I need you, to be available for functions, dinners and such."

"No." Ava swallowed. A quickie wedding was one thing. But to publicly flaunt it, to *pretend*?

He crossed his arms with a small sigh, a sure indication he'd lost patience. "Yes. Did you think I'd just give you money and that'd be it until the child was born?"

"I thought…"

"Well, you thought wrong." His jaw tightened. "This is my stipulation."

Any hope of taking the money and keeping a low profile quietly disintegrated. "So I'm to be your arm decoration."

"My fiancée," he corrected. "You will be my wife, the mother of my child, and I expect you to conduct yourself accordingly. As I will."

She blinked. "Which means?"

"No unscripted interviews, no tell-all book deals if and when we divorce." His eyes suddenly darkened. "And no lovers while we're married."

A surprised breath tore at her throat. "I need to think." Quickly she rose and the room tilted beneath her feet. Just as she grabbed the longue, Cal's hand shot out to steady her.

The shock was so instantaneous, so unexpected, that she gasped. As his long fingers curled around her upper arm, her treacherous flesh caved. A sudden flicker of heat sparked in her belly, sending desire across her skin, making her muscles ache with want.

As if her mind could sense the thin thread of control she teetered on, that night came flooding back in hot, bright technicolor. His eager mouth on hers, on her neck. His sure, skilful hands cupping her breasts, teasing her nipples into peaking hardness. And his hot passionate breath trailing a path of seduction from her navel down to—

She pulled away, refusing to meet his eyes, barely managing a "thank you." Inside, she tried to squelch the spurt of panic but reality crashed in. If she wanted to save Jindalee, she had no other choice.

She rubbed her cheek, surprised at the heat beneath her hand. There was no denying her body's reaction to his simple touch. She wanted him. Even after just one night, after his accusations and demands, she wanted him.

With an inward groan, she crossed her arms. "Fine. After you leave for Sydney I'll keep you updated on the baby's progress. Of course I will—"

"No. I'm flying home this afternoon. You're coming with me."

"Today? That wasn't part of the deal."

Cal paused, as if chewing back his words with infinite patience. "Being my wife means social functions, outings, the whole shebang. Starting immediately. I've also booked you in to see a top paediatrician on Tuesday."

She frowned. "Do I have any say in this?"

"On this, no. Which reminds me…" he flipped open his phone and dialled, exchanged a few words, then hung up. "We'll be back here next Sunday with my team," he said. "They'll need a tour, plus your existing marketing and advertising strategy. I assume you do have one?"

She straightened her shoulders with an indignant glare. "Yes."

"I've also authorised payment of your loans and any other outstanding debts." He shoved his hands on his hips. "Anything else?"

Howsabout you build a time machine and go back about nine weeks? The words bubbled up in her throat but she quickly swallowed them. Mutely she shook her head.

"Ava? Are we in agreement?"

She nearly whimpered as Cal's deep voice flowed over her, kicking up her pulse another notch. *Stop. Please stop talking, before I completely lose it.* Her feet rocked, her heart hammering in her chest.

"What happens after the baby's born?" she said hoarsely. "What if we…decide it's not working?" *What if you decide playing daddy isn't fun anymore? What if I end up hating you? What if you fall in love with someone?* Her heart twisted for a second, surprising her.

"Thinking about divorce before we're even married?" He quirked one eyebrow up and she flattened her mouth until her lips hurt.

"Yes."

He gave her a slow, considering look. "If that time comes, I'm open to discussing it. Not before. I've put a clause in the prenup to address that. But regardless of what we decide, I'm still that child's father."

The underlying thread of possessiveness was undeniable. If that didn't drop her stomach, then the "if the time comes" bit did. Of course the time would come. A country girl and a big-city billionaire were no more suited than chalk and cheese. No one these days based a marriage purely on financial gain. No one except her, that is.

She nodded, even as perverse disappointment rioted through her. "So you're asking me to marry you?"

Cal dragged his eyes away from the hollow of her neck to focus on her eyes. "Does this mean you're saying yes?"

"Are you asking me to marry you?" she repeated, crossing her arms across her chest. Unfortunately, it only drew his attention to her breasts, which were now pushing seductively up from the deep V of her buttoned shirt.

Cal's words inexplicably stuck to the roof of his dry mouth. Then he suddenly recalled their earlier conversation. *He hadn't asked her.* He cleared his throat. "Ava. Will you marry me?"

She took a breath, almost as if drawing in strength. "Yes. But with stipulations."

"Go on."

She flushed but kept right on going. "Any major decisions, any changes concerning Jindalee must be first approved by me."

Cal frowned. "My team is better equipped to decide—"

"This is my land, Cal." She levelled an unwavering gaze at him. "I get the final say-so."

"Okay," he conceded, finally seating himself on the

arm of a sturdy one seater. "I'll have my solicitor put it in the contract."

Ava stilled, waiting for a sign, anything that would let her know she was either making a colossal mistake or doing the right thing. Nothing. And as the seconds ticked by, she took another breath, then sat.

"I plan to be a hands-on mother, which means I won't be handing this baby over to a nanny just so I can swan off to parties with you."

His brief flash of surprise quickly disappeared with a cool nod. "Understood."

"And…" She faltered. "One more thing. The sleeping arrangements." One eyebrow kinked up but he said nothing. Under his scrutiny she felt the traitorous heat bloom across her skin. "I don't think it would be a good idea to…well…"

"Have sex?" He leaned back, carefully crossing his ankle over one knee as his mouth twitched. His nonchalant amusement only deepened her embarrassment.

"Well, yes."

He shrugged. "If that's what you want."

Ava nodded, mortification clogging her throat. Of course it's what she wanted. He thought she was a woman who got herself pregnant just to blackmail him. She had more self-respect than to jump into bed with a man who believed she was a common criminal.

Yet his quick acquiescence seared the edges of her womanly pride. As she studied him, she recalled an article she'd once read…something about pregnant women being a huge turn-off for some men. She'd never pegged Cal for one of those men. But then, they'd been lovers for only one fleeting night—what did she really know about her husband-to-be?

She felt the blood drain from her face. Her husband. To be.

"Then it's settled." He leaned forward, hand outstretched and for a second she just stared at him. At his questioning look, she quickly took his hand, sealing the deal and her fate with one firm handshake.

Yet her mind wasn't on the deal they'd just struck— it was on the way his long fingers wrapped around hers, enveloping her in heat and…something more, something almost protective. Something that tugged at the deepest part of her, that spoke to every teenage yearning, every wish list of happy-ever-afters she'd ever made. Here was a man in every sense of the word—strong, determined, a provider. The sheer command of his very presence took her breath away.

"Ava?"

With a jolt she realized she still held his hand and worse, she'd been stroking it with her thumb.

With a gasp she tried to pull back, but he refused to let her go. Instead she stood but he followed her, his hand still imprisoning hers.

"Ava…" he trailed off, almost as if rethinking his next words.

"Cal, please." Please don't? Or please do? Her head said one thing, her body another, and from the sudden awareness sparking in his dark eyes, she knew which one he'd chosen to hear.

Please do.

He drew her to him with all the skill and confidence of a man who knew she wouldn't refuse. He cupped her elbows, pinning her to his chest, to that warm, hard wall of muscle beneath soft cotton that cried out to be touched, caressed. Kissed.

She closed her eyes as heat and desire turned her brain to mush, waiting in willing anticipation for his lips to claim hers. A tremble started up in her belly, looping and swirling as she felt his warm breath gently swoop over her mouth. Her heart kicked up the tempo, beating hard in her throat, in her head. In a sharp rush, she exhaled, then…then…

Nothing.

"Look at me."

His sinful voice sent a flutter of goosebumps over her skin. Slowly, she did as he asked.

Danger. She felt it crackle in the air as his chest pressed intimately into her breasts. His eyes held the re-membrance of mutual pleasures, everything she'd walked away from, everything in her tortured dreams.

A deep, burning need seared Cal a thousand times over as he stared into her upturned face. To his stunned amazement, he realized he wanted her, right here, right now. After weeks of denial, his body ached for her like he'd been cloistered in a monastery for years. He shouldn't want her. Damn, he didn't even *trust* her.

Pride nipped at his heels, giving him the strength to release her. With regret dogging his retreat, he gritted his teeth.

"If you want me, Ava," he growled, unable to disguise the lust in his voice, "then you'll have to say it."

Three

Her eyes, heavy with arousal, suddenly flew wide open. "What?"

She looked so different from the first time they'd met—more earthy, more sensual. Yet he could still see a glimpse of the woman he'd bedded underneath the denim veneer: the way her eyes tilted up at the corners, the ripe lush mouth that was heaven to taste. Lord, he just wanted to peel off that snug shirt, yank down her jeans and take her with that sexy midnight hair falling around her shoulders, her lips whispering his name.

With a soft curse, he shoved a hand through his hair and gave her his back.

"You want me to ask you for sex?"

The disgust in her voice had him whirling back to the angry indignation tightening her face.

"You actually want me to beg?" She breathed, incredulous. "Of all the conceited, arrogant…! Yes, I've agreed to marry you but I am *not* going to pander to your ego by—"

"Hang on." He put up a hand in alarm. "I never said—"

"—begging you for anything! First you accuse me of blackmail and now this. I get it—it's some sort of punishment for—"

"Stop!"

His command only angered her more. She pulled herself up to her full five-foot-three and jammed her hands on her hips, her face tight with passionate fury. "I will not stop! And just because I'm having your baby doesn't mean—"

"Would you stop yelling at me?" Cal grabbed her arms, shocking them both into silence.

"Let's get something straight," he managed to grind out. "We both know we're attracted to each other—as evidenced nine weeks ago." He thought he detected a glimmer of something in her blue eyes but couldn't be certain. "But I'm not about to force myself on you because some piece of paper says I'm your husband. If you want me in your bed, then it's your decision and yours only. Understood?"

"And what," she whispered hoarsely, her eyes wide,

"makes you think I'd want you when you so clearly don't trust me?"

They remained still for a second, then two. Then, as if she realized he still held her, her arms tensed beneath his hands.

He swiftly backed off, abruptly changing the subject. "We have a flight to Sydney in a couple of hours. You need to pack."

"I have a business to run."

"You also have a family to meet. Don't you have an aunt who can look after this place for a few days?"

"How—" Ava stopped. Cal finding out about the baby was one violation she'd get over. But digging into her past without even giving her the option of what she wanted to reveal? Her mouth felt bitter and dry. Dear lord, what had she gotten herself into?

As if she was standing outside someone else's life looking in, Ava sat on the balcony of Cal's Circular Quay penthouse suite, taking in Sydney Harbour spread out like a picture-perfect postcard thirty floors below.

His place was something out of *Architectural Digest*. The elevator doors had swooshed open to reveal a massive living room in varying shades of cream and white, a warm chocolate couch opposite a solid rustic coffee table in the centre. Along the right wall, separating the bedrooms, ran a stunning tropical aquarium. In silent awe she'd barely registered Cal's brief tour, until they'd walked through the dining area and into an immaculate kitchen. Too immaculate.

"Do you cook?" she'd asked him. He'd just shrugged and said, "I eat out, mostly."

There was something here for all the senses, she realized. Even on the balcony, the decadent cream cashmere couch felt like heaven against her bare calves, just like the expensive cotton sheets on her guest room bed. The briny ocean breeze left a salty tang on her lips, tainted warmly by the patio heater glowing in the far corner. And through the double glass patio doors floated the soft strains of James Taylor on the CD player, mingling with the faint bustle of Circular Quay below. All that marred the perfection was the absence of an active kitchen. Something simmering on the stove…a lamb roast, she mused, some garlic potatoes, fresh carrots and green beans. Or a Greek salad. Her stomach rumbled in agreement and a small grin tugged at her lips.

Her good humour faltered as Cal appeared at the door with two wine glasses. He'd changed into a dark navy suit, light-blue shirt and a precisely knotted sapphire silk tie, while she had to be content with the cherry-red dress he'd first seen her in. It was a little snug across the breasts but the best she could do on short notice.

"Magnificent, isn't it?" His quiet confidence made it sound like he'd painted the harbour view himself, and she couldn't help but smile.

"Yes."

He studied her, almost as if assessing her against some unspoken criteria. She must have finally passed muster when, with a glint of remembrance in his eyes, he said, "Nice dress."

"My *only* dress," she replied and recrossed her legs. The floaty chiffon hem slid over her skin, baring a long expanse of thigh. Surreptitiously, she rearranged the fabric, but when his shrewd gaze followed her hands, the warmth began to rise again.

To fill the uncomfortable void, she took a grateful swallow of the bubbly lemon, lime and bitters, then grabbed up the paper he'd shoved across the glass table.

It was a briefing paper, not only outlining his business deals but some personal details, details she'd be expected to know as his fiancée. She scanned down the page, unable to stop that rush of morbid curiosity. She knew nothing of him—at least, not the things that really mattered. Deep, personal things she always thought you should know about your husband-to-be. Little intimacies that indicated you were a couple, in love and happy to spend the rest of your lives together.

"You'll be thirty-four on New Year's Day." At his nod, she asked half to herself, "What do you get a man who can afford to buy anything?"

"Something simple. My mother bought me the fish tank last year." At her raised eyebrow, he added, deadpan, "But I can always use a tie or a nice bottle of Scotch."

"A pair of socks?"

She returned his grin with one of her own and for the

first time since arriving in Sydney, Ava felt his full and complete attention. The gentle tug of desire unfurled inside, but with ruthless efficiency, she shoved it back.

On his private jet he'd been engrossed in paperwork and phone calls. The journey to his apartment hadn't been much better. She should have enjoyed the decadent opulence of driving in his shiny black hybrid Maserati Coupé, blanketed in the luxurious smell of leather seats, the throaty purr of the powerful engine as they smoothly glided along Anzac Parade. Yet she couldn't shake the awful thought that this was a premonition of things to come—she silent and immaculately groomed and he the workaholic with always one ear to the phone, one eye on a business deal.

She didn't want to be the wife who paraded about in designer dresses and jewels, a perky, dolled-up hostess serving only to entertain her husband's business colleagues. She shuddered at the thought of putting on makeup day after day, having her hair teased and primped, dressing up like Corporate Wife Barbie.

And stupid, stupid her—she was going to sign a contract that gave him carte blanche.

You have to remember this is just temporary. She'd be at Jindalee most days, focusing on her business. She'd be with Cal only when he needed to show her off and make a good impression. He'd said so himself.

His own personal show pony.

With self-anger dogging her thoughts, she glanced away, back to the darkening sky.

Instead of taking a seat next to her, he sat on the couch directly across the coffee table, thankfully on the outer edges of her personal space. Yet anything short of another city was still way too close. He was simply too commanding to ignore, let alone be comfortable with. It was a combination of the dark, knowing look in his eyes, the sensual flow of his voice and the annoying memories that surged up to goosebump her skin.

She quickly returned her attention to the paper. "You started working for Victor at seventeen and now you're a managing director. Did you…" she paused, mentally rephrasing the question. "You never felt the urge to start your own business?"

"VP Tech *is* my business."

She remained silent at his cryptic statement until he elaborated with a small shrug. "I dropped out of school to work in Victor's software development division. A few years later I had the idea for One-Click and Victor supplied technical staff and financial backing. Today we're the only Australian company with integrated Internet, phone and software technology in the one office program. It brings in billions."

After a brief second she changed gears. "What's your mother like?"

His reply was instantaneous. "Loyal. Generous. Supportive."

"And your stepfather?"

Cal paused, allowing himself the opportunity to study her features, the uptilted nose, the elegant sweep of her cheek. The way she looked genuinely interested in his answer. "Commanding. Immovable. Astute."

"And he won't figure out our newly engaged bliss is a front? Or are you planning to tell them the truth?" she said, her voice in complete control. Yet her eyes gave her away, deep pools of turmoil. Abruptly she glanced down, breaking contact.

"Are you worried about what people will think?" he asked slowly. The small crease between her eyes indicated he'd hit the truth.

"About what your parents will think, yes."

Despite that ever-present distrust that lingered like an early morning fog, the air suddenly shifted, stirred by a gentle wave of something Cal didn't want to explore, let alone acknowledge. Not even to himself.

He barely heard the catch in her breath, but he couldn't miss the struggle etched in the gentle curves of her face. Shoving down that sliver of unfamiliar guilt, he instead focused on his purpose. He'd had one moment of weakness, and it was his responsibility to make it right. He'd learnt that from Victor. He didn't welcome this deep, burning need to have her skin on his, to have her body hot and writhing beneath him.

Yet for the first time in months, he simply wanted.

He ground his teeth together. *Christ.* Now he was hard.

With a determined slant to his jaw, he refocused. Things with Ava were business. They had to be.

The silence stretched until the need to fill it with something, anything, became unbearable. Cal finally broke it.

"If they ask, you can just say we met over cocktails at the Shangri-La, kept in touch and met up again recently."

"But isn't a sudden engagement out of character for you?" she pressed.

"Trust me, they won't ask. At least, my mother won't."

"And Victor?"

He paused, twirling the glass in his hand. "It's none of his business whom I chose to marry. Let me handle him." As his firm command lingered, their gazes clashed, one curious and bright, the other shadowed and dark.

Ava severed it and reached for her glass. "So we're going to fake it."

The unintentional double entendre curved his mouth. "That a problem?"

She looked discomforted by his scrutiny. "I'm not good at deception."

Interesting. "Oh, I'm sure you'll manage. Just think of the money."

He could've kicked himself when an injured shadow passed over her face. But then she turned back to the view and it vanished.

What was with him? He preferred women who understood the demands of his lifestyle, women who were polished, sophisticated, who weren't looking for promises or commitment. Women who could elegantly fake a parental inspection with ease. They'd graced magazines, television, catwalks. They met his needs sexually, socially and mentally, although not one woman had met them all.

But Ava…what was it about her and just *her* that compelled him?

Sure, she was a hot package. Their one encounter still haunted his memory. His eyes dipped to her neckline, to the silky material stretched taut across her breasts. Ava Reilly was also stubborn and proud, qualities that alternately fascinated and frustrated him.

Don't forget she bargained her baby to save her business.

That should be enough to extinguish his craving, but inexplicably, it still simmered. And below that, an unfamiliar urge to know more about her, to unravel the pieces of what his brief report had missed, surged up.

"How long have you been at Jindalee?"

His sudden question snapped her gaze back to him.

"Pretty much my whole life." At his frown she added, "Don't you have all this in a report?"

"No."

She held his gaze, as if trying to work out if he was telling the truth or not. Finally she gave a small sigh. "Jindalee used to be a sheep station, built by my father in the late forties."

"How old are you?"

"I'll be thirty in December. My parents tried for ages to have kids, then they had two girls barely a year apart." She clicked her mouth shut and looked away, indicating that line of questioning was closed.

He frowned. When they married, he'd get sole control of VP Tech, everything he'd ever wanted. He should be focusing on that and only that, not sharing intimate details of their lives. She was just a convenient means to that end. He'd done the right thing, the *only* thing by claiming his child. He didn't need to know the intricacies of her past—just like she didn't need to know about Victor's ultimatum.

"So when is the happy day?" Ava said.

For a second, Cal remained wrapped up in his thoughts, in the remnants of anger still clinging to him like ethereal cobwebs. That anger was a constant confirmation never to fully trust anyone, never to let his guard down. But when he snapped his eyes to Ava's, he felt those spidery webs slowly evaporate.

Quickly he gained control. "As soon as possible. How long does it take to organize a wedding?"

She shrugged. "I don't know."

"Isn't it something women always obsess about?"

She gave him a look. "Sorry, I missed the memo."

She took a slow sip of her drink and his attention zeroed in on those cherry-painted lips as they met the rim of the glass, the small ripple under her smooth skin as she swallowed.

"Money's no object," Cal added with more calm than he felt. "If you want a particular place, a certain church—"

"It doesn't matter."

He studied her with interest. "If you could get married anywhere, where would you choose?"

"I haven't given it much thought."

"Okay." He placed his glass on the table with firm decisiveness. "St Mary's Cathedral for the ceremony," he said, naming Sydney's most prominent historical church. "Then my private cruiser on Sydney Harbour for the reception. How does August the first suit you?"

"That's less than…" she calculated in the pause, "two months away. Why the rush?"

"You have a problem with that?" He eyed her stomach, then nodded. "You'll be five months pregnant, obviously showing…"

"That's not the point," she said tightly. "Aren't there waiting lists?"

"Probably." He quirked up an eyebrow. "I can organize a wedding planner."

That threw her. "No! Okay, August the first it is," she finished lamely. "So, getting back to tonight. Tell me more about your parents."

He let her change direction without comment. "My mother, Isabelle, lived in the Hunter Valley. She met Victor when I was eleven and they married a year later."

"You have a brother," she said.

"Stepbrother. Zac." With all traces of amusement gone, he felt the sudden need for distance. He rose, went to the railing, then turned to face her, his back against the cold metal. "He's three years younger than me and Victor's real son."

She smiled tentatively. "I'm sure your stepfather thinks you're just as—"

"Don't."

Her smile slowly faded. "I'm just trying to—"

"You don't read the tabloids, do you?"

Mutely she shook her head.

"Zac left VP Tech a few years back," he said less harshly. "From what I hear he started up his own company on the Gold Coast."

I stayed. I remained loyal. And yet Victor still insists on playing this stupid game with the future of the company.

"Have you spoken to him?"

"What?" He shook his head, trying to dislodge the remnants of bitterness.

"Have you spoken to Zac since he left?" She studied him way too closely, a thread of concern in her bright blue eyes. "You're brothers. Don't you—"

"No. We need to get going if we're to make our reservation," he said gruffly, glancing away with an odd sense of guilt.

Ava hesitated for a brief second as he held out his hand. When she finally took it and he gently pulled her to her feet, she sucked in a breath. There it was again—the jolt of heat, the quickening of her heartbeat, the low ache of desire in her belly. When she instinctively placed a hand on her stomach, his eyes followed.

"Can you…feel anything?"

The sudden flash of wonder in his face was a low, primeval blow, leaving her breathless. What she felt had nothing yet everything to do with the life growing inside her. Her body was changing, growing, and hot, dark need throbbed through her veins. Her skin itched to be touched, to be kissed. By this man.

And there was no way she'd admit that, not when it'd taken all the control she possessed to recover from that near kiss.

"Just a few…flutters," she managed. "It's normal in the first trimester."

"Do you need anything?"

You. "No."

Ava swallowed thickly as he placed a hand on her back, guiding her into the apartment. *Great. Just great.* How on earth was she going to survive another thirty-one weeks of this?

"Do you have a special diet?"

She closed her eyes briefly as the warm brand of his palm seared through her thin dress. "No caffeine or shellfish. Lots of greens, water. And sleep. I've been spending a lot of time in bed…"

She glanced up, caught his flash of amusement and felt her skin prickle hotly.

Get a grip, Ava! It was just…biological. Hormonal. He was a great-looking guy and her body instinctively responded to that. That's all.

When she reached to grab her wrap draped across the back of his leather couch, she noticed a small velvet box perched on top. Her eyes flew to his.

"To add reality to our newly engaged bliss," he explained, plucking the box from her fingers and flicking it open.

Despite herself, she gasped. There, nestled on a bed of black velvet, was the most gorgeous ring she'd ever seen. It was stunning in its simplicity: a claw-set single teardrop diamond, the gold band studded with tiny emeralds. It must be worth thousands…or more. She hesitated, almost afraid to touch it, until Cal eased the ring from its nest and held it out.

"It's beautiful," she sighed.

"I know." She glanced up, only to lose herself in the dark drug of his unfathomable eyes. Quickly she refocused on the ring, willing her hand not to shake as he slid it over her knuckle. It sat there, winking at her, teasing with its carat-laden sparkle.

"A little loose," he murmured, still holding her fingertips as he ran his thumb over the band. Shivers tripped down her skin and she gently eased away.

"Not for long." At his questioning look, she added, "Weight gain."

"Ahh."

When his mouth tilted, the overwhelming need to kiss him stunned her. It shouldn't be. But there it was.

Her whole body tingled with awareness, making her skin burn from the inside. She'd read about pregnancy hormones heightening a woman's sexual appetite, had laughingly listened to the explicit stories her married girlfriends had revealed. But were those hormones supposed to be *this* intense? Like she had a sudden need to rip off her clothes and demand he ravish her on the floor?

She wanted him. Craved him, even. Like she was a chocolate addict, and one taste just hadn't been enough.

A groan rattled in her throat. She couldn't give in to a moment of weakness, no matter how amazing it promised to be. Sleeping with a man who thought her capable of blackmail would leave a deep and lasting scar, and she'd had enough of those to last a lifetime.

With supreme control she took one step back, away from the warm intimacy that had enveloped them as they stood almost touching. She drew her wrap around her, wishing it were solid armour.

"Shall we go?"

A shutter fell over his face, his nod cool and curt. And just like that, the moment was broken. But damn, a part of her wished it hadn't, wished she possessed the worldliness, the detachment to make the first move and bring relief to her growing need.

But as Cal coolly guided her out the door, she'd have to instead focus on the night ahead, and put all her energies into getting through it.

Four

Determined to follow Cal's lead and ignore the whispered glances that accompanied their journey through Tetsuya's, Ava lifted her chin and kept walking, fully aware of his warm, possessive hand on the small of her back guiding her forward. Then they were inside the private dining room and the door was closed with a discreet click.

She got a glimpse of the interior—sparsely elegant, with delicious aromas coming from the warming station at the far end—before Cal looped an arm around her waist. It was an intimate brand of ownership, one that did nothing to quash the butterflies in her stomach, and she itched to squirm away. But then he was saying,

"Ava. I'd like you to meet my mother, Isabelle," and her fate was sealed.

A deep breath calmed her panic, leaving behind nervous anticipation. Isabelle Prescott had to be in her fifties at least, but moved with the grace and charm of someone decades younger. Outwardly, she looked perfect, from the hem of her elegant black knee-length shift dress to the top of her perfectly made-up face, surrounded by a fashionably choppy blond bob. As Ava expected, the woman was manicured, perfumed and dressed like a million bucks. Yet when she tilted up to greet Cal with a kiss, her smile radiated genuine joy.

To Ava's relief, when she turned to Ava that smile never faltered.

"Ava, I'm delighted to meet you. I'm so happy for you both."

She barely had time to be surprised by the older woman leaning in to bestow a kiss to her cheek before Cal introduced Victor and a steely handshake engulfed her hand.

Cal was a man who oozed natural command and confidence, a man used to giving directions and having them obeyed without question. Now she knew where he'd learnt it from. The persona of Victor Prescott was just as large as the real-life man himself. His broad, imposing presence was immaculately suited, his grey hair precisely cut, his moustache trimmed. A pair of intelligent blue eyes summed her up in half a second and, determined not to wither under that gaze, Ava returned his handshake firmly and met it. When he smiled the action didn't quite reach his eyes.

"Congratulations, Ms. Reilly."

What an odd thing to say. She shot a glance at Cal. "For…?"

"For being the woman to finally catch my son. He's been notoriously single for too many years."

A tense look passed between the two men before Cal broke it. He took Ava's arm with firm gentleness. "Let's be seated."

With Cal seated next to her and Isabelle and Victor directly opposite, the meal began. To Ava's surprise, there were no menus, just a discreet waiter serving the first of what was to be ten courses from the restaurant's famous degustation menu.

"Venison, beef." Cal named the tiny helpings on her plate, his murmur soft and intimate in her ear. "The others are fish."

"So, Ava," Isabelle began as she dipped her spoon in the gazpacho. "Are you from Sydney?"

"Born and bred near Dubbo, actually."

"A country girl…I like that." Isabelle smiled. "So a city this size would seem a little crazy to you."

Ava slid a glance to Cal, who seemed intent on her answer. "It's large. Noisy. But," she added quickly with a smile, "very beautiful. Sydney's harbour view is like no other."

As she finished the rest of her bio, Ava was acutely aware of the attention she commanded. The scrutiny that worried her most, though, was Victor's. Reputation aside, the man had a way of intimidating with just a look and the slight raising of an eyebrow. He let Isabelle ask all the questions, only interjecting to question her about Jindalee's past incarnation as a sheep station.

As the meal wore on, and despite the glorious food—Ava had never tasted beef so wonderfully spiced before—she sensed an underlying tension settle over their table. She frequently caught a guarded sharpness in Cal's eyes, as if he was waiting for something to happen, for someone to say something. She glanced over at Victor. The man eyed them both with speculation, a look that had frequented the meal. One that had first alarmed but now just plain irritated her.

On the flip side, Isabelle was a genuinely lovely woman. Cal's obvious love and respect shone through like the sun on an overcast day. It was the way her whole face creased with humor when she spoke, the way his expression softened. She was obviously the catalyst between two equally forceful and stubborn males.

"And the poor man was covered in Béarnaise sauce!" Isabelle concluded her anecdote with a laugh, prompting Cal into a deep chuckle. Ava smiled through the tiny pang that speared her, forcing her eyes away. They landed on Victor, only to find him studying her with sharp intensity.

Quickly she dropped her gaze to her plate.

"You don't like seafood?" Victor said suddenly. All eyes went to him, then to Ava's plate, where she'd eaten the salad but left the shellfish.

Ava gave Cal a startled look. "I…"

"No, she doesn't." Cal answered smoothly, placing a warm hand over hers on the table. *Calm down*, the small gesture seemed to say. *I'm here.*

Victor snorted. "Well, I've never known a woman to refuse dessert." His gaze became perceptive. "Chocolate cognac mousse…"

"Ava doesn't drink alcohol," Cal said smoothly.

"…and a superior cappuccino."

"Or caffeine."

Victor slowly raised the napkin to his mouth, dabbed, then folded it precisely on the table.

"I see. So to summarize this evening—you're attractive, single, have no discernible indulgences and run a small business while supporting your aunt and the local community. Do you have any vices, Ms. Reilly, or can I assume you're—" he held her panicky gaze in calculating summary "—absolutely perfect for my son?"

Cal's hand tightened over hers. "Oh, for God's sake, Victor, that's enough. She's—"

"Cal, no," she murmured, urging the well of panic back down.

He glanced at her then continued calmly. "Ava hasn't been well the last few days."

Victor's chair screeched across the floor as he abruptly stood. "Cal—a word?"

Cal nodded, rose fluidly to his feet and followed Victor across the room, out of earshot. Even knowing Cal for just a few days, she could still see something simmer below the well-groomed, polite surface. Something angry and resentful.

Ava's stomach sank, aided by Victor's cynical words, loaded to the brim with innuendo. She stared at her plate as the meal congealed in her stomach. It shouldn't matter what that man thought of her, but it did. Painfully so.

"I hope you're feeling better." Isabelle's hand on her arm startled her and when she met the woman's warm brown eyes, they were fraught with concern.

The little white lie twisted inside. "Just a bug."

"I'm sorry if what Victor said upset you. He's just being protective of Cal. It's nothing personal."

"Well," Ava cleared her throat, emotion clogging it, "it sure felt like it."

Isabelle gave her a small smile. "I know. Victor can be a little…autocratic. Abrasive, even. But he's a man used to running a billion-dollar business. Sometimes it's hard to—" she gave an elegant shrug "—shut that off."

"Can I ask you a personal question?" Ava said impulsively. At Isabelle's nod, she said, "You and Victor are so different…" She paused, not wanting to offend, but the other woman's smile drove her onward. "How did you and Victor meet?"

Isabelle laughed. "We are different, there's no doubt about that. Cal was six when his father ran out. We never married, so there I was, five years later, a single mum and working at a winery on the north coast. Victor was looking to buy it, he saw me serving in the café and—" She trailed off, her face soft with remembrance.

"We fell in love. People scoff at love at first sight, but truly, that's what it was. As you probably know," she added with a sparkle in her eyes. "Like you and Cal, I had no idea who Victor was. He didn't know about my life, about my son. But we fell in love and that was it. We were married a year later, when Cal turned twelve."

Ava couldn't help but smile at the woman's misty-eyed reminiscence. "He swept you off your feet."

"And he didn't take no for an answer—not that I didn't make him jump through a few hoops first." She arched a brow in a woman-to-woman look before taking a sip of her wine.

Ava nodded with a smile and finished the rest of her water. It surprised her that this warm, intelligent woman was married to a man like Victor Prescott. Yet there'd been a few times she'd spotted the cracks in the man's ice-hard facade: When Isabelle had reached out to squeeze his hand and he'd returned the grip firmly. Her animated retelling of a story that relaxed his craggy face, softening the controlled lines. Yet in the next moment, the mask returned and he was back to studying Ava like she was a particularly fascinating bug under his microscope.

Isabelle tapped her hand on the table, bringing Ava's attention to the sparkling wedding set on her ring finger. "Ava, I know it's short notice, but would you like to go shopping with me tomorrow?"

Shopping? She glanced over to where Cal and Victor were still talking in hushed animation, then returned to Isabelle.

"We can buy heaps of shoes, drink cappuccino and people-watch," Isabelle teased, with a gleam in her eye. "Uh!" She gestured with mock severity when Ava opened her mouth. "Don't tell me. You're a handbag girl instead."

Ava laughed then. She wanted to know more about Cal, so what better way to get a handle on him than through his mother? "Sure. Shopping it is."

"Excellent!" Isabelle beamed. "Do you have any preferences?"

"Somewhere…inexpensive?"

Isabelle laughed and laid a hand on Ava's. "Think of it as Cal's treat. He can afford to indulge his fiancée, after all. And I promise we'll find something you love."

"Are you ready to go?" Cal said suddenly. Startled, she glanced up, only to find his expression shuttered down tight. She nodded and rose to her feet.

"No coffee?" Isabelle asked, surprised.

"Can't—early start tomorrow. I'll see you later, Mum." Cal placed a quick kiss on his mother's cheek then nodded curtly at Victor.

"I'll send a car for you at eight," Isabelle said as Cal placed Ava's wrap around her shoulders. "Retail therapy," she added at her son's questioning look. And then Cal was gently but firmly guiding her from the room.

The ride back to Cal's apartment was heavy with expectancy. Ava waited for Cal to reveal what he and Victor had discussed in muted anger at the restaurant, but she was still waiting by the time they'd entered the apartment elevator.

"Are you going to tell me what Victor said?"

As the elevator doors slid closed Cal swung his loaded gaze to her, holding it in silent analysis. Despite the awkward, drawn-out moment, she refused to back down.

He jammed a finger on the top-floor button again. "Victor had doubts about our marriage, our…" his gaze lingered on her mouth, "compatibility. I rebutted them."

Ava felt the sudden urge to lick her lips but instead nibbled on the inside of her cheek. "It looked pretty heated."

He shrugged and went back to staring at the blinking numbers as they ascended. "That's Victor— can't stand people disagreeing with him." He crossed his arms, still focused on the floors. "I suppose you'll need some money."

Ava frowned. "For what?"

"Tomorrow. For shopping."

"If that's your way of offering, then no, thank you."

"I can afford it." He reached into his jacket pocket, pulled out his wallet and flipped it open. "Here."

When she remained still, he impatiently waved the card under her nose.

She blinked then drew in a sharp breath. "Platinum Amex?"

He shoved the card into her hand as the doors slid open.

"Don't get too excited." He indicated she go first. "There's a limit."

"I don't need an allowance," she said tightly. "I'm not some kept woman."

"I didn't say you were."

She slapped the card to his chest as she walked past him, but he snared her arm, forcing her to stop. "Let me make this clear to you, Ava. After tomorrow, the public will know you're my bride-to-be. And the first thing you'll be judged on is your wardrobe."

She frowned and pulled free. "What's happening tomorrow?"

"I'm releasing our engagement announcement to the press. What?" he asked calmly as panic flushed the blood from her face. "The sooner we announce it, the less chance of a leak."

A soft melodic jangle permeated the warm apartment and with a shaking hand, Ava reached into her purse. Pulling out her mobile phone, she turned to the kitchen.

"Hi, Jillian." She tried for nonchalance but after she hung up from her aunt's "just checking to see if you're okay" call, she knew she hadn't fooled either of them.

From the sound of it, Cal was also engaged in a call in the living room. He may have given her privacy but he'd pointedly placed the offending credit card in the center of the breakfast bench. It sat there, glinting in the subtle mood lighting, teasing her with its shiny newness.

She reached out, fingering the bumpy numbers. It wouldn't just be small-town gossip this time—Cal's announcement was sure to make national news. People would be talking, and not just about how she and Cal had met and who "the real Ava Reilly" was. They'd focus on her clothes, her hair, her figure.

She rolled her eyes. Following fashionable trends wasn't an option when she had a business to keep afloat. The clothes and makeup she *did* have were at least three years old. Sunscreen was about as close as she got to moisturiser.

But now…the sudden and inexplicable desire to indulge, to splurge on something impractical and feminine, made her insides ache with longing. Many years ago—a lifetime ago—she'd given in to the frivolous call. When Grace was alive.

"So you've changed your mind?"

As if the card had bitten back, Ava snatched her hand away. Cal stood in the kitchen doorway, his jacket off, sleeves rolled up to reveal tanned, muscular arms. The glow from the track lighting barely brushed him, illuminating the golden hairs on his forearms, glinting across the angular face, throwing him half in shadow, half in light. With a sharp movement, he stuffed his hands in his pockets, patiently awaiting her answer as she stood there like a gawky teenager.

The man was beautiful. Her mind emptied, tongue suddenly dry. As if sensing the small war waging in her head, his mouth tweaked.

"Should I alert the media?" Cal said with deliberate nonchalance.

"What?"

He spread his hands wide, outlining an imaginary

billboard. "'Woman turns down all-expenses-paid shopping spree.'"

Finally, a smile. Despite the brief pleasure that small action gave him, he noticed the sadness that accompanied it.

"Once upon a time I would've jumped at the chance." She shifted from foot to foot before reaching down to pull off her high heels. Two inches shorter, she seemed tiny, more vulnerable somehow. She barely met his chin.

"Grace and I…" she paused, shook her head.

Cal recalled her conversation with his mother. "Your sister."

"I thought you and Victor were deep in a business discussion."

"I have an uncanny ability to multitask."

Her tiny snort of laughter surprised them both and for one moment, the tension lifted.

"Your sister died young," he stated softly.

Her smile dimmed. "She was nineteen." She made to turn away, hesitated and instead fixed him with a steady look. "My mother died three years ago of cancer, my father had a heart attack seven months after that. It's been just me and my aunt ever since." She glanced away so quickly that Cal barely had time to distinguish any emotion in her expression. Vulnerability? Sadness? Her voice reflected neither with her next statement. "Don't you already know everything about me?"

"Not everything." He knew her skin shivered when he kissed that sweet spot on her neck, the way she gasped when he nibbled her earlobe. He knew the way her eyes darkened to a stormy blue when she was all fired up about something, in the throes of passion. But suddenly that wasn't enough.

"I don't make a habit of digging into people's private lives," he said firmly.

The moment lengthened as Cal steadily held her gaze, until he shifted, taking a step closer and the air suddenly flared hot.

"Why did you run?"

He was far from touching distance but Ava's whole body still vibrated with anticipation. She remained motionless, holding her breath. He couldn't know how she'd regretted walking away that night, wondering if things would've turned out differently had she stayed.

She decided on an offhand shrug. "To avoid an awkward morning?"

"Really?"

At his slow, dubious eyebrow raise, irritation flared. "Yes. Despite what you think of me, you were my first and only one-night stand. I thought you'd be relieved not having to deal with the morning after."

"You didn't give me a choice," he said softly.

"Well, welcome to the club."

Ava knew she'd struck a nerve. Surprise flitted across his face before he swiftly smoothed it out. Slowly he crossed his arms, bringing the defined muscles in his shoulders, his biceps, into relief.

Under his gaze bravado seeped out, only to end on a

gasp when her belly fluttered. Her hand flew to her stomach.

"What?" He was by her side in an instant, his hand covering hers in sudden shocking familiarity.

She didn't know what made her more breathless, the tiny life moving inside or Cal's warm palm scorching her belly. When she looked up their eyes locked. And held.

In those seconds, his eyes echoed sheer amazement until he dropped his hand and moved away. Yet the undeniable truth lingered, lengthened into a realisation she'd be a fool to ignore or misinterpret. Cal was emotionally involved in this baby. And in that flash of intimacy, she knew without hesitation that she wanted—*ached*—for him to kiss her.

She dragged in a breath, rough shards of frustration, before stepping back. "It's late. I should…"

"Yes."

Still he just stood there, filling the doorway until she was forced to meet his eyes again.

"Excuse me."

Through the haze of conflicting emotion Cal finally registered her questioning eyes. When he silently moved aside, she brushed past him, the warmth of her body drifting by on a wave of tantalizing perfume. Captivated by her gently swaying hips as she crossed the lounge room, his eyes lingered long after she disappeared into his spare room and shut the door with a decisive click.

He cursed softly, still rooted to the spot. If reality mirrored fantasy, she'd be pulling him towards the bedroom, begging him to make love to her just about now. Instead, he was left with a raw taste in his mouth, a small fire burning a hole in his gut.

With a growl, he stalked out the kitchen, through the living room and down the hall. When he reached his bedroom he began to unbutton his shirt, cursing under his breath when the buttons stuck and he ended up ripping one free.

Ava Reilly was no innocent—she knew exactly what she was doing, from her gentle charming of his mother to the steady gaze she'd given Victor when they'd been introduced. But then this...this pure wonder would practically shine from deep within her and knock him for a six.

Trust your first impressions, Cal, Victor had told him the first day he had started work at VP Tech. *They're there for a reason.*

Grudgingly he had to admit that over the years, Victor had been right on that one. Apart from making his mouth water, Ava had an air of charming, almost old-world innocence. A far cry from the decadent things they'd done weeks ago in his bed. Things he still wanted to do.

What, a small voice rationalized, *if she wasn't pretending?* What if their night together had been as mind-blowing as he'd remembered?

With a swift jerk he pulled his shirt free of his pants.

All his ideas on how to prove—or disprove—his theory involved various stages of getting Ava naked. Something she'd no doubt object to, given her current frame of mind.

Pity.

Five

Ava blinked awake in the darkness, the unfamiliarity panicking her for one second before realization crashed in. She was in Sydney, in Cal's apartment. Today she'd be his official wife-to-be.

With a groan, she reached for her phone to check the time. Five-thirty. If she were home, she'd already be heading outside to watch the sunrise, coffee in hand.

She flung off the sheets and shoved her feet into her sheepskin slippers. Just because she was suddenly living someone else's life didn't mean she should drop her early morning ritual. Yet when she opened the bedroom door into the darkened living room, surprise gave her pause.

Where was the nausea? The morning sickness? She

ran through a mental checklist. Aching breasts—to be expected. A mild twinge in her lower back—probably the strange bed. But her stomach? Nothing.

Thank you, pregnancy gods. With a small sigh, she padded across the room into the kitchen, the watery aquarium's blue glow sending shards of light across the apartment. After inspecting the cupboards, full of gleaming cookware and barely used crockery, she finally found the cups. She chose an elegant bone china teacup and saucer, decorated with tiny blue flowers and totally out of place in Cal's bold apartment. With smooth efficiency, she turned on the water jug and finished her inspection of the kitchen while the water boiled.

The state of the art coffee machine clicked on with a soft beep and her brows wrinkled. Coffee was out unless Cal used decaf…which she seriously doubted. She scowled at the shiny appliance as if it was the manufacturer's fault her daily cup was suddenly off-limits.

"It's on a timer, not telepathy."

She whirled, picking out Cal's large shape in the muted glow.

"You're up early," she blurted out.

"So are you."

When he stepped into the kitchen Ava swallowed. The sudden desire to smooth down his sleep-rumpled hair, stuck in spikes over his head, forced her fingers into a tight fist behind her back. She wanted to run her hands over that broad, cotton-clad chest, to see if the well-worn T-shirt felt as soft as it looked. Instead she turned back to the counter and busied herself with jiggling her caffeine-free tea bag furiously in the cup.

"We country folk get up at the crack of dawn," she said.

"So do we corporate types."

She glanced up with a smile and to her surprise, Cal returned it. Surprise turned to relief as the tension lightened.

She sniffed the air. "Is that butterscotch?"

"Guilty," he reached past her, way too close, to snag a cup from the cupboard above. The aroma of warm man mingled with coffee had her inhaling sharply. "Java Butterscotch, to be exact. I also have Hawaiian Mocha, Blueberry Morning and Cinnamon Hazelnut. I like the variety," he added defensively at her amusement.

"I bet you keep that Gloria Jean's on the corner in business."

When he chuckled, something hot and intimate sent her body into its own little hum. Yet Ava didn't have time to savour the warmth, the delicious anticipation, because following on its heels came a familiar well of nausea.

No! With a quick swallow of her now-tasteless tea, she nodded to the patio. "I'm going to sit out on the balcony."

Cal watched her pad across his lounge room. Dressed in a neatly knotted, fluffy red robe and a pair of absurd slippers, her hair in curly disarray down her back, she couldn't have turned him on more if she'd greeted him in black satin lingerie.

Remembrance assailed his senses, the hint of floral scent innocent yet paradoxically seductive. He knew exactly how that hair felt between his fingers, across his skin, and couldn't stop a small curse escaping as the tangle of memories sparked in his brain.

With his coffee poured, he made his way to the balcony. Yet when he saw her profile, cup raised to her lips, something gave him pause.

He must have made a sound, caught the corner of her vision. She whipped her head around, her shadowed eyes landing squarely on him at the exact moment the sun speared across the balcony. Glints of gold crowned her, a radiant halo for her soft lush features. But it was the expression in her eyes that sent shards of desire straight into his manhood.

Her study of him was intensely personal. Arousing. He felt the burn of her gaze as if she'd run a slow hand over his body, leaving tiny flames in her wake. Her eyes roamed leisurely, first across his shoulders, then his chest. He remained frozen in her commanding grip, taking perverse enjoyment in her unabashed exploration, a hint of a smile kinking the corner of her mouth. Then her eyes dipped lower, much lower, and he instantly hardened.

In a blink her eyes flew to his, full of stricken mortification, before she whipped her head back to the view.

And damn, if he didn't take that as a challenge.

He slid the door open and the gentle warmth of the patio heater rushed him.

Her nose twitched and she suddenly turned, eyeing his cup like it was a redback spider. "Can you…not…?"

"Drink coffee?" He took a sip, smiling.

She swallowed thickly. "The smell…I was fine a moment ago but now…"

"Morning sickness?" His smile fell as she nodded, her eyes panicky as she took another convulsive swallow. Her vulnerability chased away the gentle teasing on his tongue. Swiftly he placed the cup on the floor behind him, then closed the patio doors on it.

She took a ragged sigh. "Thanks. I'm a coffee drinker but apparently this baby hates it."

Cal automatically glanced to her waist, then back to her face. The soft morning light still bathed her, lingering on the tinge of shimmer in her curls. Seeing her this way, devoid of makeup and fancy clothes, a blush still evident on her cheeks, she truly was beautiful. Not like the over-sexual, half-dressed bodies the media portrayed as "perfect," or the expensive, skinny socialites who frequented the few glittery events he'd reluctantly attended. No, Ava's beauty was subtle and seductive, a hint of innocence in those blue eyes, combined with a lush mouth that tilted like a siren's call at the edges.

He remembered her smile, the way her throaty laugh had taken hold of his libido and squeezed.

"What?" she asked curiously, breaking his dangerous train of thought.

With ever-decreasing efficiency he reined himself in. "I'll be home at seven with the papers for you to sign."

Had he just imagined her flinch? It had come out

harsher than he'd intended but when she merely nodded in acknowledgement, he mentally shrugged it off.

"Have a good time today, Ava," he added softly before reopening the patio door, scooping up his cup and leaving her there.

Wrestling his body into submission took longer than expected, but subdue it he did. When he finally left the apartment a half hour later, he'd dressed with a lot less care than he usually reserved for his morning ritual, aided by the tingling recollection of Ava's perusal. The now-familiar irritation of being unable to switch off his thoughts put him in a bad mood for the rest of the day, flaring up whenever he was alone with only memories for company.

Finally, at 7:00 p.m., after a long, frustrating day of meetings, product reports and several cryptic messages from Victor which he'd ignored, Cal stalked into his apartment with precious little patience left.

A wall of delicious aromas slammed into him, stopping him dead. Garlic. He sniffed experimentally as his mouth began to water. Tomatoes, frying meat. He tossed his briefcase on the couch and walked into the kitchen.

The sight of Ava, barefoot in jeans, sweater and an apron, humming a melody as she stirred something in a simmering pot on his cooktop, speared him on a primitive level.

My woman. Mine.

It churned up emotion so surprising, so intense that

it slammed the breath from his lungs. The cliché—barefoot and pregnant, in his kitchen no less—no longer seemed amusing. Because when she threw him a smile and said, "Dinner's ready in five minutes," he wanted nothing more than to drag her into his bed.

"You didn't have to cook." His words came out sharp, borne from frustration and his apparent lack of control.

"I like to cook," she said calmly, her attention resolutely on the pot. "If you don't want it, you don't have to eat it."

Swallowing his retort, he sighted the groceries on the kitchen bench. "Did you order that in?"

She gave him an odd look. "No, I went to the supermarket."

"Did you carry all this?"

She rolled her eyes at the dark suspicion in his voice. "No. Your mother pushed the cart then your doorman delivered it upstairs."

"I thought you went clothes shopping."

"We did." When she offered him a platter of carrot sticks, he took one, crunching it thoughtfully. "You also needed food in your fridge."

"I have food."

"Wine, water, juice, coffee, cereal." She ticked the items off on her fingers. "No fruit, meat, dairy or vegetables."

She turned back to the pot and gave the sauce another stir, but when he remained silent she threw a look over her shoulder. "What?"

He shoved down a myriad of conflicting thoughts, smoothing his expression. "How's the nausea?"

She handed him a knife with a smile. "Gone until the morning, I suspect. Make yourself useful and cut the feta?"

At his round dining table they ate in silence, an odd half tense, half expectant silence. Cal was fully aware of every move, every sound as they devoured the spaghetti and Greek salad she'd made. The tiny scrape of fork on plate, the gentle swallow of water being sipped only amplified the quiet. When he spoke, it was like a shot.

"What did you buy today?"

She downed her fork with deliberate care. "Yes."

Cal eyed her well-worn attire but said nothing.

"A few dresses," she said stiffly. "Some jeans, shoes, skirts. A few tops and a jacket. Don't worry," she added in a small voice. "I won't embarrass you."

Damn. He'd hurt her but didn't know how to fix it, so he did the only thing he could. He let silence do the mending.

"We've had some interview requests," he finally said, placing the cutlery across his plate.

She sat back in her chair, digesting that information. "Do you expect me to give interviews?"

He shrugged. "Only if you want. There's also a bunch of glossies angling for a spread—*Vogue, Elle, Cosmo,* for starters."

"Fashion shoots." She shook her head. "That's just…surreal."

"You're now a news item. You're in demand."

"But only as your fiancée," she countered.

"I thought," Cal said slowly, "women liked getting pampered, dressed up and photographed."

"I don't do 'pampered and dressed up.'" She stood abruptly. "I'm practical, a simple country girl who wears jeans and steel-capped boots. I clean the kitchen, I cook, I wash up. I work with dirt and dig a veggie patch." In quick jerky movements, she began to clear the table. "I'm not glamorous, I'm not model material…I…I have crow's feet and dry heels!"

Her delivery was so frustratingly honest that Cal swallowed his snort of amusement. He couldn't tell if she was simply explaining herself or warning him off.

"So doing girly things scares you."

She shot him a look that lacked venom. "I didn't say that."

"Why not give it a go? You might like it."

"Do you think I might also like some interviewer digging around in my personal life for a couple of hours?"

"That," he returned, following her into the kitchen with his plate, "is where my press office comes in. I can prep you." Decision made, Cal rinsed his plate.

Needing movement, Ava wiped the sparkling benches while he stacked the dishwasher. But when everything had been cleared, tidied and returned to its drawer or shelf, there was nothing left to occupy her hands.

"Go sit outside," Cal said as he reached for the cupboard. "I'll bring you some tea."

Once alone on the balcony, the rigid composure she'd been battling drained. The warmth of the patio heater brushed her skin, a delicious contrast to the sharp bite of cold wind. She grabbed up the throw rug and wrapped it around her shoulders, tucking her feet beneath her bottom as she sat.

Like Alice down the rabbit hole, everything had changed. Gone was peace and quiet, replaced by the shiny boldness of newly acquired fame and fortune. Over lunch at a North Shore café, Isabelle had bluntly described what to expect leading up to the wedding.

"You'll be on everyone's invitation list," the older woman said in between bites of her smoked salmon sandwich. "Parties, social appearances. Requests for fashion shoots and interviews. That's the upside. The downside is less delightful but just as important."

"Rumor and innuendo?"

At Isabelle's serious nod, Ava's smile had dropped. "Yes. Imagine your worst doubts, your deepest fears plastered on the front page of every newspaper in the country. If there's anything you've ever done but don't want the press to know, they'll find it." She leaned back, fixing Ava with a steady look. "It's how you handle it that matters."

Ava shuddered. It was one thing to think the worst of herself, to harbor that black cloud of failure, but to have her insecurities publicly aired for everyone to see?

That was not going to happen.

The moment was broken by the door swooshing open. Cal stepped outside with two steaming cups and a sheaf of papers.

The contract.

He placed it and a pen in front of her, then the cup. With outward calm, she picked up the papers and flicked through them. He'd efficiently tagged the places for her signature but instead of blindly signing, she tucked them beside her on the couch. "I'll have to read this over."

He nodded, settling in the one-seater across from her, a casual version of the previous night. "Of course."

Ava snagged her cup and for a few minutes they remained silent. She'd never felt the need to fill a lull with inane chat, but Cal's presence made her acutely aware of her own, the way she looked, dressed, acted. He made her as nervous as a teenager on her first date.

"Your mother loves to shop," Ava ventured lamely.

"My mother believes shopping is a great icebreaker." He smiled, shifting his large bulk more comfortably in the seat. "It's her great people leveler."

"We *did* talk a lot."

"About?"

"Mostly me. The wedding." She deliberately omitted the topic of Cal's childhood, unwilling to betray Isabelle's generous openness. "I had no idea there were so many bridal magazines on the market."

He couldn't hide a wry grin. "I always suspected Mum was a closet wedding freak. Sorry."

"I don't mind," Ava said truthfully. The woman's enthusiasm had been appealing when she'd gifted her with a bunch of current bridal magazines in the car. *Cosmopolitan Bride, Vogue Bride, Australian Bridal Direc-*

tory, The Bride's Diary…the sheer volume of what Ava had assumed was a narrow topic made her head spin. At first it had taken all her acting skills, pitiful as they were, to smile and thank her for the gift. But Isabelle had sensed her less than enthusiastic response and had clamped a lid on her excitement, instead changing the topic to their day ahead.

And as the day passed, Ava had managed to banish the heavy reality that had settled like cement in her chest and instead found herself enjoying the outing. The subversive shine of the city had already begun to leach in, the bustle and movement exciting her in a way she'd not felt in ages.

"We have two formal functions Thursday and Friday night," Cal said, bringing her back to the present. "I assume those dresses you bought are appropriate?"

She took exception at his tone. "Cal, I'm not completely clueless. I *do* know how to dress."

"Yes." His eyes ran over her, warming her more thoroughly than the tea ever could. "I believe you do." Then he glanced away. "It'll be your first public appearance as my fiancée, so be prepared. There'll be cameras, as well as questions."

"What kind of questions?"

"Ones you'll be expected to know as my fiancée."

"Like what?"

"Well, what would you want to know?"

That threw her for a second and she scrambled. "Umm…why don't you have a computer at home?"

He shook his head. "Don't need one when I have this." He pulled the phone from his pocket and handed it to her. "The new V-Fone. It's a computer, scheduler, GPS and phone in one, all operating with One-Click software. It integrates with my work computer so I'm always contactable. We've had a one-hundred-percent customer satisfaction rating since its launch three months ago."

She ran her hand over the smooth, cold surface, marvelling at the power in such a tiny device, before handing it back. "What are your working hours like?"

He made an offhand gesture. "Long and filled with meetings, budget reports, investment strategies."

"Do you like what you do?"

"I get to travel the world and make million-dollar decisions."

"But do you *like* it?" She probed. "I'm assuming one day you'll be doing Victor's job. That's pretty different than developing software."

His smile was brief and humourless. "I've worked damn hard to earn the right. VP Tech has been my goal since I was seventeen."

"I see." He still hadn't answered her. And was it her imagination or did she sense hesitation in that smooth reply?

"I work twelve- to fourteen-hour days, Monday to Saturday," he added, almost as if trying to justify his non-answer.

"Not Sunday?"

"Sundays are for…relaxing."

She flushed at the deep timbre of his voice. "What's your favourite meal?"

"Lamb roast." The muscles in his face relaxed. "My turn." He paused, assessing her, and for a moment Ava's insides twisted at his complete and utter focus.

"What is…" he paused, "your favourite childhood movie?"

Her mouth tilted. *The Sound of Music*. Yours?"

"*The Great Escape*. What did you want to be when you grew up?"

"A ballerina—but I wasn't skinny enough."

His eyes grazed her and even beneath the throw rug, she felt her body leap in response. "You look perfectly fine to me."

He was flirting with her. But why? He'd made it perfectly clear she wasn't to be trusted, yet here he was, handing out little snippets of his inner self like party favours. It wasn't in her to question why the sudden good fortune. She just went with the flow.

As the hour ticked by into the next, they shared personal likes and dislikes—he liked action movies, she romantic comedies, they both hated cabbage and pumpkin but loved tropical fruit. After retouching on Cal's career highlights, they landed on the topic of exes.

"I've dated, no one serious," Cal said, swirling the dregs of coffee around in his mug.

"Your mother mentioned Melissa…" She paused at his sharp look.

"What did she say?"

"Just that you were engaged but called it off."

"I see." He placed his cup on the table and leaned forward, elbows resting on his knees. His face became stony and she wondered what the other woman had done to make him so defensive. "And what about you?"

Ava shrugged. "A boyfriend in high school, a couple more when I was working in Jillian's coffee shop. Since I moved back home there's been no one. Gum Tree Falls isn't exactly teeming with eligible bachelors, not like…" She snapped off, too late.

"Like Sydney."

When his eyes narrowed, she could've kicked herself. *That's a record for you, Ava. Undoing all that good work in two seconds flat.*

Cal did not trust her. The sooner she realized that, the easier this would be. Yet pride couldn't let her escape without clearing this ridiculous preconception.

"I came to Sydney for a girlfriend's birthday," she said stiffly. "It was my first time in the city. We had dinner at the Shangri-La then went on to their cocktail lounge. I wasn't looking for a boyfriend or a one-night stand or anything else that night."

"But you found me."

She rose, her face warm. "You approached *me*."

"True. But you didn't say no."

Cal watched the way her face flushed as she threw off the rug then folded it with swift efficiency.

"So now it's a crime to be flattered by a man's attentions? I just wanted one weekend, *one night* to forget about the money, the pressure, the responsibility. For one night I wasn't Will Reilly's daughter, the disappointment, the screwup. The reason for—" She bit off the rest of that sentence, as if realizing she'd said too much. Her eyes, panicky and wide, met his for one fleeting moment, then away.

"It's late," she finally mumbled, refusing to meet his gaze as she reached for the door. "I'm off to bed."

"Ava."

His command fell on deaf ears because with one small click, he was suddenly alone.

Cal remained still for what felt like hours, although his sleek Urwerk watch indicated only minutes. When he'd caught her in that slip there'd been indignation, and hurt. Could she be that good an actress?

Reluctantly, he cast his mind back to that night at the bar, searching through the events to shed some light on his confusion.

At first she'd been wary, even suspicious. His smooth offer to buy her a drink had been met with reluctant acceptance. As they'd shared flirtatious but cryptic details about themselves, she'd gradually warmed to him, enough to have her willing and eager in his bed.

For one crazy second, he let himself indulge in the remembrance of her smile that tilted her mouth into kissable curves, her husky feminine laugh.

What the hell was he supposed to believe?

With a low curse he sprung to his feet and slammed

back inside. The cool shower didn't bring clarity, nor did lying in bed, staring at the LED clock hands as it ticked off the minutes until sunrise.

Six

At one-thirty the next afternoon, Cal braked his car with an irritated yank out the front of his apartment building. He may have stopped grilling Victor about this marriage ultimatum but the man wasn't off the hook yet. Throughout their mid-morning meeting Cal had been icily distant, and as a result the other board members had picked up on the tension. Yet afterwards, instead of calling him on it, Victor had left as swiftly as he'd arrived.

Dammit. With a grunt, he rubbed his temples then glared across at the double glass doors. His normally austere doorman was chatting with a gorgeous dark-haired woman, the old Scotsman sporting a look of rapt adoration on his weathered face.

Then Ava glanced across and spotted him.

All thoughts fled as last night came crashing back, rolling waves breaching his temporary sandbank.

If he'd been enthralled yesterday in the early morning light, now he was riveted. Like some slow-motion teenage movie close-up, the afternoon sun captured her in its singular glow as she walked out to greet him. She looked like every man's fantasy, from the toes of her black knee-high boots up past the flippy hem of the black skirt barely grazing her knees to the scooped neck of her clingy black sweater. A bright sky-blue trench coat flapped loosely like she'd just flashed someone and her hair bounced over her shoulders in twin shiny black waves, catching the sunlight in raven glints.

His throat went dry, his mouth curving into an automatic smile until he caught sight of an expensively suited man unashamedly eyeing her butt as she walked past. A fierce bolt of ownership surged up, ending in a possessive growl as he glared at the man. The starer merely shrugged, smiled apologetically and kept right on walking.

Ava's glossy smile curved shyly as she reached for the door handle. "Hi."

"Hi, yourself." Even with eyes hidden behind fashionably round sunglasses, he sensed the unease as she buckled up. "You look…"

"Acceptable?"

"Gorgeous." Cal checked his rear vision mirror, barely catching her flush. "You should dress like that more often."

"Unfortunately, Jindalee isn't too kind on dresses and suede."

"Then it's a good thing we're in Sydney until the weekend. Give those jeans and steel-capped boots a breather."

Her cautious laugh warmed him and they grinned at each other, staying that way for seconds too long, too long to maintain the neutrality of the mood. Cal finally broke the moment, swiftly glancing back over his shoulder before pulling into the traffic.

Ava held her breath, unwilling to break this fragile truce. The man not only developed powerful computer programs, his mind *was* a computer. No doubt he remembered every detail of their conversations, every word both spoken and implied. Yet as Cal shifted gears and the car smoothly eased into second, her jangling nerves began to relax. It was a calming flipside to the last few days' hostility and distrust.

Ava didn't believe in blind optimism, but when she turned her face towards the warm sunshine as they sped across the Harbour Bridge, hope began to spark deep inside. It was…encouraging.

"Based on what you've told me, your due date is the ninth of January." Dr. Wong smiled as he lifted the wand from Ava's stomach. "We can usually tell the baby's sex from about eighteen weeks." He paused, turned a few buttons on the foetal monitor and then pointed to the screen. "Right now, we're just ensuring everything's on track and the baby's forming at the correct rate. There you go."

The exam room was deathly silent, the cool air-conditioned cavern punctuated only by the tiny bleeps and clicks as Dr. Wong took stills from the monitor.

"Just look at that," Ava finally breathed.

Cal remained transfixed on the monitor, at the grey and white snow that indicated a tiny life grew within Ava's belly. He hardly heard the doctor's murmur, the soft snick of the door as the man gave them a private moment alone. His heart was beating way too hard, his blood pounding through every vein in his chest.

Come the new year, he'd be a father. An unexpected flash of something so big, so powerful jumped him from the shadows and left him floundering under the weight. Blindly, he glanced down and Ava's eyes, full of wonder and amazement, undid him all over again.

She was lying on the table, half-covered in a sheet, her skirt rucked up high beneath her breasts. And below that, the soft white skin of her belly, the gentle curve almost imperceptible. He was drawn to her, almost as if he couldn't help himself. It felt natural, right, that he bend down and cover her trembling mouth in a gentle kiss.

And the oddest thing happened. Everything stuttered to a halt.

It seemed like the world had stopped for one amazing second. Ava's breath caught in her throat, astonishment rendering her limbs immobile, until she felt her eyes close, her limbs languidly relaxing into the tender kiss.

Cal had kissed her with bruising urgency before, with uncontrollable passion specifically designed to arouse. But this…this…soft pressure of his warm mouth on hers, almost loving in its gentleness, tightened something deep within until she felt the telltale prick of tears behind her lids.

She barely had time to breathe in the scent of leather, shaving cream and coffee that was so uniquely Cal before it was over, too soon. When he drew back, her eyes flew open, a tiny sound of disappointment rattling in her throat. "Cal…"

His answer was throaty and hoarse. "If you want me to apologise for that—"

"No." She shook her head. "No. It was—" *Amazing. Wonderful.* "—fine."

In the cool, sterile room, she was acutely aware of her semi-nakedness, of her uncovered belly, still wet with the remnants of the ultrasound gel. "Can you pass me a paper towel?"

As if grateful for movement, he turned to the dispenser, grabbed a few towels and handed them over. "I'll wait for you in the lounge." He swiftly pulled out his mobile and in record time was out the door.

Ava frowned. One minute he'd been kissing her, the next he was gone. It was like flicking off a switch, the way he could tease her emotions into tentative expectation then firmly close the door in her face.

With a sigh she finished cleaning up, straightened her clothes and scooped up the pictures the doctor had printed out. The damnable truth was she wanted him to kiss her, wanted him to touch her. Wanted him to ease the aching throb in her body and make sweet love to her.

She opened the door, silently watching Cal as he clicked through his messages. He didn't trust her, they both knew that. Yet she couldn't stop herself wanting him. And therein lay the paradox—how could she want a man who didn't want *her*?

The riddle stuck in her brain for the rest of the day, until she finally forced it away while making cheese-and-pickle sandwiches for dinner.

"Don't cook tonight," Cal had said after he'd dropped her back at his apartment. "I'll be late, so I'll grab something on the way home."

It didn't take a genius to work out the subtext. Ava speared the pickle with vicious intent. *Don't get too comfortable, and don't expect to play happy families.* Well, she wouldn't. For the best part of the afternoon she'd moped around the apartment until her lower back had demanded movement and she'd finally turned off Oprah. Dressed in a blue designer tracksuit that Isabelle had declared matched her eyes, she'd gone for a walk.

The massive spread of suburbia, concrete and noise still overwhelmed and she quickly bypassed the white majesty of the Opera House and headed for the Botanical Gardens instead. For an hour she strolled the lush green lawns and abundant flora until it became clear her presence had attracted unwanted attention.

Being surreptitiously pointed out in loud whispers,

followed by the click of cell phones, was a novelty she didn't care to repeat. Now, as she sat on the balcony and bit into the sandwich, the sharp tang of pickle juice jolted her taste buds. It shouldn't matter that she was low on Cal's priorities, yet it still didn't stop her insides from twisting. He was a businessman and had made an offer based on pure business.

But a child wasn't a business deal.

The sandwich churned in her stomach and she dropped it back on the plate. She may not be top on his list, but instinct told her this baby was. Even if Cal didn't realize it, his reaction at the doctor's gave her hope. It meant that it was a start, however tiny.

It was Saturday night and Ava ignored the throbbing ache in her high-heeled feet and instead pasted a smile on her subtly made-up face. Last night it was a charity event, tonight a glitzy book launch. Two completely different causes yet identical undercurrents, identical partygoers. Decked out in jewels and couture, the women were mostly blond, always tanned and perennially skinny, despite the champagne many downed like seasoned drinkers. The men were expensively attired, oozing privileged wealth and indulgence.

On Cal's arm, Ava felt like the new guppy in the fishbowl, a thousand curious eyes directly squarely on her. Their curiosity had taken many guises—some disbelief, some barely hidden animosity. A few, like tonight's guest of honor, had expressed actual happiness and like a much-needed gulp of water to her drought-stricken mouth, she'd returned the congratulations with genuine warmth.

"You need to do more of that," Cal murmured, a soft rumble in her ear that sent quivers across her skin.

"What?"

"Smile more."

"I am," she replied tightly, her smile still firmly in place.

Cal rolled his eyes. "Now it just looks like you ate a bad prawn."

She snorted out a laugh, one quickly engulfed in the buzz of the fast-growing crowd.

"I can tell you're faking, even if everyone else is fooled," Cal added, his mouth close to her ear. She could feel his warm breath on her sensitive flesh and she clamped down on her bottom lip, stifling a groan.

"I've been to more parties this last week than in my whole life, not to mention the primping and preening and smiling at complete strangers," she muttered back. Many of whom were shallow, appearance-obsessed and way too interested in her cleavage, she realized with a sinking stomach. "And my feet hurt," she added for good measure.

"Do you need to sit?"

Contrition gnawed as she caught the flash of concern on his face. "No," she sighed. Her head still whirled from the million congratulations and curious questions about how and when they met, to the inevitable wedding day. If she heard one more barely dressed woman coyly ask Cal, "When's the big day?" while pointedly ignoring her, she was going to scream.

"Congratulations, Cal. Have you set a date?"

Through the fabric of his Italian suit, Cal felt Ava stiffen, her fingers tightening imperceptibly on his arm. Her face, however, creased into politeness as he introduced the two women.

"Charmed, sweetie." Shannon Curtis-Stein smiled insincerely, her tanned ice-blond figure poured into a black flapper-style dress. Although, Cal conceded, the plunging neckline was hardly in keeping with the era.

Next to all these sleek peacocks, parading their finery and gym-honed bodies with utter confidence, Ava was a breath of fresh air. There'd been a moment when they'd walked into the Hilton's function room and she'd hesitated, staring at the assembled throng as panic skittered across her face. As usual, the women were wearing variations of a familiar theme—short clingy dresses with shoestring straps that showed heaps of leg or toned, muscular backs. Sometimes both. In comparison, Ava's long, floaty strapless silver gown was distinctly elegant. Regal, even. Ignoring the buzz under his skin that had become second nature whenever Ava was around, he'd linked his hand in hers and gave it a reassuring squeeze. And when she'd met his eyes with jaw set, clear blue eyes serious, he knew she wasn't going to buckle.

That's my girl.

He started. Where the hell had that come from? Admiration, yeah, okay. Facing this crowd was a daunting prospect for anyone, let alone a girl from the bush. But laying claim like she was something to own, something exclusively his when they both knew the real truth?

She glanced up at him now and gave him that familiar smile, a shy lip-tilt full of barely hidden apprehension. Even with her body ramrod straight, shoulders back, that smile gave her away every time.

This wasn't a woman in control—she was petrified.

Her hand tightened in his, her breath whooshing out as she breathed deeply. She was way out of her depth, and she knew it. How the hell had he missed that? Her eyes revealed more than she realized from the deep, burning anger at his demands to the desperate control when she'd faced Victor.

It had taken days to realize she couldn't hide her emotions any more than he could stop himself from touching her.

And just like that, his mind cleared. Man, he could stare at her for hours, the way her bare shoulders curved, the elegant sweep of her neck, displayed by her hair piled high. Under his scrutiny, a wayward curl fell, brushing her shoulder in a gentle, teasing kiss.

"You need a necklace to complement your dress," he murmured. "Something that would sit just about—" he drew his fingers sensuously across her collarbone and she gasped "—here."

He paused, his palm a brand on her warm décolletage, unashamedly laying claim. A satisfied smile tugged at his mouth as her eyes widened and her heart-beat upped tempo beneath his hand.

He leaned in, propelled by a desperate urge to follow his hand's path, barely registering Shannon's derisive snort and departure in a whirl of expensive perfume. If he remembered correctly, Ava made the most erotic sound when he licked that sensitive flesh…

She shifted back, a small protest quelling his intent, bringing him back to the present. The noise from the party hit him full-on, as if he'd spent the past few minutes in a sound void and someone had just cranked up the volume.

"What do you think?" He recovered swiftly, only slightly annoyed by the huskiness in his voice.

"I think I feel like an overfed, ruffled sparrow."

At his confusion, she added with a small gesture to the crowd, "Not enough gloss, not enough sophistication."

"You're kidding, right?"

She looked irritated. "No. These women are all perfect. Perfect straight hair, perfect bodies, perfect smiles."

At a loss, he captured her arms and firmly turned her to face him, her back to the crowd. "Name one."

"Lisette Warner," she returned without hesitation.

"She cheats on her husband."

Ava's eyes widened. "Joy Falkner."

"Shallow and bitchy."

"Shannon Curtis-Stein."

"Oh, that's obvious. She's had a boob job."

Her mouth tweaked. "I thought men liked boobs."

"I don't know about 'men,' but fake doesn't do it for me." He couldn't stop himself from eyeing her neckline, modest by the crowd's standards but still affording him a gentle swelling tease of her creamy flesh.

Memory flashed. He recalled the familiar softness of her skin, the way it tasted beneath his hands, his mouth. He didn't have to close his eyes to picture the way her nipples had puckered as he'd gently sucked on them— and as he stared, he saw the imperceptible outline of them now, tightening beneath the snug satin of her dress.

Good Lord. He snapped his eyes up, barely catching her flush of embarrassment before she offered him her profile.

"Trust me, Ava, elegance and style beat skin and bleach every time. Not that there's anything wrong with a little skin…" his voice dipped lower as he leaned in, his mouth temptingly close to her ear, "at the right time."

She slid him a glance, her eyes wide and dark, pupils dilated. Then in the next second, she looked away, her soft breathy intake confirming his suspicion.

He knew arousal when he saw it. Hell, he could practically smell it on her, above and beyond that now-familiar innocent/seductive fragrance she always wore. Despite the thousand reasons why he'd convinced himself to keep his distance, his body began to throb in earnest.

He'd set the boundaries of their relationship and Ava had agreed, so when had the chains of that restriction begun to chafe? Last night he'd had to stop himself from testing the softness of her hair, had paused halfway to place his hand on her belly, a belly that had gently rounded in the past few days. That doctor's appointment had only exacerbated his awareness of his baby growing inside her.

He'd been hell-bent on keeping a physical distance, yet like every big mistake, his downfall had started out small. Last night, as they'd walked into their first official event as an engaged couple, she'd tentatively linked her fingers in his and the blast of guilty pleasure had staggered him. A touch reluctantly given, yet initiated in a moment of desperation, to give her courage. A touch more intimate than a kiss. Her vulnerability simultaneously humbled and aroused him.

So he'd tested his boundaries as they'd mingled with the cream of Sydney society, waiting for her withdrawal as he'd stroked her arm, played with the hair at her nape. She'd jumped the first few times, surprise reflected in her eyes, but eventually that had melted into acceptance. Even welcome, judging by her body's response.

He snaked his arm around her waist now, bringing her hip firmly against him as his hand gently cupped her elbow.

"Cal…"

"What?" He briefly glanced across the room before coming back to her. "We're a happily engaged couple. We're expected to—" he paused, his fingers stroking the sensitive flesh in the crook of her elbow "—touch."

She attempted a laugh, but it came out all shaky and nervous. "You're giving me goosebumps."

He grinned, enjoying her discomfiture way too much. "I hope so. What perfume are you wearing?"

When Cal's voice came, deep and sinful in her ear, Ava trembled.

"Nothing," she managed to croak. "I don't wear perfume."

"Then why," he paused and dipped his head, his jaw barely grazing her neck and sending her eyelids into languid descent, "do you smell so delicious?"

Her body flushed hot, heart kicking hard. "It's called layering…" She ended on a gasp as his murmur of appreciation rumbled over the sensitive spot just below her earlobe. "Body wash," she continued bravely, barely forming the words. "Lotion, body spray. It's…" a sharp intake of breath as his lips gently nibbled on her neck, "Jasmine and peach. Cal, please."

"Mmm?"

She darted her eyes around the crowd. "People are staring."

"No, they're not." His arm tightened around her waist, pinning her to him and she gasped, feeling the evidence of his arousal beneath their clothes.

"Cal," she said firmly, pasting on a gentle smile to appease any casual observers to their exchange. "As much as I appreciate your 'happily engaged couple' act, you really need to stop."

His whole body went completely still.

"I didn't realize you were uncomfortable with my attentions."

And just like that, there was a universe between them.

He may have left his arm around her waist but Ava felt the exact moment he mentally withdrew. The set to his jaw, the cool way his eyes glanced at her then back to the party, made her want to reverse time and take everything back.

She lifted her chin, refusing to let her disappointment show. This was real life, not the movies. He wasn't about to fall desperately in love with her just because she was having his child. If anything, their circumstances only exacerbated distrust, and given what Isabelle had revealed about his past, she didn't really blame him or—

Shock and confusion caught in her throat, rattling around for a few agonising seconds before she slowly exhaled. *No, no way. Cal Prescott didn't fall in love, least of all with someone he didn't trust.*

She eased her weight from one foot then the other, a movement Cal's eagle eyes didn't miss.

"Tired?"

A second ago he'd been aloof, even angry. Now he radiated nothing but solicitousness. A shard of emotion pierced her composure, shocking her. Was she actually *jealous* of her unborn child? It was irrational and shallow but there it was. The baby in her belly—not her—provoked awe, tenderness, concern. She might just as well be an incubator.

"Ava? Are you okay?"

She nodded, unable to speak past the emotion clogging her throat.

"Okaaay." His gaze became unreadable. "Our flight's at eight tomorrow. You want to go home?"

Home. She glanced around the crowded room, at the warm press of strangers laughing, drinking and talking, and felt a pang of homesickness so deep it made her chest ache. "Yes. I want to go home."

He gave her an odd look before placing his hand on her back. "Then let's go."

Seven

The next morning, parked outside VP Tech in Cal's car, a call of nature forced Ava into the foyer in search of a bathroom. His "I'll be a few minutes" was well on its way to fifteen by the time the smiling security guard directed her past the elevators to the restrooms at the far end.

Ava stared at herself in the full-length bathroom mirror. Money shouldn't change who a person was, but right now, seeing this unfamiliar glamorous woman staring back at her, she wasn't so sure. Her hair, usually tied back in a simple ponytail, was now glossy and loose around her shoulders. The faded jeans had been replaced by a long-sleeved shirtdress, the short hem showing off her legs in fashionably high heels. Her face, her skin…she leaned in and blinked under the unforgiving lighting. Her eyes were wider, expertly emphasised with the help of Napoleon Perdis and Isabelle's personal makeup stylist. Her mouth was positively pouty, the rich berry shade matching her dress.

Ava pulled back with a frown. She wasn't Ava Reilly, daughter of William and Bernadette, owner of Jindalee. She was…

"Cal Prescott's fiancée." She paused, then gave an overly bright smile to her reflection. "Hello, I'm Ava Prescott." She took a breath and stepped back. "I'm Mrs. Ava Prescott. Mrs. Ava Reilly-Prescott. Oh, ugh." With a moue of distaste she whirled and shoved the door open with her shoulder.

But just as she was about to round the frosted glass wall, Victor's angry voice pulled her up short.

"You ignore my calls and now you're off back to the bush," Victor was saying, the tinge of derision unmistakable. "The woman's bankrupt. Surely that should tell you something?"

Ava held her breath, cheeks flushing. When Cal spoke, the sharp edges in his clipped reply were unmissable.

"What I do with *my* money is none of your business, Victor."

"But your time is. We have a dozen important meetings coming up this month, not to mention courting those American buyers." Another pause, then Victor added more calmly, "You know your time is money. You can't go jetting off to the back of beyond when you're CEO. It's neither acceptable nor necessary."

"Pot calling the kettle, Victor? You've been absent at least three times in as many weeks."

There was a long, awkward moment. "That's got nothing to do with the company," Victor finally said stiffly.

"And who I'm marrying does?"

That was it. Ava straightened her shoulders, shoved on her sunglasses, then closed the bathroom door with a loud click.

As expected, Victor and Cal had fallen silent when she came into their line of sight. From behind her sunglasses, Ava ignored the thick tension and gave a breezy smile. "Hello, Mr. Prescott," she acknowledged coolly. "How are you?"

"Fine."

For once, his curt reply didn't intimidate her. She'd learned a lot about handling rude people these past few days so instead, she looped her arm around Cal's in casual intimacy. After the debacle of last night, her skin jumped with unexpected joy.

"Bathroom break," she said, holding out his car keys.

Despite the layers of clothing, she felt the unmistakable heat from honed muscle just before his arm bunched beneath her touch. Yet his expression was unreadable, as if he'd shut everything down.

Victor finally spoke. "Take another week to finalize this…project." He barely flicked a glance towards Ava. "But remember VP Tech is your first priority."

"You don't need to remind me about priorities, Victor."

A look passed between the two men but Ava was too disturbed to pay it any attention. *Of course the company was his first priority.* It was a fantasy to think she'd actually pondered giving in to her body's demands, that some time in the last few days she thought Cal had begun to believe she was incapable of the deceit and that they'd had a chance of making this sham marriage work.

She swallowed the throbbing hurt, taking a few seconds to gather her racing thoughts, to smooth her expression into something resembling neutrality.

Victor's gruff voice brought her back to the present.

"Isabelle wants to throw you an engagement party."

Cal grimaced. "I don't have—"

"You're getting married and your mother wants to celebrate it."

Ava felt Cal tense again just before he nodded and turned, steering her towards the door. "Fine. Jenny will let you know what day suits. Now if you'll excuse us? We have a plane to catch."

Two hours later, Ava watched Cal take in Gum Tree Falls, seeing it through his eyes for the first time as they drove through: the single main street in all its unapologetic outback glory, old weather-beaten stores, cracked guttering that flanked the potholed bitumen road. The rolling hills in the distance, covered with native gum trees and bushland scrub, and the grazing sheep that were the lifeblood of the small country town.

Sydney felt like a century away, not just a half-hour flight and twenty minute drive from Parkes, the closest town that could pass for civilisation.

The ties of the past reached in, entwining around her chest, constricting her breath. And suddenly she was seventeen all over again, desperate to escape the chains of her youth. If she closed her eyes now, she could hear the gentle whispers starting up, a thousand buzzing flies swarming in her head.

"What does 'Jindalee' mean?" Cal asked, breaking through her thoughts.

She studied him as he drove, a picture of wealthy, sunglasses-clad confidence at the wheel of this top-of-the-line hire car. "It's Aboriginal for 'one-tree hill.' See?" She pointed to the main house, then the massive gum tree a hundred meters away. "My father built on the one hill he didn't have to deforest."

"He was a conservationist?"

Her mouth twisted as they pulled into Jindalee's parking area. "No. Less labour, therefore, less cost."

Cal said nothing, instead dragging on the handbrake and killing the engine. Last time he'd barely had a chance to notice his surroundings. Now he swung open his door and took a long sweeping look.

From the outside, the homestead fitted every sense of the word—walls made from large slabs and roughly mortared, topped with an olive-green corrugated roof. A wooden porch that ran right around the house. Two large plant pots with wild greenery flanked the wooden steps that led up to massive wooden double doors. A small wrought-iron table and two chairs sat to the left of the entrance; and on the right a wooden loveseat covered in a long, colourful cushion.

As Cal reached in to remove their bags, the doors opened and a small, elderly woman emerged. When he straightened, the woman and Ava were deep in conversation, their heads side by side in comfortable intimacy.

The woman gently swept her hand across Ava's belly and said something, prompting Ava to laugh. That small, simple reaction seemed to relax her body and for one moment, he felt a shot of something race through his chest. Yet when Ava turned to include him in the welcome, he remained rooted to the spot. Since last night the strain between them had been palpable and he was unwilling to exacerbate that by intruding on the moment.

Ava's half curious, half confused frown finally propelled him forward.

"Cal, this is Aunt Jillian."

Jillian's welcoming hug was like being wrapped in a comforting blanket. Like Ava she only came to his shoulder, but the genuine warmth in her embrace shone through, creasing her face into a smile.

"Welcome to Jindalee, Cal. I just wish you had more time to settle in before…" She looked at Ava apologetically. "Sorry, darling. Lord knows how she knew you were coming. I couldn't get her to leave—"

"Don't worry, Aunt Jill." Ava stroked her arm. To Cal

she added, "You're about to get a crash course in small-town curiosity." Then she glanced over his shoulder, pasting on a too-bright smile. "Anne! How are you?"

Cal turned to see a thin, middle-aged woman descend the stairs. Her greying hair was wound up into a wobbling bun as she fast-walked over to them, her long face split wide with a smile.

"Look at you, Ava! All dolled up like some fancy city wife-to-be! I heard you'd gotten yourself engaged to a Sydney man and came to see with my own eyes."

Cal noticed the way Ava suffered the cheek kiss before pointedly pulling back. The woman didn't notice anything amiss though, because she turned to Cal and kept right on talking.

"I'm so thrilled Ava finally managed to find herself a man. I don't have to tell you what a wild little thing she was. Born and raised in the Falls, just like me, but Ava, well, she's been a little cracker from day one. It's kept the whole town entertained, wondering what she'll get up to next!" She paused to laugh, oblivious that she was the only amused one. "Let me see, when she was five, she was bitten by a redback, then the following year, a cattle dog—"

"Anne," interrupted Jillian, but the other woman was on a roll.

"Oh, and skinny dipping in Reilly Dam when she was twelve. Then of course, there was the Dean incident," she added sotto voce, "and let's not even mention—"

"Let's not," Ava said sharply.

Startled, Anne blinked then quickly stuttered, "but you came good in the end!" She beamed, giving Ava a shoulder hug and shaking her firmly for good measure, unaware of Ava's frozen expression. "I'm Anne Flanagan, by the way."

She offered her hand to Cal and he shook it. "Cal Prescott."

"Prescott?" Anne smiled indulgently at Ava. "I read that but thought it was a typo. 'Surely that can't be our Ava,' I said to Jillian. 'Isn't that the name of the VP Tech billionaire?'"

Cal couldn't quite hide a self-satisfied smile. "That's me. Victor Prescott is my father."

For one amused second he thought the woman would faint but Jillian swooped in to take Anne's arm, steering her to her car. "It's nearly nine. Don't you have to open the café?"

"Oh, yes!" Anne fluttered, digging in her purse for her keys. "And after you're both settled in, come on over and I'll fix you up coffee and scones, on the house. No, Ava, I won't take no for an answer!" She opened the car door and beamed at them both. "Fancy that—a billionaire. You did well, Ava! Toodles!"

And then she was gone in a roar of dust.

Cal noticed Jillian had moved back towards the house, giving them privacy. Ava stood stock still, her back to him, facing the now-empty road as dust settled around them, until finally another car crested the rise, destroying the awkward moment.

"Well." Ava suddenly turned. "There's your team. Let's go in and get started, shall we?"

The too-polite smile stretched her mouth wide, emphasising the odd sheen in her eyes before she blinked it away. She looked so alone yet so defiantly rigid that the urge to wrap her in his arms was almost like a physical ache.

"Ava."

"What?" She reached into the hire car and retrieved her handbag, swinging it onto her shoulder before facing him. She just stood there, looking gorgeous and classy in that red dress and black coat, brittle control barely holding her expression together. He recognized the familiar act, the one where you pretend everything's normal even when it was damn well not.

"We'll have to use my office," she said brightly. "No doubt Jillian's already seen to lunch and the tea breaks."

Her gaze held his, challenging him. With an inward sigh, he let it go with a nod.

Yet as she clicked up the front steps, his eyes followed her. He'd get an explanation from her. Later.

They're guests, Ava told herself as Cal and his team followed her down the path to Jindalee's guest houses. *Just guests asking for a tour.* No need to panic, no need to get nervous. She managed to remain calm and professional as she led them through the rooms, the kitchen, the dining area. But when it came time to settle into her office and pick apart just exactly where she'd gone wrong, those butterflies rushed up, fluttering crazily in her chest.

After the meeting paused for lunch, Ava sat in her chair, her brain buzzing from everything they'd discussed. As the others gathered outside to debate the value of the amazing view, she and Cal were alone, the only sound the nervous in-out-in click of the pen beneath her thumb. When he pointedly glanced up from his papers, she flushed and shoved the pen across the table.

Had she actually worried about losing control of the one thing that was still hers? Cal's staff—Judy Neumann, Margie Mason and Jack Portelli—were professional and experienced, from suggesting color schemes and menu changes to creating a larger Internet presence and a membership incentive card.

Her head spun with information overload and, lethargy forgotten, she scraped back her chair, went over to the low filing cabinet and poured herself a glass of juice. Cal had confidently presented this multi-million-dollar overhaul with the bottomless pockets of the Prescott name behind him. His team had enthusiastically gone through the proposal and she'd found herself seduced by their ideas, their energy. And when she'd glanced at Cal, she had been struck by his encouraging nods and satisfied smile at their presentation. He entered discussions but knew when to step back. He made suggestions and then let her make the final decisions. He had a way with his staff that didn't stifle their creativity, didn't step on toes and more importantly, let them take the lead while still maintaining control.

He may be a tech geek, but the man was a natural with people, too.

"What do you think?"

Ava looked up, startled to find Cal standing beside her. "I'm amazed they came up with all this in such a short time. I'm very impressed, but—"

"What?"

"Do you really think marketing Jindalee as an exclusive health spa retreat will work?" She palmed the bottom of her glass, fingers wrapping around the cold condensation. "Wouldn't the rich and famous rather party all night in a big city?"

His mouth quirked. "There are some who're interested in an authentic outback experience."

"With feather canopy beds and spa treatments?"

"Our focus group wants the facade without the gritty reality. At Jindalee they'll be fed, pampered and waited on, with this as their backdrop." He swept his arm wide to encompass the unfettered view from the huge window. Mile upon mile of gently undulating hills backed him up, stark against the bright blue sky. The gum trees swayed as grey storm clouds massed in the far distance, threatening rain.

"But what you're suggesting…" She turned back to the table and picked up the floor plans. "Treatment rooms, mud baths, indoor spa and sauna—it would double Jindalee's size. We'd have to apply for building permits, not to mention shutting the place down for months."

Cal shrugged, unfazed. "The permits aren't a problem, not when we'll be creating local jobs. And it's not as if you're making a profit, so shutting down isn't an issue."

Her face flushed. "It's not just about making a profit, Cal. This place is more than bricks and mortar to me."

With one fluid movement, he crossed his arms and put his shoulder to the wall. His long fingers gently tapped one defined bicep, his expression thoughtful. She could get lost in those eyes—intelligent, assessing eyes that constantly reminded her of the decadent hours they'd shared.

"So let me make Jindalee into something unforgettable," he finally said.

She turned back to the window, placing the forgotten juice on the cabinet. "It's already unforgettable."

"But not profitable, which is what you need."

She frowned, studying her reflection in the tinted glass. "What's it all going to cost?"

"Don't worry." She glanced back and his eyes locked onto hers. "I don't renege on a deal, Ava. I said whatever it takes. This is it."

Before she could say anything further, he straightened and reached for his jacket. "Let's take a break and you can show me the town."

"Tell me I wasn't in the Twilight Zone back there."

Ava gave him a pained look as he guided her back up Jindalee's front steps, his hand a now-familiar warmth on her back. "Welcome to my life."

"They're like a bunch of gossiping high schoolers. Can't they talk about anything else than what you did ten years ago?"

"Like rising feed prices, the continuing drought…. The latest brand of stock whip? Not half as much fun as placing bets on what I'll do to screw up next."

Her footfalls echoed on the decking as she went over to the long wooden bench. Cal recognised the tension pulling at her shoulders as she sank into the cushions with a sigh. She was wound up enough to make his own muscles ache in sympathy. Not the type of person tough enough to play out a ruthless game of blackmail. In fact, if he were completely honest, her whole demeanour under pressure had been contrary to every assumption he'd made.

Irritated, he said shortly, "So why didn't you leave?"

"My father built Jindalee from nothing."

"That's not an answer." He leaned against the porch railing.

She sighed, a deeply troubled sound. "I lived with Jill in Parkes for a few years, working at her café, but I still missed this place. Just look around." She indicated the scenery with the small lift of her chin. "This place is…powerful and humbling. It's extreme—flash storms one day, glorious sunshine the next. It's welcoming, familiar. Beautiful." She fixed her eyes on him, stormy and honest. "Why do I stay? Because of this." Her arm swept out, encompassing everything around them. "It's about the glory of a morning sunrise, when it feels like there's no one else in the world. It's about the tranquillity of a warm summer night. It's something—" she paused, struggling to find the words "—almost spiri-

tual." She gave a small smile. "I'm not very good at describing it, am I?"

"It's about finding peace within the land."

Dumbfounded at his perception, Ava nodded. "That's
right. It's about the land, not those people in town."

"So why not give them something positive to talk
about? Let me make Jindalee that something, Ava," he
added seriously.

Ava swallowed a throbbing heartbeat as her breath
caught. The sheer command, the utter confidence in his
intense gaze was dangerously hypnotic. *So this is how
it feels.* To be rescued. Like she was a fifteenth-century
damsel saved from marauding invaders by the powerful,
heroic knight.

All she could do was nod again until the threatening
rumble of distant thunder forced her gaze skyward.

"It's going to rain." She rose to her feet and reached
for the door. Every inch of her skin seemed to tingle as
he followed her in, her body leaping to life despite her
desperation to ignore it.

If the morning had been a whirlwind of emotion, the
rest of the day was torture, like her senses were playing
some horrible game of "I told you so." When she looked
at Cal, she not only remembered those lips kissing her.
Now she recalled the way he'd used his daunting
presence to preempt all those nosy questions in town.
Staring at the conference table only brought his hands
into her eyeline—hands with long, teasing fingers that

knew how to touch, stroke. Caress. She couldn't even block him out by focussing out the window because she could still hear that sinful, liquid, caramel-chocolate-honey voice, constantly reminding her of erotic whispers, satisfied sighs.

The meeting finally broke up at six. With Cal finishing up in the office, Ava showed everyone out, shaking their hands with a bright smile and thanking them for their efforts. But the instant she closed the door, exhaustion rushed in.

Cal found her there, sagging into the heavy door with her forehead against the dark wood. Her shoes had been replaced by comfortable slippers, her sleeves were rolled up and her lipstick was long gone. She'd swept her tumble of hair into a sloppy ponytail and it now dragged down her back with a few tendrils loose and curling over her shoulder.

The present suddenly slammed into the past, creating a sharp, aching desire that went straight to his groin. He'd felt her eyes on him all afternoon, as if he were part of some intensive study. Yet when he'd glanced her way, she'd avoided his questioning gaze.

"Are you okay?"

She jerked upright, almost guiltily, before turning to him and smoothing back her hair. "Just tired."

"Then come and sit down."

She looked at his outstretched hand, then quickly back at him as if waiting for the catch. The doubt on her face twisted his gut.

"Come on."

With obvious reluctance, she took his hand. As he folded his fingers around her cold ones, warmth sliced into him.

"Are you hungry?" she asked faintly as he led her down the hall towards the living area. He could feel the pulse beat steadily beneath the delicate skin on her wrist.

"Not really. You?"

She gave him a quick smile. "Starving."

He made a detour and they ended up in the kitchen. Cal pulled out a chair and encouraged her to sit as he opened the fridge.

"You don't have to cook for me. I can—"

"No," he said with a decisive shake of his head. "I think I can manage a microwave."

She smiled back, an innocent response that still succeeded in kicking up his heart rate. "There's soup on the bottom shelf."

Ten minutes later he presented her with hot tomato soup and thick toast before settling in the chair opposite. Since last night he'd begun to recall more things, disturbing things that were contrary to his original assessment of this woman. It wasn't only the inbuilt elegance, the expressive eyes. It was in her tiny, unselfconscious movements, like the way she nervously shoved her hair back, or when she straightened her shoulders in firm determination.

If it was all an act, he should've seen the cracks by now.

"Something's been bugging me."

She paused, the spoon half way to her lips. "About?"

"You."

She flushed and placed the spoon back in the bowl, waiting his next move.

"Tell me about your sister," he finally said. "What was she like?"

Her eyes spilled sudden emotions before she efficiently gathered them back up. "Grace was…" She smiled. "Beautiful. Poised. Well-mannered. She wanted to be a fashion designer, a painter, a vet. She finally settled on psychology, of all things. And she would've been damn good at it, too. She radiated humor and joy. Everyone adored her. She was the good one, the angel."

By her own omission, Cal drew the assumption. "And you weren't."

She stirred her soup absently. "I was her polar opposite."

"You got the blame for her death."

Her eyes snapped to his. "I wasn't charged," she said almost defiantly.

He met her probing stare head-on and a moment later, she nodded, as if coming to an important decision. "The crash was my fault. It was dark and I was speeding."

Underneath her brittle expression he recognised the desperate need to belong, to be accepted for who she was, not defined by what she'd done or who her father had been. With a start, Cal realized that was him at twelve, uprooted from his mediocre life and transported into a different universe where wealth and privilege ruled. Yes, Sydney society had its gossipmongers, but money talked louder. The Prescott name demanded respect. Here they treated Ava like a misfit child, pointing out her screwups under the guise of humour, not allowing her to forget.

Once he'd given a damn what others thought of him, once he'd been desperate for a father figure, to make his own way, to be someone. It stunned him to realize that thanks to Victor's ultimatum he was still trying to prove himself.

"My father stopped speaking to me," she said now. "I lived with Jillian for five years until my mother got sick."

"He kicked you out because of an accident?" He scowled.

"No, he kicked me out two months before when I refused to stop seeing a boy he disliked. The Dean situation," she clarified, crossing her arms on the table. "One day I convinced Grace to sneak out and go shopping. I was driving her back home, it was late and we came across the back paddock after dark. I took a crest too fast and crashed in a ditch."

Ava took a breath, noting the scowl on Cal's face had deepened, but she was too caught up to stop the tumble of words erupting from her mouth. It wasn't the memories that made her sad, it was her inability to change them. But he'd started this conversation and she didn't know how to stop it with anything but the cold hard truth.

"I don't remember anything after slamming my head on the steering wheel." She rubbed her temple, refusing to let those gut-wrenching memories take hold. "But when I woke up in hospital I had a broken arm and Grace was dead."

"And your father cut you from his life."

Ava shook her head. "You have to understand that this was a man who ruled his family with loads of discipline and little emotional reward. He was ex-army, a man who never showed weakness or affection and thought apologies were for sissies. He and I clashed from the very beginning." She gave a small smile. "And I did a lot of things just to piss him off. Grace…" She shook her head. "Grace was the peacemaker. She hated conflict and tried to convince him to talk to me. Then the accident happened and that was it until my mother was diagnosed with cancer."

"He asked you to come home?"

She nodded, the memory of her proud, gruff father brought low and humbled by the uncomfortable reality of her mother's death sentence. "Whatever Dad's faults, he loved Mum. He'd do anything for her and the only thing she wanted was a truce before she died."

The gentle ping of the kitchen clock echoed in the cooling stillness, ticking off the seconds until Ava spoke again.

"Are you sure you're not hungry? Do you want a drink? Coffee?" She smiled wryly. "It's not up to Sydney standards but still pretty good." She rose to her feet but ended up stifling a gasp.

Instantly Cal's hand shot out, grabbing her arm. "What?"

"Pins and needles."

"You need to put your feet up." His command brooked no refusal and Ava was exhausted. She let him lead her into the lounge room, push her gently into a chair and shove an ottoman under her legs.

With a deep sigh, she muttered her thanks, leaned back and closed her eyes.

Eight

Hours later Ava woke with a start. Someone had stoked the fire and it burned away merrily in the darkness. She shifted, noticing for the first time the blanket tucking her in.

"You're awake."

Cal sat on the couch opposite, firelight flickering over his broad shoulders. His shirtsleeves were rolled up, collar and buttons askew where he'd yanked off his tie. Paperwork lay forgotten on the coffee table as he leaned forward, elbows on his knees. Had he been watching her sleep? She felt the flush across her cheeks and shoved the blanket down.

A languorous warmth spread into her legs, making

them tingle as he continued to watch her. It was like he was trying to figure something out but the answer continued to elude him.

"Can you stop that?" she finally said.

"What?"

"Staring at me."

His mouth spread in languid pleasure, causing her to flush again. "You don't like me looking at you?"

"It's disturbing." More than that, it aroused her. She tried to rein in the memories, refuse their hold, but it was like swimming through mud. She swallowed thickly, forcing her breath to even out.

This deep, aching desire was excruciatingly familiar. It had seized her common sense once before, nine weeks ago, when she'd been lulled by a sinful voice and seductive eyes.

She rubbed a hand over her eyes.

"Have you eaten?" she asked.

"Yep."

She dropped her feet to the hardwood floor welcoming the cold shock. "You didn't have to wait up. I can show you to your room if you—"

"Ava," he interrupted, "you don't have to do everything yourself."

Confusion spread across her face but it was the hint of sadness, carefully masked, that drew Cal in. "But I have to."

"Why?"

She hesitated. "Because no one else will."

In the darkened room, the peace broken only by the gentle hiss and crackle from the fire, Cal rose.

"Well…" She shoved her hair back from her face with a tentative smile that didn't quite work. "Good night." He caught her look, vulnerability tinged with steely determination, before she stood and severed eye contact. She looked away as if her feelings were somehow shameful, something to be hidden.

He didn't think, didn't hesitate. He just moved.

When he pulled her into his arms, she stiffened, resisting at first. But she was no match for his insistence. Her small sigh shuddered into him, contracting something buried deep inside his chest.

"I'm not going anywhere," he murmured.

For now. The unspoken truth lay between them, something intangible that still commanded a physical presence. Ava let herself wallow in the moment of weakness. It felt good to be held by a man, to have strong, warm arms wrapped around her. It made the world safe and right, it made her feel protected and loved. She wanted to stay this way forever.

Something shifted inside, something that she couldn't describe. For the first time in forever, she felt like someone else was on her side. She felt championed. Wanted.

Ava couldn't pinpoint the moment everything flipped, only that it did. His embrace was meant to comfort, and for a few moments it did just that, but when she lifted her head from his shoulder something changed. It could've been the way his eyes held hers, dark pools of intense complexity. It could have been her will, desperately tired of the front she'd thrown up against this emotional onslaught.

Whatever the reason, everything shorted out as she tipped her mouth up to his and whispered, "Kiss me."

Her soft words crashed into his mouth, then rolled back on his sharp exhale. She barely had time to regret, rethink, before his groan hit her and his mouth was suddenly covering hers in deep, searing possession.

Sensation collided in her brain, sparking a rush of blood through every secret corner of her body. Her half-groan, half-sigh against his lips only seemed to encourage him, because he angled her mouth to taste deeper, his tongue firmly pushing her lips apart. If it was hormones or just hot-blooded desire, she didn't know. Didn't care. She wrapped her arms around his neck and strained forward, offering herself. When her breasts, now full and throbbing, mashed up against the hard wall of his chest she groaned at the sweet, aching bliss.

It was what she'd wanted, what she'd burned for, ever since he'd turned up on her doorstep.

A low pulse began in the pit of her belly, fanning upwards and heating her skin. He seemed to sense that, because he released her face to skim his hands across her collarbone, then down her arms before coming to rest on her hips.

She shivered, skin prickling with eagerness, desire making her bold. She dragged her hands across his shoulders, then eased her fingers under his sleeves, ending on a sigh when she encountered honed, hot muscle beneath the soft cotton. She kneaded, she stroked. She craved. Like a drug thickening her blood, making her limbs languid, she felt desirable, wanted. And she wanted him.

His flesh beneath her palms sent a myriad of sensations bursting behind her eyes, only to ratchet up higher when he groaned low in her mouth, sending a primeval thrill into every bone. With one swift movement he grabbed her bottom, pulling her sharply up against him, against the hard, throbbing arousal separated by only two thin layers of clothing.

Cal's iron-grip control began to slip. All he could feel were the luscious curves of her butt beneath his hands, her hard nipples digging into his chest like two tiny pebbles. Her amazing scent teased his nostrils, his senses, coupled with the glorious musky sweetness of warm woman.

His blood pulsed quick and hard, threatening to demolish the promise he'd made. Yet like a sudden match sparking in the pitch black, reality flared. He didn't want it, didn't need it, but he couldn't ignore it.

When Cal suddenly broke the kiss, breathing hard, Ava murmured her disappointment. But when she leaned in, seeking the warmth of his mouth again, he tilted away then released her, the way barred. Rejected, she stepped back.

His eyes bored into hers, mysterious and unfathomable. Then he dragged a hand across his chin, the grating rasp of his five o'clock shadow echoing in the dark, intimate silence. "I'm trying, I'm trying to keep my word, but dammit, don't start what you're not going to finish."

That last word came out husky and hoarse and she opened her mouth to protest, but no words came. Instead, with heat flushing her cheeks, she backed away until there was nothing but cold space and air between them.

"I feel…I want…" She paused, her head whirling. It felt like someone had bundled up all her raw emotions, magnified them a thousandfold and was now pegging them back at her. And Cal just stood there, silent, waiting.

She took a deep breath and straightened her shoulders. "The truth is, I have a billion hormones racing around inside me. Morning sickness, fluid retention—" she picked up a lock of hair and it curled around her finger "—even my hair has changed. Yes, I'm attracted to you, but I didn't expect…" *To want you this badly?* How on earth could she admit that?

"I see." Under his slow, excruciating perusal Ava wanted to escape so badly her calves began to tense. "So what do you want to do?"

"I don't know."

Cal nearly groaned aloud. It'd been so long since he'd believed in honesty, in the goodness of someone who didn't demand something in return. If her agonised whisper hadn't got him, the look in her eyes did—eyes normally so clear and wide, now cloudy with confusion.

Cal wasn't a man who denied himself much of anything: if something was offered he went after it. Ava was offering but amazingly, she hadn't convinced herself yet.

With the ache in his jaw echoing the throb in his groin, he gathered up the files and turned for the door, envisioning a long, cold shower.

"Good night, Ava."

"Cal, wait."

Her words washed over him, her gentle plea stroking along his sensitive flesh, stopping him dead. He tried to force his body to settle but all he wanted to do was reach out and finish what they'd started. His skin ached in anticipation, every inch humming in earnest.

"What?"

He turned then, to her flushed face, fingers threading uneasily through her hair. She looked so unsure, so ready to bolt yet so absurdly beautiful that his tongue stuck to the roof of his mouth. And suddenly, everything became clear.

"You know what I think?"

Nervous and still sluggish with passion, Ava could barely get out a whispered, "What?"

"I want you."

She held her breath as he paused, dangling the moment like a tempting prize. "I want you in my bed. Under me." His mouth curved, a sensual sculpture in warm flesh as his voice took on a throbbing, hypnotic rumble.

"Above me," he drew out every syllable for maximum effect, punctuating with measured, predatory steps. "I want to hear you moan, to kiss you…everywhere."

"What—" her voice came in low and rough and just a little bit hoarse "—are you doing?"

"I got fed up waiting for you to ask."

With a low moan she met him in the middle and gave herself up to his mouth. She suffered the bittersweet torture of his lips feathering over hers, testing then tasting her bottom lip while her breath kicked up. It took almost superhuman effort not to plead, to beg him to take her right here, right now.

Cal could feel her tense beneath his hands but focused on the kiss, tenderly sweeping his mouth over to the corners of hers, tracing the edges with his tongue. Even though he knew her body intimately, had kissed every inch of it, they'd never shared a kiss like this. Not something so incredibly gentle that still succeeded in arousing him from go to whoa in seconds flat.

His lips trailed away from her mouth, across the curve of her cheek before ending at her ear.

She gasped, her hot breath skimming across his jaw, making him shudder.

"Where's your room?"

Somehow they made it down the hall, to Ava's bedroom at the back of the house. No sooner had she closed the door behind them than Cal swiftly took control, pushing her up against the wall and mashing her breasts against his chest. Her nipples peaked against his shirt, sending hot, urgent need surging through his body. He grabbed her face and kissed her again.

Ava felt the effects of that mind-numbing kiss explode through her veins. All this time she'd been denying the sinful indulgence of his lips, his mouth, and for what? His arms pinned her but she felt safe. His mouth devoured but she felt wanted. His arousal dug into her stomach, and she felt desirable.

His mouth eased hers open in a deep growl as if the thought of denying him entry was possible. It wasn't. She wanted his mouth, his tongue, his touch. Caught up in the kiss, she nearly jumped out of her skin when he plucked open the buttons of her dress. His hot hands quickly replaced the blast of cold and with a groan she angled her head, opening her mouth wider to his invading tongue.

His instant husky murmur shot white-hot need straight between her legs. She remembered how perfectly they fit. No awkwardness, no fumbling. Just pure poetry in motion, two dancers in unison, following the steps they knew by heart. Their one night together hadn't just been a crazy, larger-than-life event she'd promoted in her mind as the pinnacle of pleasure. It had been everything and more.

She ached to touch him, to feel the texture of his skin, the way it heated beneath her fingers, her mouth, her tongue. Feverishly, she grabbed his shirt, fumbling with the buttons until he took pity on her and just yanked it off.

At first she gasped as the buttons popped, flying

across the room, hitting her dresser with a tiny ping. But then he smiled, a wicked, sensuous smile full of knowledge, one for her and her only, and suddenly, something deep inside burst.

It must have registered in her eyes because he tumbled her to the bed, mouths locked in a renewed bout of frenzied kisses. Quickly her dress came down, pooling around her waist and then his mouth was on her breast, covering one painfully peaked nipple through the satin fabric of her bra.

Sensation exploded through her nerve endings, sending her back arching, her breath gasping. It was intense, unbearable, and she grabbed him, prepared to shove him away, but he preempted her, pinning her hands above her head.

"You like that?"

Ava panted, her eyes wide as she stared up into that sensual smile. "Too much."

His smile widened. "So if I, for example, did this—" he bent and dragged the bra aside with his teeth and she gasped as her nipple sprang free "—then this—" he licked at the tightened bud then blew gently, peaking her tender flesh into almost unbearable hardness "—that wouldn't be good?"

God, that voice. That deep, slow, seductive voice making her limbs melt, promising hours of wicked joy. Ava whimpered, gently rocking her hips, but all that succeeded in doing was settling his hardness more comfortably between her legs.

"You know it's more than good," she whispered, tilting her head back as frustration and arousal raced through her veins. But avoiding his eyes didn't ease her throbbing desire. Instead, Cal's deep, rumbling chuckle flooded over her skin, a second before his mouth covered her nipple.

She bucked, but it was futile. Need roared through her skin, burning, unbearable. Her whole body trembled as his lips and tongue worshipped her flesh, his teeth rasping gently, teasing, peaking. Her eyes snapped down, only to find him studying her, his mouth claiming her breast as he boldly teased her other nipple into hardness with his thumb.

"Cal, please." The plea slipped out but she was past caring anymore. "I need you."

"Wait."

Hot, desperate desire clawed through Cal, burning his body from the inside out. But still he continued his exploration, cupping the new fullness of her breasts before kissing a path between the erotic valley, stroking her warm, fragrant flesh before ringing his tongue around the nipple then taking that rock-hard bud deep in his mouth.

He was enjoying seeing her squirm, caught up in the familiar wave of white-hot passion—until he heard her gasp, followed by a frustrated groan. And suddenly, need bubbled over, scorching him with its intensity.

"Cal…please!"

He clenched his teeth, desperate for control, as he swiftly reached under her dress and dragged her knickers down.

She managed the buttons of his pants, then his zipper, before he stood and yanked his pants and boxers free. Then with a groan he sank back down into Ava's welcoming body.

"Hurry." Her breathy demand echoed in the thick stillness and he needed no further urging.

With one smooth thrust, he parted her legs and buried himself inside her.

Their breaths hissed out in simultaneous wonder, the air congealing around them and meshing with the scent of warm arousal. Then Cal cupped the warm flesh of her bottom and began to move.

They spoke in murmurs and sighs, their rhythm at first hesitant, then growing in familiarity. A glorious wave swept Ava, her entire body humming and hot. Cal was large and a tight fit, but she accommodated him like they were two pieces of the same puzzle. A perfect match.

He'd trapped her hands above her head in a sensuous prison, their fingers linked in fragile intimacy. And when he upped the pace, she threw her head back and gave herself up to him.

Their ragged breathing punctuated the air, mingling as he dipped down to kiss her briefly once, then again. Farther down, between her throbbing legs, she felt the sensuous glide as he filled her, pulled back, then thrust again. He'd been gentle at first, as if testing his welcome, and when she finally dragged open her eyes and focused on his, they were almost black and seriously intent on pleasuring her.

She angled her hips upward and on the next thrust he went deeper. She was rewarded with his groan, which came from the most private places inside, and she murmured her satisfaction.

Cal was nearing the edge, too quick. The need for release clawed inside, sending a wave of sweat beading across his skin. Their bodies were already shiny-slick with it, and when Ava leaned up to nibble gently at his shoulder, he nearly lost it then and there. With a soft command he pushed her back before gritting his teeth and picking up the rhythm.

He sensed just before he felt the buildup of Ava's climax. All around him her tightly wound muscles squeezed and with a groan, he held on to the thin skein of his control, determined to make sure she took pleasure first.

Wait...wait...

Their heartbeats mingled, pounding insistently for precious seconds. And then it happened. Her eyes widened, her breath coming out in tiny, almost amazed gasps, before her warmth flooded him totally, completely. He released the breath he hadn't realized he'd been holding and with relief thrust once, twice.

As Ava gave into the glorious sensations, shudders wracking her body, she felt Cal's hot breath in her ear, his groan as he, too, reached his climax before collapsing, stealing the breath from her body in a deliciously crushing embrace.

She became aware of their breathing, echoing loud and

harsh, as she floated back down to earth. Unwilling to break the afterglow, she slowly stroked her hands down his body, taking illicit enjoyment in the curve of his well-honed shoulders and the erotic dip of his lower back before it flared out into an exquisitely beautiful behind.

"Victor and I have little in common," he said suddenly in the darkness. "So I relate to him through the company. Like boys who play a particular sport just to please their fathers."

She pulled back, seeking his eyes in the muted glow of the moon. "It's your connection. There's nothing wrong with that."

Dimly she was aware he'd squeezed his eyes shut, knew a denial hovered on the tip of his tongue. She held her breath as the seconds stretched interminably. Would he actually voice something that intensely private aloud?

His phone trilled, breaking the moment. With a sigh, he gently disengaged himself from her arms. *Time's up,* the phone continued to mock. *Back to the real world.* As air rushed in to cool her skin, to pebble her nipples, she shivered.

The bed dipped and his feet landed with a soft thump on the carpeted floor and she suddenly realized how she must look—dress bunched at her waist, breasts bare. With a flush she sat up and shoved her hands through her sleeves, barely managing the buttons with stiff, fumbling fingers.

Cal hung up. "I have to go back to Sydney."

"Tonight?" She cringed at the awful, naked neediness

in her voice and ducked her gaze to focus on the last button. Only when it was done did she finally glance up.

They stared at each other, teetering on that finely balanced tightrope as the seconds ticked by. And with those awkward seconds came the inevitable regret and doubt.

Why didn't he say something?

"Okay, you have to go. I understand," she managed as calmly as she could. Yet the clouds of worry that had been temporarily blown away by their lovemaking began to gather in ominous shadows once again.

"Ava, I'm—" He paused, sighed, then started again. "Look, what we—"

"Don't. Don't say anything." Spying her knickers on the floor she quickly snatched them up, cheeks burning. *So help me, if you apologise…* "We had sex. It's no big deal." She forced her voice to sound casual, but her fluttery insides told the real truth.

"Rubbish."

She nearly crumbled then, but pride forced her to remain calm. "It has to be. Look, Cal, let me make this easy. What we did doesn't have to mean anything. We were just two people enjoying sex."

Frustration tinged the edges of his expression, his dark eyes rife with something she couldn't quite fathom. Still he remained silent, just studied her in a way that felt too intense, too intimate, too…*everything* after what they'd just done.

"You have to go," she reminded him.

In uncomfortable expectancy she padded her way over to the en suite. Would he stop her? To her relief, he let her go.

As Ava stepped into the shower and the jets of hot water streamed across her skin, a thousand conflicting thoughts battled for attention in her brain. What on earth had she done? One night of forbidden passion was forgivable, even understandable given the pressures in her life, but twice? And with a man she knew better than to get emotionally entangled with.

She couldn't change him anymore than she could stop herself from wanting him. Their lovemaking and Cal's phone call proved that. And it wasn't her place, her right to try and change him. Women who believed they could were just kidding themselves. Love meant accepting the other person's faults as well as their qualities, not being unhappy with—

The bottle of shampoo dropped from her stiff fingers as realization hit her like a wrecking ball—solid, inevitable and twice as devastating.

No. Nooooo…

She loved him. How the hell had that happened?

Amazingly, Ava's burden became heavier, not lighter, under the weight of distance. His absence forced her to rethink everything.

Doubt and uncertainty rolled around in her head for days, only easing off when Cal's interior design team arrived to discuss Jindalee's makeover.

All too soon it was Thursday night and the luxurious car service was depositing her at Cal's apartment. Standing on the footpath staring up at the shiny apartment complex, she finally allowed the emotion to surge up. And surge up it did, nearly choking her in the process.

She gritted her teeth, clenching her fists inside her coat pockets. She'd had two e-mails since Monday, the first from Jenny, Cal's assistant, seeking confirmation that his design team had arrived. The second was sent at some ungodly hour, him asking how the baby was and confirming her return. No phone call so she could wallow in the delicious warmth of his voice, no personal queries about her health, her feelings.

Work had once again taken him away.

With a groan she screwed her eyes shut, blocking out the apartment lights that now seemed to taunt her.

She wouldn't go to pieces. She had to think of the baby. Her and Cal's baby. A baby he wanted, a baby she already loved. If she couldn't have Cal's love then at least they'd be bonded by this tiny life they'd made together.

But would that be enough?

"Ms. Reilly?"

She glanced at the chauffeur, who was holding the doors open for her. A frozen breeze rushed down the street, sending a shiver over her skin, propelling her forward.

It was time to focus on what she was here for. Jindalee. Her baby's future. If Cal wanted a perfect wife, if that meant dressing up and playacting, so be it. If it also meant ignoring the pleasures they'd shared and squashing those more frequently disturbing urges to touch, to taste…?

She couldn't answer that, not until she was faced with it again. And she sure as hell would not lower herself to scheduling in sex like it was some kind of business appointment.

She absently thanked the driver and pressed the elevator's top-floor button.

When the doors swished open, the apartment's only light came from the aquarium's muted glow.

"Cal?"

The silence was complete. Perversely disappointed, she dropped her bag beside the couch, then swept off her coat.

From inside her handbag, her mobile phone beeped. It was Cal's office.

"Ms. Reilly? It's Jenny."

"Yes?" Ava sat gratefully on the couch arm and unzipped her suede boots.

"Mr. Prescott will be late and told me to tell you not to wait up."

"I see."

"Also, your engagement party is scheduled for the third of July."

"Okay."

Jenny paused as if waiting for something more, then said gently, "Have a good night, Ms. Reilly."

"Wait! Jenny?"

"Yes, Ms. Reilly?"

Ava hesitated, but the desire to know overrode everything else. "Is everything okay? I know One-Click is currently virus-testing and I heard there's a new one doing the rounds…" She bit her lip at the leading question, hoping Jenny would fill in the blanks.

She did. "Yes, we managed to contain it but Mr. Prescott's working 'round the clock to find a cure."

The answer should have allayed her doubts, but when Ava hung up, she knew they hadn't even made a dent. Cal wasn't just avoiding her, he was at work and she was alone and waiting—an eerie portent of things to come.

Automatically she went through the motions of making hot chocolate, the familiar task soothing her troubled mind. She had no right to be angry, but it still didn't stop the aching throb in her heart. What they'd shared at Jindalee was just sex, two people mutually attracted doing what came naturally. A spur-of-the-moment thing. A one-off.

It didn't change the fact that work came first with Cal and he was only marrying her for their child. She needed to get that through her head if she was to get through the other side of this marriage with her heart intact.

She'd survive if she had to. And it was really too soon to determine if this was a permanent thing. If it was…

Her child would not have an absentee father. No way. She'd rather suffer the unimaginable but momentary pain of divorce instead of putting her child through years of heartbreaking disappointment.

Nine

Two weeks later, on the eve of his engagement party, Cal stared out the window of VP Tech at the storm obscuring his view. The Harbour Bridge was barely visible past the slashing sheets of rain pounding down, the Opera House only a well-studied memory beneath the iron-grey sky.

He jerked his gaze from the window to take in the expansive hush of his air-conditioned office.

There was no sudden screech of rosellas, no gentle ping of a kitchen timer. He breathed in deep. Coffee brewed an hour ago left its lingering mark, but besides that, nothing. No baking biscuits, no roast. Compared to Jindalee, everything was filed, sorted and in its place.

Ava had been avoiding him—and not just physically. His inadequate "We have to talk" early one morning was met with a curious look and a shake of her head.

"We've got nothing to say," she'd coolly returned before rushing out the door for yet another scheduled interview.

To his surprise, she'd morphed into a media-savvy ingenue, answering all questions with grace and aplomb. Even when people began to speculate about how they'd first met and her future role in the Prescott family, her facade didn't waver; she'd deftly fielded further enquiries with the skill of a pro. It was like living with an elegant shell of grooming and poise.

He ran a hand over his jaw with a sigh. If he'd hated the parties before, he loathed them now. Ava's smile was too bright, the look behind her eyes too controlled. She was turning into everything he'd assumed she was and he hated it.

Last week she'd hired a wedding planner.

He shoved the computer mouse across his desk with a curse. The joy he took in his work, normally a source of deep fulfilment, had waned. Victor had demanded more of his time and focus while he made another international trip and as a result, Cal's working hours had encroached into his Sundays. He'd come to resent the intrusion even if Ava hadn't voiced one objection at his absence. Her silence on that topic had spoken volumes.

In comparison, Jindalee had been coming along in leaps and bounds. He slumped back in his chair, massaging his bunched neck muscles with one hand. To his surprise he'd become emotionally invested in Jindalee's progress. It was something about commanding a small team, watching them interact and bounce ideas around that gave him a deep and profound sense of satisfaction. Flying west had become filled with joy, not obligation, even if it was purely selfish on his part. Because at Jindalee he got the real Ava, the woman with the infectious excitement, the woman who moved him. She made him feel needed despite her outward show of independence. And despite it all, he *wanted* her to need him.

Suddenly exhausted, he closed his eyes, ignoring the phone as it buzzed insistently on the desk.

Ava was right. It was something about the stunning splendour of the land, the utmost peace and tranquillity that called to him. VP Tech had consumed his every waking moment yet the absence of it was like a calm, welcome lull.

The phone continued to scream and with a soft curse he yanked it up and took the call. But less than half an hour later, his mind wandered again.

Ever since their one night at Jindalee there'd been nothing to indicate Ava would welcome him back in her bed. During the week he'd been up to his eyeballs in VP Tech while Ava had returned to Jindalee. When they were together, they weren't alone. And in Sydney he'd come home late too many times to a darkened apartment and a closed bedroom door, only to shower, change, then go right back to work.

It doesn't have to mean anything more than two people enjoying sex.

Work now forgotten, he steepled his fingers and stared out the window as the rain lashed down. More than once he'd caught her watching him as they silently passed each other in the barely light morning, the longing rawness in her eyes barely visible just before she'd glanced away. She wanted him, too.

And dammit, he was tired of waiting for her to admit that.

"We're due in the boardroom in ten minutes."

Startled, Cal turned to find Victor in the doorway, a file tucked under one arm. Annoyance rushed in, flooding every part of his brain. *I'd give a thousand bucks to be anywhere but here.* Jindalee. With Ava. A strange tightness took possession—panic, frustration and regret all mingled in.

He rose, reluctance in every muscle, every limb. "I'll be right there."

"A pleasure to see you, Mr. Prescott, Ms. Reilly. Most of your guests are already here."

The doorman's warm smile never wavered as he swept open the large doors of the Observatory Hotel's private function room. They were soon engulfed by a party in full swing. From the corner of her eye Ava noticed the subtle glances, the way the other guests pretended not to stare as Cal led her through the impeccably decorated interior.

He made introductions with skilled aplomb, introduced her to a dozen people she'd have no hope of remembering after tonight. Still she kept a smile plastered on, tried to respond with genuine happiness at the multitude of congratulations. This unabashed luxury was so far removed from the simplistic glory of Jindalee; she'd love the opportunity to just absorb the ambiance of this heritage-listed building without the intrusion of the gathered throng, to let the smells and sounds of past history rush over her. But with Cal's hand at her back, searing a brand through her elegant sky-blue halter dress, she could do nothing but keep moving forward.

For weeks she'd perfected the charade until she'd finally managed to ignore those minor earthquakes through her body. It happened when there was skin-on-skin, when Cal casually touched her arm, took her hand, or, on occasion, leaned in to place a searing kiss on her cheek. To onlookers, all very loving and intimate but to her pure temptation buzzed through her blood like the gallons of Bollinger champagne they'd been constantly toasted with. Champagne that was off-limits, she chafed. Cal had had the foresight to fill her glass with sparkling cider and thankfully no one ever seemed to notice.

The night wore on, through Victor's formal welcoming of Ava into the family, Cal's response and a few impromptu speeches from the floor. Then the lights dimmed and someone turned up the music—sexy, energetic, heavy-on-the-bass dance music that throbbed in her temples—and people started migrating to the dance floor.

She was alone for the first time that night, standing with a half-drunk glass of cider, watching Cal as he casually chatted with an eagerly made-up brunette in a tight black dress that looked as though it'd pop if she took a deep breath.

"Not dancing?" Victor appeared at her elbow.

Ava shook her head. "I'm getting a headache, actually."

"That's not good," Victor agreed solicitously.

Ava wasn't fooled by his demeanour. His eyes were way too calculating. Cal had exactly the same look, had perfected that unnerving stare just a little too well. Her head began to throb in earnest.

"Do you need an aspirin?" Victor asked, waving to a hovering waiter.

"No, thank you. I'll just tough it out a little longer."

Victor followed her eyes to where Cal stood, still talking. "Cal hates these things, but for you, he suffers them."

Ava felt her polite smile slide into uncertainty. "Excuse me?"

Victor turned his full attention to her. "He's been courting the press since you announced your engagement, made sure you're both on the top of the invite list to a dozen parties he normally ignores. And he's devoted precious working hours to your bankrupt business. Cal's unfocused and I believe it's because of you." He flicked a glance to her stomach. "And that baby."

Blood pounded through her veins, flushing her skin deep and hot. "How…?"

"Cal told me." Victor turned to give her his full attention, blocking her view of Cal. "And given the kind of man he is, I'm not surprised he offered marriage. But you must also be aware of his commitments, his responsibilities. Tell me, do you know how much he earns?"

She shook her head. "I've never thought about it."

"Over six thousand dollars a minute. Now think about how long he's spent on your business. Time *not* spent at VP. Look at him." Victor stepped back and she drank in the sight of Cal, formally dressed in a black Gucci dress suit and a golden tie, looking way too irresistible. "VP Tech is Cal's life. One day it will be his and he'll need his wife to support him." He raised his bushy eyebrows, eyes deadly serious. "A wife who won't make unreasonable demands, one who understands the time and commitment involved in running a billion-dollar company."

"Like Isabelle."

Victor's face softened for one second before the mask was back. "Exactly."

It was Gum Tree Falls all over again. She just couldn't measure up, could she? He made her sound so…inadequate. She rubbed her temple in earnest now. "I didn't… It wasn't…"

"You look pale, Ava. Are you okay?" Cal was suddenly there, his hand on her back before angrily turning to Victor. "What did you say to her?"

The menace below that rough growl was palpably real

and Ava swiftly put a hand on Cal's arm. His muscles tightened into granite hardness beneath her fingers.

"Nothing, Cal. Just a small headache."

When he snapped his gaze from Victor to her, she caught the remnants of that simmering anger bubbling away in those dark depths before it cleared.

"Do you want to leave?"

Around them, the party was in full swing and the warm air and loud music began to pound inside her head.

I want you.

She nodded, unable to meet his eyes just in case he could somehow read her desperation.

They were out of there and into the limousine in record time, but even with the heat turned on Ava still felt the chilly edges of Victor's conversation all the way to her toes.

"What did Victor say to you?"

"Nothing."

He studied her in loaded silence, a silence that pulled at her resolve, twisting and turning until she had to say something.

"I want to thank you for Jindalee—it's more than I could've ever hoped for. But you have other commitments and it was never my intention to drag you away from them."

The muscles in his face tightened. "So he's been giving you the 'time is money' speech."

"I'm sorry."

He stared out the window as they made their way

down Castlereagh Street. "For what? Victor's been a demanding workaholic as long as I've known him."

"So why do you…"

"Stay?" She noticed the way his jaw clenched. "Sometimes I wonder."

She paused. "Look, it might be none of my business…but something's not right between you two."

He swung his gaze back to her, his expression unreadable in the muted interior. "And you're the expert in family harmony?"

She flinched as the tiny barb hit its mark. "I know when something needs to be talked over, not just ignored."

"Trust me, Victor's not talking. He's more concerned with jetting off to Europe."

They arrived at Cal's building then, cutting off Ava's reply.

She suffered the elevator ride under a cloud of thick tension, wishing for the courage to say a million things, but the mere act of breaking this awkward moment made her sweat. So the questions sat on her tongue, unspoken.

Finally inside the apartment, she watched Cal shrug off his jacket with sleek efficiency before striding into the kitchen. He removed a flat whiskey glass from the dishwasher, muttering something under his breath.

"What?" Ava asked.

"I said, sometimes I wonder why my mother puts up with him. She certainly doesn't come first in his life."

Ava smiled, recalling the night she'd first met the

Prescotts. "You don't know that. They really love each other."

"Yeah. She loved my father, too, but he refused to marry her. When he left, it destroyed her."

The unspoken subtext roared between them but Cal was beyond caring. Love hadn't destroyed him. Instead, he'd used Melissa's betrayal to drive his ambition to greater heights. And now he had everything a man could want—wealth, power, security.

Their child.

"Did your father ever contact you?"

Cal glanced away. "No. Victor went looking for him after he and Mum married." With a shrug that looked a little too casual, he added, "The guy died in a bar fight years ago."

Ava blinked. An outsider would've detected nothing amiss with his calm answer. But she saw the tight muscle in his jaw, the emotion in his eyes so expertly covered. The knife-edge control in his deep voice. And just like that, whatever fear she'd been harbouring disappeared.

"Your father—your biological father—had flaws."

His laugh was so bitter, she could taste it. "You call running out on a girlfriend and your six-year-old son just 'a flaw'?"

"I'm not defending him—"

"Then what the hell are you doing?" His eyes were furious, twin daggers of frustration and anger.

"I'm saying everyone is human. Everyone makes mistakes."

"So why can't you forgive yourself for your sister's death?"

The well-aimed jab hit its mark and she drew in a sharp breath. "That's different."

"No, it's not. You were young, you made a mistake."

"And I paid for it with Grace's life!"

She yelled the last word, startling them both. But when the echo died, the air held a sudden expectancy.

"Don't you think," he said softly, "that Gum Tree Falls has blamed you enough without you joining the club, too?"

He had this uncanny ability to cut right to the heart of her.

She closed her eyes, knowing he'd only been the voice to her own black thoughts. He'd acknowledged her deepest, darkest doubt, one she'd hidden from everyone, including herself.

Lord, those memories still possessed the power to chew her up inside.

"And if it wasn't for your father leaving, your mother wouldn't have met Victor. And you wouldn't have created something groundbreaking, something amazing. VP Tech has taken technology to every school in Australia, even the remote country towns."

His mouth twisted into a bitter smile. "So it's all fate?"

"Just like Melissa was."

He snapped his head up then cursed as his glass smashed in the sink. Gingerly he plucked out the pieces then tossed them in the trash.

"Right. So she's not to blame for faking a pregnancy just so you'd marry her?"

Clarity swept in on the tail end of that revelation. "Is that why…?"

"Why what?"

Her chin went up. "Why you don't trust me?"

Cal's body was tense and wound up tight with fury—at Victor, at this ever-present arousal, at these unsettled feelings of conflict. But her soft question washed over him, dousing his anger and yanking him up short.

She stared at the floor, the perfect-fiancée facade she'd perfected these last few weeks gone. In its place was an expression so raw that he knew she was barely holding together. She blinked, and to Cal's horror he wondered if she was about to cry. Had *he* done that? The thought shamed him.

"No!"

His rough denial snapped her eyes up to him, where she remained still, almost as if holding her breath.

His insides were all jammed up, tense and tight. He didn't want to be like Victor, unable to express his feelings and holding on to this bitter grudge he'd perfected against his stepbrother. He didn't want to be like Ava's father, forcing the ones he loved from his life.

He glanced at Ava's belly, to the draping fabric that hid the gentle roundness from view. And there it was again, a rush of incredulity rolling over him, leaving him vulnerable and raw.

"Melissa loved the attention and the money. She

didn't…" *Love me.* He bit off the words and picked out another bit of broken glass from the sink. He couldn't say that, couldn't leave himself open that way. "She lied to get into my family. I don't make the same mistake twice."

"Cal—" Ava paused, weighing up the wisdom of her next words. His ex had done more than lie: She'd taken Cal for a fool, played on his emotions. That was unforgivable. And it cut deeply that he thought she was like that. "I never intended to blackmail you, no matter what you think."

Despite her racing heart, Ava held his probing gaze steadily. *I need you to believe me.*

"I believe you, Ava."

With a whoosh of breath, she released the pressure gathered in her shoulders, closing her eyes in silent prayer. But in the next instant, they sprang open as she felt Cal's fingers brush her cheek.

Cal had leaned forward and was tucking a stray curl behind her ear. Her heart sped up again, this time with insistent, hot need.

"Cal…"

His hand stilled and when his eyes flew to hers, she caught the want, the desire, before the shutters came down.

At that moment, that exact second, her heart soared. She could have done a dozen things—pull away, stop to analyse what she was doing, what it all meant—but instead she grabbed the opportunity with both hands.

Ava leaned forward and kissed him.

It was a closed-mouth kiss, experimental and tentative. It reeked of caution and fear of rejection but when she pulled back, his hard face reflected none of her fears. His dark eyes only reflected danger, as if she'd pushed her luck too far. It sent a forbidden thrill coursing through her limbs, tingling, exciting.

Fear and desire mingled together. Funny how both emotions could bring her to a standstill. She waited for his next move with breathless anticipation.

As she stood there, looking uncertain, a little scared and so completely out of her depth, Cal's heart flipped. Man, she could destroy him with nothing more than a look from those bright blue eyes.

A rocket surge of lust sped through his blood. It had been too long. He'd practically counted the days, the hours since she'd last been beneath him, since he'd been buried inside her welcoming warmth.

He held out his hand. "Come with me."

The simplicity of his command tripped off his tongue like the most skilful of seduction lines and Ava felt herself go under. The intensity, the sheer decadence in the depths of his chocolate-brown eyes tugged at her restraint as if daring her to refuse, to deny the instantaneous pull they both instinctively felt. And in that instant, everything around them faded into obscurity.

Her fate was sealed.

Cal couldn't remember undressing but must have because he was staring down at Ava reclining on his bed, unashamedly naked with her hands behind her head.

Her lush breasts thrust forward, begging for his touch, the look in her come-hither eyes roaring blood through his veins to his groin.

He paused, imprinting the perfect erotic snapshot in his brain.

"Cal…" Her voice was breathy, proof of her arousal, and when her mouth curved into a languorous smile he didn't have a hope in hell of keeping his distance.

His breath came out on a groan as he settled over her, into her, touching and tasting the creamy flesh. She was flawless, from the curve of her cheek to the shapely legs. Dynamite packed into five-foot-three, curve upon curve of lush woman. And it was all his.

He swept a palm over her stomach, revelling in the gentle roundness before dipping his head to place a kiss over her belly button.

Ava was helpless to resist the tremble that started between her legs, a tremble that took over more than just her flesh—it engulfed her heart in a flood of emotion. *Cal, I love you.* She squeezed her eyes shut as she felt Cal's hands and mouth gently caress her belly, his hot breath scorching, branding her.

When his lips crept lower, she jerked, her breath hissing out in a shocked rush. Against her belly, she felt his mouth curve into a smile.

"Open for me." It was more demand than request yet she did as he bade anyway.

The instant Cal's mouth touched the most private part of her, she sighed, a gentle, anticipatory whisper that ratcheted up his heart and sent blood racing at a hundred miles an hour.

In slow, lazy licks he loved her with his tongue and lips, every single sense drenched in her scent, her taste. He wanted to give more, much more, but when her hips began to rock gently, a maddening yet completely perfect motion, the desperate urge to be inside her forced him up.

Her whimper of protest ended on a satisfied sigh as he quickly positioned himself and drove into her hot welcoming flesh.

And as he loved her deeply, thoroughly, he realized that he'd finally come home.

Ten

"Congratulations. You did it," Victor said gruffly. They stood in the small anteroom off the entryway of St Mary's Cathedral awaiting the arrival of the bride. Inside the church a flurry of guests seated themselves among the pews, murmuring quietly. Doctors, lawyers, property developers—the movers and shakers of Sydney society, Cal noticed. The invites included anyone who'd had dealings with Victor and VP Tech, even those Cal barely knew. In comparison, Ava's guests barely took up two rows.

Outside, the street had been cordoned off to preempt the inevitable traffic jam, but it hadn't stopped the crowd steadily growing all day, forcing the local police to serve as crowd control.

Cal tweaked his perfectly knotted cravat with unfamiliar nervousness. By unspoken mutual agreement Sydney was designated business-only—he had VP Tech, she the wedding, interviews, photo spreads. They'd come together for public engagements and frantic, almost desperate lovemaking in the thin hours of dawn before real life intruded once again.

On the flipside, Jindalee was his guilty pleasure. When he stood on the porch surveying the construction chaos against the stunning post-sunset backdrop, his satisfied smile was dimmed only by Ava's echoing one. They made sweet, leisurely love in her comfortable four-poster and afterward, in the dark, he'd stroke her belly and talk to his unborn child, floored and humbled by how simple life could be. Ava didn't talk about the past or bring up the future and Cal let it go, instead revelling in every stolen moment together.

Today, Ava would be his wife. It didn't matter how the day had come to be, just that it was. That's all that mattered. Not this painfully slow ceremony, not the scores of people he didn't know or care about. And from this day on, he'd—

"Did you hear me?" Victor said now.

"I heard you."

For weeks, Cal had kept a tight lid on his simmering thoughts but now they threatened to boil over.

Not now, not today.

He abruptly turned and caught sight of his mother through the half-open door. Beautiful and elegant in a powder-blue suit and a small-brimmed hat, she stood at the entrance and greeted latecomers with a wide smile.

He grinned, but that fell when Victor pointedly closed the door.

"You've been distracted, unfocussed." Victor continued with a puckered brow. "If you're having second thoughts…"

Cal turned back to the long baroque mirror and straightened his perfectly straight sleeves. "A bit late for that now, isn't it?"

Victor sighed. "Look, that was—"

"I don't care anymore."

"Clearly not."

Cal's eyes snapped to Victor's reflection through the mirror. Sarcasm, mixed with an odd kind of guilt, creased the older man's face.

"We need to talk."

Cal shrugged. "About?"

"The future of the company."

He snorted. "I'm getting married, Ava is having my child. Aren't I doing enough?"

"I have a brain tumour."

The world slammed to a halt. *Victor was sick?* Cal gaped. "What?"

Victor's lip tilt was anything but humorous. "A brain tumour—a slow one, which apparently is the best type to have. I've been seeing a Swiss specialist who's been monitoring it and now he's recommending surgery. It's a tricky operation with obvious risks, but he's confident. I go under the knife next week."

The apprehension eased off a bare inch. "Does Mum know?"

Victor's slight nod barely classed as acknowledgement. "She wanted to tell you weeks ago, but—"

"Damn right I needed to know! Jesus!" Anger bubbled up inside, churning futilely in the pit of his stomach. "So what will you do about…" He trailed off, blood rushing from his face as realization dawned. "So that's where you've been jetting off to. And *that's* why you demanded I get married! Sonofa—"

"You're having a baby and getting VP Tech. Tell me where you lose in this."

Cal clenched his teeth. Never before had he felt the desperate urge to deck another man, sick or not. "You didn't have to lie."

Irritation creased Victor's face. "I didn't lie—I just didn't elaborate. I know you, Cal. You needed an incentive. I wanted you committed—"

"Bullshit. You knew the company was my life, my number-one priority."

"'Was'?" Victor frowned.

"You know what I mean. And don't change the subject."

Victor crossed his arms stiffly. "I wanted you settled. The company just provided leverage."

Cal took a deep breath, forcing the fury back behind the gates. "So you have pangs of mortality and suddenly decide I needed to get married?"

Victor flushed, his eyes skittering away. "A man thinks of lots of things when he's faced with death."

They both paused, two proud men unwilling to shine a light on the dark corners of their emotions, until the panic and worry began to ebb from Cal's tense muscles.

"Did you have any intention of giving the company to Zac?" he said, less harshly.

"I knew you wouldn't fail."

Once, months ago, that simple statement would have been a welcome shot in the arm. But instead of pride, Cal only felt a low, simmering irritation.

Victor continued. "Zac's been ignoring my calls since he walked out. Which you would've known if *you'd* actually called him."

Cal sucked in a breath. Victor Prescott pulled no punches, that was for sure. "So he's not coming to the wedding."

"He declined the invite. That boy is so bloody stubborn."

"Like his father."

Victor glared at him. "Or his stepbrother. I've come to terms with Zac never speaking to me again. But you two should kiss and make up before I die."

Cal scowled. "Don't be so morbid. You're not going to die."

"I'm not planning on it any time soon. And your mother just wants to see you happy—"

"Do *not* tell me she knew about your little scheme."

Victor had the good grace to look uncomfortable. "Not at first."

"Brilliant. That's just brilliant." He raked a hand through his newly trimmed hair, mind whirling.

Someone knocked softly on the door but they both ignored it.

Victor straightened his cuffs and cleared his throat. "So. Now that that's out, I'll need your signature next week to finalise the papers."

Cal stared at him for the longest time, until Victor's brows plummeted. "What?"

"We'll be on our honeymoon."

"Oh, right. Seven days."

"Ten."

"We've got that product development meeting with the Department of Education next month." Victor glanced back to the door as the knock came again.

And this from a man about to undergo major surgery in a week? "Sorry. Can't do it."

"Why not? After today the company's yours, something you've always wanted. It will be your number-one priority and I'll need to get you up to speed with things before I leave. The workload will be crazy, of course, but that's nothing new. Your new bride will understand."

Cal strode to the door, his insides shaken from upheaval. His whole life he'd met his responsibilities, had given two hundred percent to gain Victor's approval. *Never walk away.* That vow had shaped every choice, every decision he'd made. And because of it, he'd cut his stepbrother from his life, a decision he'd never fully forgiven himself for, a decision he'd planned to make right today.

Yet Zac hadn't showed.

Cal had won the prize but at what cost? He'd been lied to, manipulated, and he'd responded by doing the same to Ava. Yes, Victor had had his reasons but it didn't mean it was right.

He'd become so damn focused on work that life was passing him by. He'd become Victor and he hated it.

That realization brought sudden clarity into stark focus. With a firm slant to his jaw he reached for the door handle and twisted.

"You blackmailed me into a marriage I didn't want. But you know what? I don't care right now." He yanked open the door, the hinges screaming in protest. "I'm getting married today—"

Victor tensed. "Cal."

"—and you can take your company and shove—"

"Cal?"

The tremulous question behind him broke through his subconscious, jerked his head towards the soft voice.

Ava stood with her hand raised mid-knock. The strapless, flowing white dress, her hair bunched up under a tiara like some fairy princess, her stunningly beautiful face— it all registered somewhere in his brain, on another level. But it was her expression that cut him to the bone, deep pools of blue set in a pale, haunted expression. Those eyes wounded him more deeply than a thousand betrayals.

She took a step backward, shaking her head. "Is it true? Did you…" Her panicking gaze drifted over to Victor. "Did he…?"

"Now, let's just calm down—" Victor began, until Cal stepped across her eyeline, cutting the older man from view.

"It's not what you think."

Her expression tightened. "But is it true?"

His nod was brief but nothing less than shattering. Ava's face crumpled for one second but in the next, she straightened, a flash of something hard and angry in her eyes as she pulled her shoulders back. Alarmed, he reached for her but she put up a warning hand.

"Don't. I thought this baby was important to you, that *I* was important. But obviously, gaining control of your precious company takes top priority."

"Now wait just a minute—" Victor interrupted but to Cal's amazement, her ferocious glare had him snapping his mouth shut.

She had guts, his Ava. There weren't many people who'd stare down the powerful Victor Prescott.

With a look of pure disgust, she backed away, the white satin skirt swirling around her legs in a flurry. And with that one small movement, she dragged the ground out from under him, crumpling hope beneath his feet. In desperation he scrambled for something to say, anything that would stop her from walking out.

"You'll lose Jindalee."

Instead of binding her to him, it drove her away. The

look she gave, pain mingled with pity, ground the rest of his words to hot dust in his mouth as she kept on backing away.

"Do you think that's all I care about—business? Then you don't know me at all."

Cal jerked forward but she was out the huge chapel doors, hurrying past Isabelle, standing open-mouthed in the vestibule.

Cal sprinted after her. It wasn't over. He could fix this, he could turn that utter horror in Ava's eyes back into the slow blooming love he suspected was lurking below the surface. He—

He came to a halt on the pathway. She'd paused at the white Bentley that had delivered her to the church, a hand on the door. With his blood pounding hard and fast, he sighed, a man spared a reprieve. "Ava. Please, let me explain about—"

"Cal…" The pain in her voice pierced his resolve, sending shards of alarm through his brain. Then she slowly turned and the pale fear etched on her face forced his heart into his throat. She clutched her stomach, her eyes huge. "The baby," she gasped. "Cal, the baby!"

He only just managed to catch her as she pitched forward in a dead faint.

"You look like death warmed over."

Isabelle's gentle voice broke through the swirling blackness of Cal's thoughts and he glanced up. Beside him, on the bed, Ava had been asleep for twelve hours.

Twelve hours in which he'd run the gamut of emotions: despair, regret, self-loathing. Twelve hours in which he'd prayed to every deity he could name, and then some he couldn't. *Let her live. Let our baby live.*

He wasn't surprised he looked like crap.

"The doctor says both she and the baby will be fine," Isabelle said now.

With a curt nod, he dragged a hand over his stubbled chin, words failing him.

When Isabelle gathered him in her arms, he held on tight, letting her rock him gently like he was once again her baby. "They're fine, Cal," she whispered. "They're fine. I'm so happy for you." She pulled back then, dabbing at her eyes with a tissue before composing herself. "Victor's outside. He wasn't sure if you'd want to see him after…well." She waved a hand, letting him fill in the rest.

"You heard."

"Victor told me. He has a convoluted way of showing it, but he loves you. He isn't proud of deceiving you, you know. You're a good man, Cal and I love you very much. But you're also stubborn and unforgiving."

"If you're taking his side—"

"I'm taking no one's side. Believe me, Victor knows how angry I am." Her face softened as she added, "Give him a break—we both had a terrible scare. Can you imagine how he's been since having to face his mortality?"

They both shared the black humour with mutual smiles until Isabelle said, "We talked for weeks—about life, family. Zac. You. We both knew you hadn't been happy in a while. I thought you needed romance and Victor assumed your work wasn't challenging enough."

Wasn't challenging enough? Cal shook his head, harsh laughter bubbling from his mouth.

"Cal?"

Ava's croaky question shot him to his feet. He barely registered his mother's departure, the gentle click of the door behind. Instead his complete attention was on the seemingly tiny figure on the hospital bed.

Her hand went to her stomach, her eyes round with panic. "The baby—"

"He's okay." He took her hand, felt the icy cold beneath his fingers. "You're okay."

"He?"

Cal nodded, too choked up to speak.

"We're having a boy," she said faintly. When her eyes met his, relief smashed down on him like a thousand bricks.

"Jesus, Ava…you…I…"

To his shame, his voice cracked on that last word. And to compound his mortification, he felt the track of tears slide over his cheeks. Flushed, he reached up to dash them away but Ava tightened her grip with a confused frown.

"Cal…did I hear you praying to Buddha?"

He went for a laugh but it came out nervous and unsure. "Yeah."

"And God and Mohammed and—" she screwed her face up in concentration. "—Zeus?"

"I wanted to make sure the message got through."

"Because of me?"

Her eyes were deep and fathomless, eyes he could happily drown in. His heart began to up its tempo, his breath shaky.

"I didn't want to lose you. Or the baby. Ava…" He took a deep breath, snaring her wide gaze in his. "I'm sorry I didn't tell you." She swallowed, the small movement drawing Cal's attention to the smooth column of her throat. "Waiting for the ambulance was the longest ten minutes of my life. And when they couldn't revive you…"

He bowed his head, panic rising up in his throat as the memory engulfed him. The soft pressure of her hand grasping his dragged him back from the edge and he looked up, only to go under again, drowning in those blue eyes.

"I didn't think you needed to know," he began again. "You were marrying me anyway and I…dammit."

Her hand squeezed his. "I understand, Cal. It's okay."

"No, it's not. An omission is still a lie. I…" He hesitated, then said, "I love you, Ava."

She drew in a sharp breath and closed her eyes, almost as if it hurt. In the long, painful seconds that followed, Cal waited, his skin prickling, nerves taut. As he waited, a small tear trickled out and curved over her cheek, before her eyes flew open.

"I love you too, Cal. But…" She paused, took a deep shuddery breath that seemed to come from the depths of her soul. A shard of deep pain crossed her face, wounding him square in the chest. "How can this marriage work? I want to be with you, Cal, because I love you. But your life is VP Tech, it's not with me."

"Sweetheart, I don't want the company. I want you."

Confusion flitted across Ava's face. "But I thought—"

"Yes, I originally wanted to marry you to get the company. But things have changed. I've changed." He massaged her hands gently between his. "I am one-hundred-percent, completely and totally in love with you. And I am one-hundred-percent positive that I don't want VP Tech. I want a life. With you."

Oh. Everything ground to a slow, breath-stopping halt. Ava couldn't move, couldn't speak. In her head, thoughts began to zip crazily around, sending her brain into a whirl.

"Ava?" He smiled, a tentative smile that got her heart racing, her blood pumping. "You're in shock."

"No…yes…I…" Her heart pounded in fury, sending a wonderful tingle through every vein, every limb. This was more, so much more than she ever expected. Ever hoped. Ever wanted.

"Nod if you can hear me," Cal said, his voice dipping low, making her shiver.

She nodded.

"You love me."

Nod.

"Do you want to marry me?"

Nod.

"How does a March wedding at Jindalee sound?"

Nod.

His slow, generous grin melted her bones. "I'm going to kiss you."

She finally managed to breathe. "Wait. Does this mean Zac gets the company?"

"Oh, so now you have a problem with marrying a guy who's unemployed?" he teased, his mouth so close to hers that it made her tremble.

Her lips curved. "You should call him. He walked out on Victor, not you."

"I was planning to. But first you need to shut up so I can kiss you."

"Yes," she managed just before his warm breath feathered into hers and their lips met in a long, languorous kiss.

Epilogue

Two months later

"**W**ell? What did Zac have to say?" Ava said from the bedroom doorway as Cal hung up the phone.

He glanced up, then did a double take. "What on earth have you got on?"

She looked down at her attire, then back up at him with an innocent grin. "Your boxers are nice and roomy. And your T-shirt smells like you. Mmm," she purred, rubbing the sleeve against her cheek with exaggerated delight.

He laughed, tossed the phone onto the couch and crossed the room in long, purposeful strides. As he reached her, the setting sun spread through the window, bathing her in red and gold ribbons. The light bounced off her shoulders and the glints in her freshly washed hair, illuminating her pregnant belly in all its glorious roundness.

He exhaled, slowly and shakily.

"Lord, you're beautiful."

He'd never get tired of seeing her blush. And when he reached out to cup her belly, their eyes met, both acknowledging the joy and power of the life growing inside her.

She tilted up her chin, her lips seeking his, and without reservation he gave himself up to the pure pleasure of their kiss. Her peach-and-vanilla fragrance, now as familiar as the silken skin beneath his fingers, never failed to turn him on. Her willing mouth, her long-limbed beautiful body, now lush and plump with his child... Senses exploded and in record time he was hard, the familiar thump-thump of arousal speeding up his heartbeat, forcing his breath out in ragged gasps.

Ava abruptly pulled back. "What did Zac say?"

Cal groaned, his arms tightening around her. "I'm ready and raring to go and you want to talk about my brother?"

"Hey, mister, you were the one who started kissing me."

"Yeah, but you wanted it." His hand swept down her back and over her butt before coming to rest on her belly. He grinned when he felt her shudder and a tiny groan escaped her kiss-stung lips.

"Cal!"

He sighed with exaggerated grief. "Fine. Zac didn't believe Victor would give up VP Tech or I'd given up the CEO's position." He leaned in and resumed his exploration, placing soft, seductive kisses on her warm nape. Her small pleasure-laden sigh sent a shot of pure male satisfaction through his veins.

"But he's taking the position?"

Cal grunted noncommittally, his attention and mouth now focused solely on where her neck met her earlobe. "That's not clear. He's coming down to Sydney on Friday to sort it all out."

"That's great!" Ava pulled back, breaking contact midkiss. "With Victor now fully in remission it'd do them both good to sort out their differences and—"

"Wife-to-be," he growled, tightening his embrace, "do you want to talk about Zac and Victor or would you rather I take off that ridiculous getup and kiss you all over?"

"Oh."

Ava swallowed. If a girl could melt, she'd be doing it right about now. The hot, possessive look in Cal's eyes made her entire body sing with anticipation, the insistent press from his groin proof positive he wanted her. But more than that, he loved her. Every day he showed her—and not just with gifts she suspected gave him more pleasure to give. It was in the thousand little ways that a commanding, proud man such as Cal Prescott demonstrated love—in the sudden looks, the constant, gentle touching. And in the middle of the night, when they lay spent and satisfied from lovemaking, he'd caress her seven-month bump and talk to their child with such reverent adoration that it brought her to tears every time.

"I have something for you," Cal said with a grin as he turned her around and steered her into the bedroom.

She blinked now, forcing the emotion back. "Cal, really. You don't need to keep buying me things. I've got more than enough clothes and jewellery to last... What's that?"

He'd removed a scrap of black material from his jacket pocket and was dangling it from one finger with a wolfish grin.

"Are those my...?"

"Black satin knickers from our first night together." He hooked two fingers around the delicate waistband and pulled. "Care to try them on?"

Ava rolled her eyes. "They'd hardly fit."

He nodded seriously. "I guess not."

"Cal!"

He laughed as her punch landed on his arm, her balled fist making absolutely no impact upon the knots of honed muscle. With a mischievous gleam in his eye, he wrapped her in his arms and they gently fell to the bed, his body cradling hers.

As their laughter subsided, his face became serious, an expression she'd come to know all too well. Slowly, sensuously, he locked his fingers in hers and pulled them over her head. "I love you, wife-to-be."

She'd never get sick of hearing those words from his

lips. That low, throbbing declaration flooded her senses, filling her with love, clogging her throat with brimming emotion.

"And I love you, husband-to-be." And then with her whole body, her whole heart, she proceeded to show him.

She looked up and saw his smile.

It should carry a mental health warning: one glimpse and you'll forget your own will. She held frantically to hers. "You said one dance and then I was free to go." Yet she left her hand on his shoulder.

"And you are free to go. But you'd rather stay and dance with me."

She met his gaze, looked into eyes that were the green of a forest river, and for a moment everything within her stilled in a kind of recognition. She struggled to recall what he'd said, struggled to hold on to her own sense of who and where she was. "That's quite an ego you have there," she said, with a lightness she didn't feel.

"Perhaps." The smile left his lips but it lingered in his eyes, sought a response in hers. "Am I wrong about you wanting this next dance?"

"No."

HAVING THE BILLIONAIRE'S BABY

BY
SANDRA HYATT

All the characters in this book have no existence outside the imagination of
the author, and have no relation whatsoever to anyone bearing the same name
or names. They are not even distantly inspired by any individual known or
unknown to the author, and all the incidents are pure invention.

Published in Great Britain 2010
Harlequin Mills & Boon Limited,
Eton House, 18-24 Paradise Road, Richmond, Surrey TW9 1SR

© Sandra Hyde 2009

ISBN: 978 0 263 88183 7

51-1010

Harlequin Mills & Boon policy is to use papers that are natural, renewable
and recyclable products and made from wood grown in sustainable forests.
The logging and manufacturing processes conform to the legal environmental
regulations of the country of origin.

Printed and bound in Spain
by Litografia Rosés S.A., Barcelona

After completing a business degree, traveling and then settling into a career in marketing, **Sandra Hyatt** was relieved to experience one of life's "Eureka!" moments while on maternity leave when she discovered that writing books, although a lot slower, was just as much fun as reading them. She knows life doesn't always hand out happy endings and figures that's why books ought to. She loves being along for the journey with her characters as they work around, over and through the obstacles standing in their way. Sandra has lived in both the US and England and currently lives near the coast in New Zealand with her high-school sweetheart and their two children.

You can visit her at www.sandrahyatt.com.

For Scott.
For everything and for always.

Dear Reader,

Welcome to this, my very first Desire™ book. Callie and Nick's story came to me as I played around with the idea of a hardworking "good girl" who, just once, ignores her master plan and acts on impulse—with far-reaching repercussions. Nick, another of life's planners (and whose plans definitely didn't include fatherhood), seemed like the perfect hero for her. It just took the two of them a little while to figure that out. I've occasionally heard the process of writing a book compared to having a baby. At first there's the merest glimmer of an idea, the almost impossibility of it ever becoming anything, then the gestation period where it grows and develops, and then finally, all going well, you get to hold your baby in your arms, or hands, as the case may be.

This book is the end result of that very first glimmer of an idea and I hope you enjoy reading it even half as much as I enjoyed writing it.

Happy reading,

Sandra

One

Life is too short for this. Callie Jamieson stepped onto the dimly lit balcony and let the plate glass door swing closed behind her, gladly trading the glitz of the New Year's Eve wedding reception for the silent reflection of lights on Sydney's Darling Harbor.

Relaxing her grip on her champagne flute, she moved away from the pulsing beat of the music to the shadowy corner that offered not only the most privacy, but the best view of the glistening water. She shook her head and allowed herself a smile. What had she been trying to prove? The exercise regime, the new dress, new hairstyle. And at the end of it all she'd rather be walking barefoot along the water's edge. Alone.

She made her resolution then and there. Stop searching for a future or wallowing in the mistakes of her past, and start enjoying the present.

The music washed louder over her and she tensed with the knowledge that someone else had come onto the balcony. She stayed still, facing the water, hoping that the night and the slender potted palms positioned in front of the handrail would screen her from the casual observer.

"Rosa wanted me to call." A deep, resonant voice carried to her. "She insisted I do it right now. So, how's it going?" There was a long pause. "Congratulations. I guess we really do have to excuse you for not making it to the wedding." Did she imagine the catch of emotion in that warm voice? Curiosity got the better of her and Callie turned her head. A man stood midway along the balcony. With the light behind him, the only thing she could be sure of was that he was tall and that his crisply cut dark hair had a hint of a wave. With one hand he held a phone to his ear, and in his other he carried a glass of champagne the match of hers.

"Give me the details so I can pass them on to the family. We'll do the cigars when we get back." His accent was predominantly Australian, but with an underlying hint of something more exotic.

Callie glanced from her unknown companion to the balcony door and back again. Hopefully, he'd finish his call and be the one to go. She just needed a little peace, a little space before she reentered the fray and then made a discreet exit from this entire fiasco. Tomorrow morning she would be on the plane back home to New Zealand.

"Give Lisa our love." From the corner of her eye, Callie saw him start toward the door. A sigh of relief welled within her, but was cut short at the ringing of his phone.

"Nick speaking."

Nick? Brusque. Strong.

"What is it, Angelina?" The warmth she'd heard

earlier was gone. His deep, measured voice was resigned and somewhat displeased. The contrast intrigued her, and Callie turned a little more. He'd stopped partway toward the doors, and the light spilling onto him revealed broad shoulders tapering to lean hips. In the stark lines of his profile—the strong jaw, the nose with the slight bump midway along—she recognized one of the groomsmen.

There had been plenty of time during the hour-long service to contemplate the bridal party: the striking, petite blond bride, the five rose-pink, ruffled and frilled bridesmaids and the equal number of groomsmen, most of them dark-haired, and all of them good-looking.

This one's mix of careless elegance and intensity had piqued her curiosity. Was he naturally serious, did he have a problem with the wedding, or would he, like her, just rather be somewhere else?

During the second scriptural reading she had imagined a moment's eye contact, as though he'd sensed her study of him, and her mouth had run dry. Logic told her that, from her position at the rear of the cathedral, that sensation of connection, of heat, was surely impossible.

Now, as she had then, she looked away. He wasn't a friend of Jason, the groom, so his link had to be with the bride.

"You ended it, Angelina, and it was the right decision. I hadn't realized how much your expectations had changed." It wasn't as easy to stop listening as it was to stop looking. There was a long pause before he spoke again. "We agreed at the start that neither of us was looking for that sort of commitment."

Callie focused on the city lights, and though she knew she shouldn't be eavesdropping, still, a part of her waited for him to speak again. There was another even longer pause. "I'm sorry." His voice had gentled. "But no. You know this is for the best." With a heavy sigh he snapped his phone shut. "Damn," he said quietly into the night.

Callie felt for the unknown woman. She had done her time with a man who didn't want to commit. She knew the pain and sense of inadequacy that brought. She wouldn't ever go there again.

Today, she had watched the man she once thought she would marry pledge his love to another woman.

She glanced over her shoulder, and between the arching fronds of a palm saw Nick rest his forearms on the balcony railing. A warm breeze sifted through her hair. It was no hardship to wait him out. Taking a sip of chilled champagne, she looked back at the play of lights on the ink-black water. For long, restful minutes she considered how she could re-create the effect with oils.

"Solitude is one thing and loneliness another. Which is it for you?"

The words were so quietly spoken, Callie wasn't sure they were directed at her. She looked over to see that the stranger had turned in her direction. Dark eyes were fixed on her. But how to answer? Was this solitude or loneliness?

A phrase of her mother's popped into her head. "If you're choosing between bad company and loneliness choose the latter." Except, that wasn't quite right. The loneliness had been inside the dazzling reception, surrounded by others. Outside was the blissful solitude. Callie was suddenly struck by how insulting the remark could seem. Especially by a member of the wedding party. Her mother would have softened the remark with a toss of her head and a gurgle of throaty laughter.

Callie, who usually prided herself on being nothing like her mother, could carry off neither.

The man assessed her anew, curiosity rather than affront in his gaze. "Should I ask about the bad company or the loneliness?"

She sought to deflect that interest. Hopefully, he didn't know she was the ex-girlfriend, here only because she and Jason were determined to keep their relationship amicable. "Perhaps like you, I came out to take a phone call."

A half smile lifted one corner of his mouth and his amused gaze flicked over her, bringing a frisson of awareness as he took in the sleeveless, red sheath that skimmed her curves, finishing at her ankles. It was a dress she never would have worn if she'd still been with Jason. He preferred muted colors and conservative styles. There was no place on this dress for even the slimmest of phones, and her evening bag still lay on her seat between Jason's overly friendly uncle and his unfriendly cousin. Dark eyebrows rose appreciatively. "Technology is a marvelous thing."

She smiled reluctantly. "Or perhaps I just came out for some fresh air." Surreptitiously, she returned his assessment. The cut of his suit whispered tailor-made rather than off-the-rack. And no distortion of its classic lines betrayed the phone he'd slipped into a pocket.

"Or solitude?" he asked.

Her smile widened. "Definitely that."

Holding her gaze, he lifted his glass. The pale liquid shimmered golden in the light from inside, bubbles glinted like tiny jewels. "To solitude."

She raised her glass in return. The irony of toasting solitude with someone else wasn't lost on either of them.

He touched his glass to his lips and took a sip, and Callie watched the slide of his Adam's apple, then looked away, conscious of her awareness of him. For a time they remained silent. Out on the harbor a launch motored toward the bridge, the low murmur of its engine drifting across the water.

"So, is there someone waiting impatiently inside for your return?"

The undisguised spark of interest warmed her ego. "No." And for the first time that evening it didn't seem such a bad thing that Marc, her colleague, had bailed on her at the last minute. The guests and the bride and groom were supposed to have seen her dancing gaily with a gorgeous man. It was meant to demonstrate how well she had gotten on with her life.

"Then I propose another toast. To new beginnings, new lives. To freedom."

Is that what he felt over the end of his relationship? Callie lifted her glass. "To freedom." She tested the concept. And in saying the words she recognized the feeling that of late had been unfurling within her. They both took another sip.

"Unfortunately, however, I'm not as free as I'd wish tonight." He glanced inside. "Duty calls." In three strides he was at the door. He paused with his hand on the saucer-size silver disc that served as its handle and turned back to her. "Perhaps a dance later?"

His gaze, full of promise, held hers as she answered. "Perhaps." She got the feeling he wasn't often refused.

He smiled, teeth gleaming white in the night, his eyes reflecting the glitter of light from inside. It was the first smile she'd seen from him, and Callie revised her opinion as she gripped the railing for support. Merely intriguing when he wasn't smiling, he was knee-weakening when he was. He even had a dimple.

Just one, low on his left cheek. He probably had a litany of faults, but certainly none of them were obvious to the eye.

Nick pulled open the door and disappeared. Mesmerized, Callie watched the glass panel swing slowly shut behind him. She gave her head a quick shake, trying to dislodge the schoolgirl sensation of enchantment that had enveloped her while they'd been speaking.

Reality returned.

"Perhaps" was no commitment on either of their parts. She was free to go. She had come, seen Jason married, and felt almost nothing. Certainly no pain, only regret that they had stayed together for as long as they had. If he'd told her the truth—not that he wasn't ready to get married yet, but that he wasn't ready to marry *her*—they could have parted sooner. Six years seemed such a colossal waste.

She gave herself a few more minutes of the view and the peace, then crossed to the door. Blinking against the bright lights, she stepped inside. The high-ceilinged ballroom was hung with crystal chandeliers and brimmed with women in shimmering dresses and men in tuxedos. Laughter and music filled the air.

Callie glanced toward the dance floor in front of the head table and saw Nick expertly leading a plump woman in a waltz. Grinning, he lowered his head toward her silver curls and said something. The woman laughed and slapped his shoulder. Nick laughed back.

With an unexpected twinge of regret that she would never know what it was like to be held in his arms, Callie sought the exit. The doors beckoned on the far side of the room. Surely no one would either notice or care if she left now. Tonight, thoughts were turned to celebration and new beginnings. And she'd got that much herself. Closure of a chapter, a fresh page to start her life on. Tomorrow a new year would begin. She had proved, at least to herself, that she was well and truly over Jason. She wished him and Melody only the best.

She would retrieve her evening bag then slip away. But as she got closer to her table she found her way blocked by a cluster of bridesmaids, heads conspiratorially close together.

Callie tried to edge behind them, there was just enough room.

"It's not public knowledge yet," one of the bridesmaids whispered dramatically. "But Melody and Jason are both over the moon about the news. Jason hasn't stopped grinning since they found out."

Callie froze, her hips pressed against the back of a chair swathed in linen and gold.

"He's almost mollycoddling her," the whisperer continued. "Of course, she loves it."

"When's she due?" asked another.

"Six months."

Despite how much Callie wanted children, Jason had insisted that he didn't. Not yet. She had persuaded herself that she was content to wait. Obviously, his denial should also have come with the same qualification as his sentiments on marriage—*and not with you*.

Her grip on her champagne flute tightened. She had been so naive, searching for the perfect life, hoping for a future where there was never going to be one. Because, in reality she had been his holding pattern—company, while he waited for the right woman. Her chest constricted. The sensation that out on the balcony had felt like blossoming freedom withered into soggy loserdom.

She closed her eyes. She had tried so hard, and it

hadn't been enough. Taking a fortifying breath, she straightened her spine and opened her eyes. The past couldn't be changed, but the present could. She had to get out of here. She didn't even care about her evening bag. There was nothing in it she needed.

Except her room key.

Her heart sank, but she rallied. Never mind. She would go for a walk and come back for it later. With a careful sidestep, she eased herself back the way she'd come, and with escape beckoning, spun around.

And collided with Melody.

Callie's champagne coursed down the intricately beaded front of the bride's designer wedding gown.

For a second they both froze in horror. Aghast, Callie snatched up a linen napkin and blotted frantically at the dress. "Melody, I'm so sorry."

"It's okay." Melody tried to help. "It was an accident." But the bride's distress showed clearly in her wide eyes and the hitch in her breath.

Two bridesmaids rushed over looking daggers at Callie. She took a step back and was about to apologize again, when a deep voice cut through the bridesmaids' dramatic squawks. "Good thing it wasn't the merlot."

Callie looked up to see Nick rest his hand on Melody's shoulder. "It'll be okay." His quiet assurance calmed the bride, who smiled ruefully. They seemed close, and Callie wondered, not for the first time, what their connection was. She guessed Nick to be maybe a decade older than Melody's twenty-four.

"I thought it would be me who spilled the wine." Melody laughed hesitantly.

"Didn't I hear you say earlier it was time to change into your going away outfit?"

Melody nodded her agreement and was escorted away by a posse of bridesmaids, two of whom cast accusing glances back at Callie as they left.

Nick turned to her, a half smile playing about his lips. "I believe you owe me a dance."

She shook her head. "I should go."

"Why the rush? The dancing has barely begun." His large, warm hand enfolded hers, and it seemed easier to follow than to refuse him. And it was certainly easier to be in the company of someone so sure of himself. He led her between the tables, smiling and nodding at various guests, but not breaking his stride. "One dance, and then if you still insist, you can go."

They reached the parquet dance floor and he turned her into his arms. The band had begun a new song, and they waltzed effortlessly among the other couples. She remembered, almost with a start of surprise, how much she liked to dance. Jason had never enjoyed it, and so it had been a long time since she'd last felt the freedom—there was that word again—of the dance floor. Slowly the tension seeped from her. This man's presence was so potent, his touch so captivating, she could almost forget who and where she was.

He danced well, and they fit together with the ease of couples who had danced this way many times, each knowing intuitively how the other would move. The touch of his hand was firm yet gentle at her waist, his shoulder solid and powerful beneath her palm. She breathed in his scent, a mix of expensive cologne and masculinity, and smiled.

"That's better." His voice was warm and intimate in her ear.

The music slowed almost to a stop. Reality returned.

With a sense of impending loss, Callie tried to disengage her hand. The band segued into another number and Nick, his palm still curving around her waist, began moving again.

She looked up and saw his smile.

It should carry a mental health warning. One glimpse and you'll forget your own will. She held frantically to hers. "You said one dance and then I was free to go." Yet she left her hand on his shoulder.

"And you are free to go. But you'd rather stay and dance with me."

She met his gaze, looked into eyes that were the green of a forest river, and for a moment everything within her stilled in a kind of recognition. She struggled to recall what he'd said, struggled to hold on to her own sense of who and where she was. "That's quite an ego you have there," she said with a lightness she didn't feel.

"Perhaps." The smile left his lips, but it lingered in his eyes, sought a response in hers. "Am I wrong about you wanting this next dance?"

"No," she admitted, allowing her lips to curve. She was dancing with this man not because it was the appropriate or right thing to do, but purely because she wanted to. If this was freedom she could easily get used to it.

"Good."

She felt as if she'd passed some kind of test. As they glided around the floor, Callie lost awareness of everything except Nick and their bodies, of his closeness, and his supple strength. For the first time in a long time, she felt both desirable and desired. A heady sensation. And in an unsought response, she felt, too, the reciprocal stirring of yearning deep within her. She could imagine wanting more, taking more.

One dance blended into the next. The music changed to something with a slow, steady rhythm and a Latin-American feel. And as they moved. Nick looked down at her. Those river-green eyes seemed to see right into her. *Please let him not know the forbidden territory her thoughts had ranged to.* Callie looked away and was startled to realize that, save for one other couple locked in an embrace, the dance floor was now empty and the crowd in the ballroom had thinned considerably. As if in a waking dream, she looked back into Nick's eyes and felt herself drawn deeper.

His eyes darkened. With a fluid movement, he spun her away, then drew her back into him. For a second her back pressed against him, his arms encircled her. With another turn, she was facing him again and breathing more rapidly than the dancing warranted.

Her awareness centered wholly on this man and the way their bodies moved together to the rhythm of the music. He led expertly, signaling with his touch where he wanted her to go, and she followed that self-assurance effortlessly.

She thought in that moment that she, who liked to lead in life, would follow him anywhere.

They turned and for a passing moment their thighs intertwined. Loverlike. The desire that had been smoldering all evening ignited and swept through her.

"Tell me your name?" His jaw, faintly shadowed, was only a whisper away from her face, and his voice resonated through her.

"Calypso." She chose to tell him her full name. She didn't often use it. Jason had never liked it; he'd thought it odd. But wasn't tonight about reclaiming a part of herself she'd lost? She'd been named after a boat, for goodness' sake, but at least a boat that had sailed the high seas and sought adventure.

Another turn. "It's beautiful," he said. Her gaze met his, and the masks were stripped away. He saw the desire she couldn't conceal. She saw its match in the green depths of his eyes.

He wanted her.

Her pulse leapt as her mouth ran dry. She wanted him too.

The ground seemed to disappear beneath her feet, replaced by the soaring sensation of freedom. Terrifying and exhilarating. The freedom to choose—that power heady and intoxicating. Or perhaps that was the man himself. It had been so long since anyone had looked at her like that.

He exuded confidence, strength and a barely concealed sexuality. And he tempted her. But she also knew he wanted no commitment. He was not at all what she was looking for.

But searching for what she thought she wanted had resulted in disappointment and disaster. She reminded herself of her resolution to live in the present, to seize life.

Perhaps? The word shimmered with limitless possibilities. Perhaps for tonight she could throw caution and practicality and planning to the wind, and go where fate, or lust, was leading her. Perhaps for tonight she could seize life with both hands and actually live a little. Tomorrow she would return to her real life of responsibilities and careful planning. But tonight…

"Are you ready to go?"

She knew what he was asking. "Yes."

* * *

Nick held Calypso's delicate hand in his as he led her to the elevators. She asked him no questions, offered nothing about herself. That lack of any attempt to create a basis for intimacy told him she wasn't looking for any more than he was. Perhaps it was because of that reticence that he suddenly found he wanted to know more about her—who she was, what made her laugh, what made her cry, her secret hopes and fears.

His sister's wedding was the last place he thought he'd meet someone and feel this pull of attraction. After the tensions of the last few months with Angelina, both before and after their relationship ended, he'd planned on enjoying a break, some time on his own without the demands of a relationship.

The solitude he had toasted with the woman now at his side.

But there was something different about this woman. He had felt a connection the moment he'd first seen her dark silhouette in the night. He felt a connection now, just holding her hand in his.

Some things are meant to be. His grandmother Rosa's words. He tamped down on the thought. He wasn't a believer in fate. A man created his own destiny. But this…this felt like fate. He could almost hear Rosa's soft, knowing laugh. Rosa, who had sent him outside to make that call. As though she had known…something.

No matter how often he denied it, she insisted that Nick was the only one in the family to have inherited her *gift*. And sometimes, like now, he could almost believe it. He smiled when he realized what he was doing, using mumbo jumbo to justify going to bed with a woman he'd just met.

This wasn't destiny. This was his libido awakening. He pressed the button for the elevator.

"You're smiling?"

He looked down at the woman beside him and was drawn into her chocolate-colored eyes. He lifted his free hand, fingered one of the silken curls that framed her face. He could imagine how she would look the morning after a night of passion—tousled and sleepy. The thought took him by surprise. His mind didn't usually leap so far ahead with a woman. He lived moment by moment. But he could see the morning after, could imagine breakfasts in bed. Could imagine lunches, dinners, more dancing. "I have a lot to smile about."

Her own smile in return was hesitant, but no less powerful for that. Satisfaction and desire swelled. He had wanted to make her smile, to erase a shadow of sorrow that seemed to lurk behind her eyes. He knew that, for tonight at least, he could make her forget everything. A knowing glint touched her eyes and temptation leaped. He wrenched his gaze away. If he kissed those softly parted lips now he wouldn't want to stop. He jabbed the button again, and was rewarded with the ping signaling the elevator's arrival.

As the doors slid closed, secluding them in the private space, he did what he'd ached to since he first saw her standing alone on the balcony. He curved his fingers around her slender neck, his thumb resting at the softly vulnerable juncture of throat and jaw, her hair like silk cascaded over his knuckles.

Savoring the moment, he bent his head to taste her.

It was a gentle kiss, as though they had all the time in the world. She tilted her head and the kiss deepened. Peaches. She tasted of the sun-ripened peaches that had been served with dessert. Her lips were pliant beneath his. Their bodies scarcely touched, and yet need for her arrowed through him.

He was a man who stayed in control. At all times. He was known for it. But here, in an elevator, that control was perilously thin. It was with a mixture of despair and reprieve that he realized they had arrived at the top floor and the doors were waiting open.

He lifted his head, looked again into those deep brown eyes and reached for her hands. Her hastily retrieved evening bag dangled from one slender wrist as he raised her hands to his lips and kissed each of her knuckles in turn.

They walked toward his suite. It seemed important not to rush. Time needed to be taken to absorb her, the touch of her hand, the scent of her hair, the awareness of how her body moved so close to, and so in tune with his.

Pulling the card key for his room from his pocket, he hesitated as he held it above the slot. He looked at her, wanted her to be absolutely certain. Wanted to know that this craving wasn't of his own imagination. She slid the card from his fingers and inserted it. When the access light blinked green, she pushed open the door and stepped into the room ahead of him.

She turned and reached toward him. As he took her hands in his, the thought that he never wanted to release them assailed him. He met her gaze, losing himself in eyes that seemed both brazen and innocent. With a smile that matched her gaze, she pulled him through the doorway and into her arms.

For a moment she stood pressed against his chest, fitting perfectly, as he knew they would fit in other ways. Her supple warmth flowed into him, heated him further still.

She tilted her face upward and kissed him. And took his breath away.

Again that taste of peaches, and beneath that a subtle flavor and scent that was hers alone, enhanced by the heat and longing of desire. His hands skimmed over her curves, the red fabric of her dress silken and sliding beneath his palms.

He ached to claim her. Every inch of her. With every inch of him. He needed this to be as unique and special for her as every sense told him it was going to be for him.

He wanted tonight to last forever.

He broke the kiss and rested his forehead against hers. He cupped her pale shoulders bathed in the dim city light that spilled through the window. Beneath his touch he felt movement as her hands, both delicate and forceful, pulled his shirttails free, worked buttons undone until they slid—exploring, learning and trailing fire in their wake—up his front and settled on his chest, over his heart. Did she feel how it pounded with the blood that rushed through him for her?

There was a moment of stillness, the calm before the storm, and then they were kissing again, tongues teasing and dancing, that connection remaining true as clothes were peeled away and discarded.

Her beauty and her passion staggered him, stirred something unknown within him, a primal intensity that made him want to claim her not just for now, but for always.

The *now* he knew how to deal with as they fell onto his bed.

Dawn was just beginning to lighten the sky when Callie slipped from the tangle of luxurious sheets. It wasn't till she'd finished dressing that she turned back to look at Nick. Even sleeping, he enthralled her. He was…beautiful. There didn't seem any other word for it. His dark hair was tousled, eyelashes curved above high, shadowed cheekbones. One arm was thrown up above his head, the bicep pale and curving. And the chest. Ahh, the chest. Callie took a moment for that alone.

Recalling herself, she crossed to the desk in the suite, her footsteps cushioned by the deep carpet. As she looked for a pen and paper she contemplated what to say, how to say it. Name and number alone? Thank you? Something witty about his kind of company being so much better than solitude? She looked at the sleeping man again. If she leaned down and kissed those lips he'd awaken. But she had a plane to catch.

Picking up a silver pen, she reached for one of the business cards that sat in a small, neat stack. About to turn it over she glimpsed his full name.

And froze.

Dominic Brunicadi. She dropped the card as though it burned.

What had she done? The billionaire bachelor was many things—almost a client, newly related to her ex, and way, way out of her league—and all of those things precluded her having anything to do with him.

Two

Nick strode through the crowd at Auckland Airport, and despite his best efforts, thoughts of Calypso stole into his mind. The turn of her head, the light in her eyes, the delight of her laughter.

In the month since *that* night, he'd had a hard time forgetting her. There had been incredible chemistry between them, on the balcony, on the dance floor and later. He remembered it only too well, and too often. Or perhaps the plaguing sense of something lost was only pique that she had vanished.

He'd asked a couple of people who she was, but they hadn't known. He wouldn't ask more, because he liked to keep his private life just that. Still, he felt like he was trying to track down Cinderella. She must have been from Jason's side, and he fully intended asking Jason about her when the opportunity presented itself.

He had no intention of chasing after a woman who clearly wanted nothing further to do with him. She'd left no means of contacting her, nor had she called him—though he'd noticed his business cards had been disturbed. But he needed to know who she was.

And for his own peace of mind he needed to know the answer to one small but vital question.

He scanned the crowd. Ridiculous to even think he might see her here. Milling passengers riffled through bags and papers looking for passports and tickets, frazzled parents attempted to quiet fractious children. Ruthlessly, he pushed thoughts of her aside. He had his sights set on the exit doors and was mentally assessing his upcoming appointments when his cell rang. Not breaking his stride, he pulled the phone from his pocket and checked the ID.

"Melody?" He hadn't expected to hear from his sister so soon. She and Jason only got back from their honeymoon a few days ago. "How was Europe?"

He let his sister gush about their travels as he found the black Mercedes parked outside and slid into the seat.

"Glad to hear it went so well." Nick turned the key in the ignition and the engine purred to life. "But that's not why you called me, is it?" Mel seldom called without there being a reason. She knew he wasn't one for idle conversation. There was a suspiciously long pause.

"It's Jason."

Nick sat up a little straighter. Surely there wasn't trouble in paradise already. He didn't quite have Jason figured out yet, he'd spent so little time with the man. Nick had been in Europe when the relationship started, and it had progressed so rapidly that suddenly wedding invitations were going out. All he knew for sure was that Melody was besotted and she was happier than he'd seen her in years. So far, he'd been able to like the guy for that reason alone. "What's wrong?"

"Nothing. At least, I think it's nothing."

"What is it, Mel?"

He heard her indrawn breath. "I'm worried about his ex at Ivy Cottage PR."

He recognized the name of the New Zealand–based firm that Mel used for Cypress Rise, the boutique winery associated with their family home in the Hunter Valley. Mel had met Jason through his work on the winery's account. Nick knew nothing about the other partner, Jason's ex. "What about her?"

"It's probably nothing…."

"But?" Mel wouldn't be calling if she thought it was nothing.

"She and Jason used to be more than just business partners, and he still has a lot of contact with her. He wants to buy out her share of the business and run it from here, boost up the Australian side of things." Melody spoke quickly, as though unburdening herself. "He's offered her a good price, but she won't sell. He says he doesn't want to pressure her, but it's like she won't let go of him. And now she's phoning him at unusual times, late at night and early in the morning."

"Do you think you could be overreacting?" Mel had been hurt in the past and had been wary ever since.

"I could be. I probably am."

"But you're still worried?"

Melody gave an unconvincing laugh. "Yes."

"And you'd like me to go see her?"

"You're in New Zealand. And you have such a good feel for people. You could go in your capacity as a director of the winery."

"Even though I have nothing to do with the day-to-day running of the company?"

"I'd just like your opinion. I mean, she seemed nice, but most of my dealings with the business were with Jason."

Nick sighed. Melody was the only person who could twist him around her little finger. It had been that way since she came into the world ten years after him, and the bond between them had only strengthened with the death of their mother when Melody was three. Their father had coped by immersing himself in work, largely leaving the children to deal with their loss together. "I'll see if I can fit her in." They both knew that was as good as a promise. "Where do I find her?"

"Thanks." He heard the relief in her voice. "It means a lot to me."

But when he did make time to call in at the ivy-covered cottage on the outskirts of the city, Ms. Jamieson wasn't in, and the surprisingly young receptionist, with spiky, ink-black hair tipped with red, would only say she wasn't due back in the office till Monday morning.

However, what he did spy on the receptionist's desk was an invitation to an awards ceremony taking place that evening. He recalled Melody telling him earlier about the New Zealand PR campaign for their wines being nominated for an award, and how she wouldn't be able to go, because she'd only just be back from the honeymoon. He considered his evening ahead. He could reshuffle a few things.

In the glittering banquet hall, Nick talked easily to acquaintances from the hotel and wine industry as he scanned the room. Even if, as he suspected, Melody was overreacting, the evening wouldn't be a total waste of time. He'd picked up some useful pieces of information and made contact with several colleagues he hadn't seen in a while. One of them had pointed out Kelly Jamieson, seated at a table with her back to him. Glossy brown hair was pulled into an elegant twist at the back of her head. She wore a high-necked, slim-fitting gown of a dazzling electric blue. There was something familiar about the tilt of her head, and the pale creamy shoulders.

Nick blocked the thoughts and concentrated on the business at hand. All he needed was to talk to Ms. Jamieson and assess her intentions. As he started toward her, the woman turned her head and he caught a glance of her profile, long lashes, high cheekbones and a jaw with a hint of defiance.

Not Kelly, but Callie, Calypso.

He couldn't name the feeling that slammed into him. In the first unguarded instant it was almost something triumphant.

He'd found her.

But after that brief, shimmering moment, triumph turned to doubt and a sharp sense of betrayal. He paused. Relegating emotion, he sorted through the facts. This was the woman Mel suspected of interfering in her marriage. The same woman who had slept with him at Mel's wedding and then disappeared. A woman who had given him a name that, if not exactly false, didn't seem to be the name she was known by.

What if Mel's concerns weren't unfounded? What if she had slept with him to get at his sister or Jason? He had to at least consider the possibility.

Callie sat at the large round table, idly spinning the stem of her empty wineglass between thumb and fore-finger as she listened to Robert from Harvey PR explain in detail the campaign his company had been nominated for.

She tried to be attentive, but couldn't help her relief when finally the MC, a moonlighting television presenter, stood behind the podium and gradually the conversation died away. The chair on her right was pulled out and she glanced up at the tall figure beside her. As the MC began his introduction the breath stalled in her lungs.

"Nick." His name passed her lips on an exhalation that left her feeling winded.

Over the last month she'd constantly tried, and failed, to stop thinking about him. Seizing the day—or night—had seemed such a good idea at the time. And a spectacularly bad idea in the dim light of an early Sydney morning.

"Calypso." He sat easily in the chair next to her, smiled a greeting to the others at the table before turning back to her. His gaze met hers. For long seconds she could only stare. Her heart and her head vied for control of her reaction.

She looked into the green depths of his eyes and saw…nothing, not the warmth she remembered, no surprise, either. He was studying her, looking for something, but she couldn't tell what. "You left early the morning after the wedding."

Early and fast. She'd practically sprinted from the room after seeing his business card. She lifted her chin, didn't want him to see her turmoil. "I had a plane to catch."

"Of course." He agreed easily. And yet, despite the outwardly relaxed manner, she had the feeling he was anything but.

She hadn't once seen him in her three years working with the Cypress Rise account, and she'd fervently hoped that trend would continue. All she wanted was to be able to put him out of her mind. As she looked at him now, she was forced to accept that things just weren't going her way lately.

It also didn't help that for the last couple of weeks she'd been working on the Jazz and Art festival she was organizing for Cypress Rise. In fact, with the account so to the fore of her workload, she'd actually congratulated herself for pausing only occasionally to bang her head on her desk and mutter, *What was I thinking?*

She took a deep and supposedly calming breath. "I wasn't expecting to see anyone from Cypress Rise here. Melody said—"

"That she couldn't make it. Fortunately, I could."

"Fortunately." She tried and failed to imbue the word with sincerity.

His gaze flicked over her before coming back to her face. "You're looking very demure tonight." The softly spoken words contrasted dramatically with the cool gaze. "Though I think I preferred the siren-red, with the low neck and that delectable thigh-high split in the side."

This was no wistful recollection. She looked at him, confused by his thinly veiled accusation. Where was he going with this?

"And your hair. I liked it loose against your shoulders." For a moment the sharp gaze softened. "I liked the way it brushed across—"

"This is a business function." Callie said quickly before he could call to mind images that had no place here.

He straightened. "As opposed to a seduction?"

Her confusion deepened. "Surely, you're not suggesting that—"

"I'm not suggesting anything. Just curious."

"About?"

"Several things. Your name, for instance. Everybody else seems to know you by Callie."

"It's Calypso, but I don't always use the full version." Why was she feeling that she had to defend herself for using her own name?

"Ahh." The river-green eyes were narrowed. Strange how, at the wedding, those eyes had seemed full of promise and passion. If there was promise there now, it was not of good things to come.

"We'd toasted freedom." She gave in to the urge to explain. "Calypso felt right for…then."

His face advertised his disbelief. Was she being accused of both seducing and deceiving him? Callie's spine stiffened. She lowered her voice. "Over the last few weeks I've engaged in plenty of self-recrimination for my lapse in judgment that night. And though I'm happy to heap blame on myself, I'm not going to let you do it, because there were two of us in that room—equal partners." The sense of equality in itself, something she hadn't felt before in the bedroom, had been liberating. But it wasn't something she wanted to dwell on now.

A waiter came to stand at her shoulder, offering to fill her glass. She nodded acceptance, though she seldom drank. Jason and Melody's wedding being a notable exception. Still, the wine was a Cypress Rise vintage, and she'd scored something of a coup in getting it served tonight.

The MC finished a joke about the PR and advertising business and good-natured laughter filled the room. Callie hadn't heard a word of it.

Nick leaned in, his face so close she could almost count the dark, spiky lashes framing his accusing eyes.

"It's not equal if one person has far more information than the other, and if that person chooses to withhold it."

She held that gaze. To think she'd once imagined a connection with this man. The cold reality was that he was a complete stranger. "I withheld no more than you did."

"You're saying you didn't know who I was?"

She leaned in, too, matching his stance while she made her point. "Not till the next morning, when I saw your business card."

"Despite the speeches?"

A strange heat built, as neither of them backed away or broke the contact of their gaze. Callie desperately wanted to attribute the heat to anger. "Most of which I missed." To avoid Jason's uncle and his unavuncular patting of her thigh.

"I was in the wedding party."

She fought the distraction of the familiar, masculine scent of his cologne. "There being so few of you in the wedding party, and the resemblance between you and your sister being so striking." Nick, olive-skinned and over six feet tall, looked nothing like petite, blond Melody. He gave a single, slow nod of his head. He seemed to be acknowledging, if not exactly buying, her point.

"I can't think why you're so reluctant to believe me. Aside from anything else I would never have…a relationship—" what else could she call it "—of that kind with a client."

"Company policy?" he asked in a deceptively calm voice.

Given what had happened between Jason and Melody, she could hardly insist that it was. "Personal ethics," she said instead.

For long seconds he continued to study her. Finally

he looked away and relief washed through her at the break in the tension. He took a sip of his wine, savored it before swallowing. He'd heard her defense; she didn't know if he believed it.

"Look, Nick. We shared…" She broke off as a second waiter appeared and placed a plate of mango salad in front of each of them.

"Fantastic sex." He finished for her in a voice that was low, but not low enough. The waiter's eyes widened as he looked at her. Callie glared at him and he backed deferentially away.

She transferred her glare from the waiter to its rightful target, but chose to neither confirm nor deny the question. Denying it would be a blatant lie, and confirming it suddenly seemed like a very bad idea.

"A night."

He smiled at her choice of words.

"Of freedom. But…"

"But?" There was something in his eyes. A memory?

Much as she didn't want to, she remembered too. "That's all it was." She'd had her taste of that kind of freedom, and it wasn't for her. That one night had crystallized her goals and needs. Her plans for her life centered on her business and hopefully one day finding the right man, a man who appreciated the simple things in life—like love—a man who wanted to settle down and have children. Even if she hadn't heard Nick ending a relationship that was looking like too much commitment, the research she'd done on him after she came home told her not only of his phenomenal success in business— buying up companies like she bought coffees—but also of the string of glamorous women he dated.

The MC's voice broke over them as he announced the

winner of the first category. Callie applauded as Tony, a colleague and university classmate, headed for the stage. He made a brief speech of acceptance and thanks.

As the main course—mustard-seared rack of lamb— was served, Callie picked up her fork and, from the corner of her eye, watched as Nick picked up his. She saw his hands, strong and capable, remembered what those hands had done to her. Nick leaned closer. She caught his scent again, and despite or perhaps because of her anger, it stirred something else equally primal, and equally resented. Because all they had shared was dancing and sex, all her thoughts associated with him were physical and intimate. She fought to shut down that awareness.

He nodded at her untouched wine glass. "You're not drinking."

Again she was caught off guard by where his thoughts might be heading. "I don't." She tried to sound nonchalant.

"You did at the wedding."

"Not much. Mostly I just carried the glass around." As though holding a glass could make her look like she was having a good time. "And it's not a commandment or anything. I make the occasional exception." Like, if she really felt the need to fortify herself as she had that night.

Tonight, on the other hand, she got the feeling she needed her wits about her more than anything else.

"Are you pregnant?"

Callie's fork clattered to her plate and she looked up. A frown pleated his brow. His eyes had softened as they searched her face. She looked away.

"Keep your voice down. It's not going to be good for my business if the rumor starts circulating that I'm pregnant."

The MC introduced Len Joseph, an old mentor of Callie's and an industry stalwart, who would be announcing the nominations for Innovation in a Small Business, the category she was a surprise finalist in.

"I wondered, because of—"

"I'm not." She cut him off before he could say the words "broken condom" aloud. That had been the one awful surprise in an otherwise blissful night. But it had broken early during their lovemaking, and they'd assured each other it would be okay. She closed her eyes for a few seconds. Please let this be over and then she could slip out of here and never have to see this man and all the things he reminded her of again.

"You've had your period?"

She opened her eyes and looked hastily around to make sure no one was listening in on their conversation. "Yes." She'd had her period. It had been a little late and a little light, but she'd definitely had it. "Now, could we change the subject, please?"

Some of the tension eased from Nick's jaw and shoulders. What would he do, or want to do, if she had become pregnant? He'd surely be appalled by the prospect. And she couldn't blame him. She wouldn't know what to do herself. But to get pregnant after her one and only one-night stand would have surely been both incredibly unlikely and incredibly unlucky.

And she would have had only herself to blame. She should never have acted on the compulsions of that glittering night. Besides, she'd provided the condoms. She had slipped the little box, a present from her PA, into her evening bag as she'd got ready that evening, never expecting to use them. They were a symbol of her independence, a step on her journey of liberation.

She'd decided, as she'd worried about the repercussions of what she'd done, that some kinds of liberation weren't all they were cracked up to be. What she sought lay within herself, not with someone else.

Callie turned back to her unwanted meal. And yet, there was that loudly ticking biological clock, the one that had lately started chiming the quarter hour, as well, and that little voice that, when she was least expecting it, whispered "a baby" in reverential tones. She might not know precisely what she'd do if she was pregnant, but she couldn't help sometimes wondering. After her relief at the arrival of her period there had been a quiet, fleeting disappointment.

Suddenly, Robert Harvey clapped her on the back. Applause sounded and Callie looked up to see her stunned face on the enormous screen at the front of the room.

Dammit. She'd won her category.

She dredged up a smile; but as she stood to walk to the stage, Len noticed Nick and called him to come up with her as a representative of Cypress Rise. Callie couldn't believe it. Wasn't it just her luck that the two men knew each other?

Nick's hand touched lightly at the small of her back as she climbed the stairs, and she had to fight the urge to spin around and slap it away, because even that courteous touch caused sparks of unwanted awareness.

She accepted the plaque and the asymmetrical glass award with a kiss on the cheek from Len, then turned to find Nick directly in front of her. "Congratulations," he said, and she couldn't read the expression in his eyes. Strong hands curled around her bare upper arms as he bent to kiss her briefly on one cheek. "I remember the scent of your perfume." The softly spoken words teased across her skin. "It's haunted me for the last month." He kissed her other cheek, Italian fashion. The applause increased. Fingers trailed the length of her arms as he stepped away. He was playing to the audience, the louse, and could have no idea how very much he disconcerted her.

"Touch me again after this," she said with a wide smile, knowing only he would hear her words "and I'm sure I could find a novel use for this sharp and surprisingly heavy award."

Nick's quiet laughter was low and deep and seemed to resonate at a frequency her body was attuned to, stirring…feelings. Feelings she couldn't—didn't want to name.

He stood behind her as she made a brief, impromptu acceptance speech. She could feel his presence, an aura of charisma and attraction. She hastened back down the stairs, but was stopped at the bottom by a photographer from a business publication covering the event. "Ms. Jamieson, a photo of you and your client, please? Mr. Brunicadi, could you stand a little closer?"

A flash went off as she was about to respond.

"Thanks." The man dashed off while bright spots still floated in front of her eyes.

Callie headed toward her table. The temptation to keep right on walking was fierce. She needed to get away from this man who made her think of the touch of city lights on the planes and contours of his body, who made her remember how she had been when she was with him—uninhibited, passionate—a woman she didn't quite recognize.

The real her didn't know how to handle being with Nick again. Whereas being with her didn't appear to bother him at all. Clearly, he'd had way more practice than she at seeing again someone you'd once slept with. As they neared her table, Nick slowed her with a hand on her arm. He glanced at the exit and shook his head as though he'd read her thoughts. "It'd be bad form." He pulled out her chair. "Stay. Enjoy your moment."

Callie glanced around the room—already smiling colleagues were making their way toward her. She looked back at Nick. "I'll stay because for the first time tonight you're right, it would be bad form. But you on the other hand, may as well leave, because I have nothing further to say to you."

His gaze flicked to the trophy she clutched, then back to her face. "I'll leave." He held her gaze. "Because with this win you'll be swamped for the rest of the evening. But, Calypso, we're not finished."

Three

Nick spread the morning paper out, frowning as the white wrought-iron table, too insubstantial for his liking, wobbled beneath his touch. Sunlight streamed onto the veranda of Calypso's gracious villa, promising another hot day. He leaned back in the chair and slipped on his sunglasses. It could almost be pleasant here. All he needed was a cup of good coffee. He checked his watch. Hopefully it wouldn't be too long before he could leave and get himself one.

He glanced at a vineyard not three hundred feet away. Long rows of vines stretched over the contours of the land. Even from this distance, he could see that the vines were ill-pruned and the grass around them too long.

Shaking his head, he turned his attention back to the paper. It wasn't his problem how her neighbors tended their vines. He skimmed the headlines before turning to the business pages. A photo of Calypso and him graced the second page. He studied the picture, saw her wide eyes, her full mouth, and a sensuous figure that even her seemingly modest dress couldn't disguise. Questions assailed him. Why had she really slept with him? If it was simple attraction, why had she disappeared? Why the late-night phone calls that Melody was so worried about?

They were questions he needed answered. But could he trust her? Or, more importantly, could he trust his own judgment, when every thought about her was clouded with memories, and an attraction that wouldn't abate?

He would keep her close till he had his answers, and if that closeness bothered her he'd look on it as a small measure of payback.

The bang of a cupboard door shutting sounded in the kitchen behind him. Last night he hadn't been prepared for the fact that Melody's problem woman and his mystery woman were one and the same. His resolve had been undermined by her confusion and his. And despite everything else, there had been no need to detract from her success in winning the award. She deserved that time to celebrate. So he had left.

But today was a new day and he was ready, anticipating their next clash.

A couple of minutes later the French doors at the other end of the veranda swung open and Callie stepped out. He didn't know what he'd expected, but it wasn't this.

He'd seen her in sleek red and dazzling blue, both times a mix of glamorous, elegant and sensual, but now her long legs and delicate feet were bare, she wore a white silk-and-lace negligee, but over the top of it an unbelted, soft, pink terry cloth bathrobe. The taunting contrasts of sweet innocence and seductress.

A man could slip his hands beneath that robe, cradle the silk-covered hips. He knew how her skin would feel beneath his touch. Nick swallowed, forced his gaze upward.

She held a steaming yellow mug. The scent of fresh coffee reached him. Walking to the edge of the veranda, she tipped her face up to the sun, closed her eyes and inhaled deeply.

Suddenly he wished he was anywhere but here. He didn't want to notice the rise and fall of her breasts. All he needed was answers, not to be seduced all over again. Though a part of him that wouldn't be silenced couldn't help but wishing it might be the other way around.

Callie turned and saw him and the serenity in her face transformed to shock. "What are you doing out here?"

"I didn't think you'd want me coming inside before you were up."

A frown drew her brows together. "I don't want you coming inside at all."

"It's a good thing I'm out here then, isn't it?" His deliberate calmness was a counterpoint to her flustered outrage. He'd discomposed the cool, Calypso Jamieson of last night. He knew better than to let his satisfaction show—or the fact that she discomposed him equally.

"No! It's not a good thing. I told you last night that I had nothing further to say to you." Her wide brown eyes flashed fire.

"You did. But though you may not have wanted to continue our conversation, I still have questions. And I want answers."

Callie strode the few steps to the table and set her mug down. Hot liquid slopped over the side.

With a touch of his fingers, Nick shifted the newspaper out of the way of the spreading puddle. "Mind your paper. Though, given your penchant for spilling drinks, I suppose I should be grateful I'm not wearing that."

"Given my feelings on finding you here at all, you should definitely be glad you're not wearing it." Her frown deepened. "Whose paper?"

He shrugged. "It was down by the mailbox. I brought it up for you."

"Make yourself at home, won't you." Color suffused her face and her deceptively sweet voice was heavy with sarcasm. "Can I get you a drink? A cup of coffee? Perhaps you'd like a bagel?"

Nick glanced at her coffee, then the damp patch on the table. "No, thanks."

It might be pushing her too far to take her up on her offer, though it would almost be worth it to see her reaction.

He wanted to rile her, to unsettle her as she had him, as her proximity continued to do. But that wasn't what he was here for, and he needed to remember that. He closed the paper and folded it in half, pushing it to one side. "Why won't you sell your share of Ivy Cottage PR to Jason?"

Those brown eyes widened. "What?"

"You heard me."

"Yes, I heard you, but I can't quite believe the question."

"Believe it."

Her hands clenched into fists at her sides. "What I do with *my* business is just that, my business, not yours. I suggest you stop wasting your time, and mine, and leave."

He folded his arms. "I'm making it my business, and

I'm not going anywhere till I have some answers. We can get this over and done with through this one, simple conversation, or we can drag it out as long as you like. The choice is yours."

Her fists stayed clenched, but she shifted them to her hips. "What I want is for you to go. Leave, please. Now."

He didn't have time to be curious, but he didn't think anyone had ever tried to order him from a premises before. Nick slid his sunglasses from his eyes so he could meet her gaze directly. He wanted her to see just how serious he was. "I'm booked on a flight back to Sydney this afternoon. I'd like to catch it. Answer a few questions and I will. Choose not to answer and I'll be in your office on Monday morning, and then Tuesday and Wednesday…. You get the picture."

She didn't answer.

"Of course you can still refuse to speak to me, even at your office, but with you being the PR expert, you can imagine what the press would make of a rift between your firm and the client you've just won an award for. Quite an interesting tidbit. They do so love those stories with a human interest angle."

She stared at him and the silence lengthened. He didn't mind. He was good at silences.

"I'm getting changed." She stalked away.

Nick took her response as a concession. She would be coming back. He spread out the paper again and wondered if she'd make him wait endlessly. But she returned quickly. So at least she wasn't playing games. She wore slim-fitting jeans and a snug white T-shirt. Thankfully, now his focus wouldn't be splintered by expanses of creamy skin. Although her curves beneath the worn denim and soft cotton were their own definition of temptation. He focused on her face. It was just as bewitching. Only the righteous anger in her eyes helped ground him.

"I'm starting to see a picture," she said, her head tilted to one side. "Last night's insinuation of seduction and deception, this morning's ill-founded accusations." She pulled out the chair opposite him and sat down. "This has something to do with Jason and your sister, hasn't it?"

"You tell me. Explain the late-night phone calls, explain your reluctance to sell."

She continued studying him, but didn't answer his questions. "You were very quick to believe I had an ulterior motive in sleeping with you." Humor suddenly danced in her eyes. "Do women usually need one?"

He suppressed the smile that threatened. "It's not been my experience." He turned the tables back on Callie. "So you're saying it was attraction, pure and simple?"

Her eyes widened as she realized the trap she'd fallen into. "A *passing* attraction," she said quickly.

This time he let his smile show. Because, despite what either of them said, the attraction was still there, sizzling in the air between them.

She looked away. He used the opportunity to study the curve of her neck exposed by the ponytail she'd pulled her hair into, the delicate ears that had turned a pale shade of pink.

"Who told you I wouldn't sell my share of the business?" Her gaze seemed to be directed at the distant vineyard. "It wasn't Jason, was it?"

"No," he admitted. And his chagrin was as much for the fact that it was Callie who'd recalled him to the business at hand when his mind had wanted to linger on other thoughts, as for the fact that she was right.

"Do you always rely on second-hand information?"

He wasn't going to let her make this about him. "I have no doubt about the credibility of my sources."

She studied him thoughtfully for a few seconds before speaking again. "I'm sure you trust your sister." It was no great surprise that she'd figured that much out, and he quelled the flare of admiration. "But either she's drawing inferences that are incorrect, or Jason isn't telling her the full story." She paused, thinking. "I don't think he would outright lie to either of you, he's not dishonest, but he's extraordinarily skilled at not revealing information that reflects badly on himself. It comes down to a kind of insecurity, and a need for control."

"Spare me the psychoanalysis of your ex-boyfriend." The thought of her with Jason bothered him more than it should. "Are you saying you *are* willing to sell your share of the business?"

"No." Her answer was quick.

"Then he is telling the truth?"

"No."

Nick raised an eyebrow.

She folded her arms across her chest, full breasts lifted beneath the soft cotton of her T-shirt. Had she done that deliberately? As a diversionary tactic it was incredibly effective. He trained his gaze on her narrowed eyes, could see no duplicity, only indignation.

"I don't have to explain myself to you. I suggest you talk to your new brother-in-law."

Her weary frustration wasn't going to sway him. Nick pulled his phone from his pocket. "Should I cancel my flight?" He almost wanted to. It would mean more time sparring with her. But he knew once again that that was his libido speaking.

"Put the phone away, the intimidation attempts are growing tiresome."

He hid his surprise. If circumstances were different, he could enjoy crossing swords with this woman. She was quick, insightful and definitely no pushover.

Callie uncrossed her arms and placed her palms flat on the table, making it rock and threatening her drink again. "Check your facts," she challenged. "Ivy Cottage PR is *my* business. I started it, I built it up. Jason came into it later and was a big part of the business—the front man, keeping in good with the media, the suave salesman charming the clients." Nick thought of Melody and how Jason had swept her off her feet.

Callie continued. "But I'm the creative side. I do the planning and the actual work. The agreement I had with Jason was for him to sell his share of the business to me. Only, he's changed his mind about the price we agreed on and now wants far more than his share is worth. The business is doing well, but I can't carry that kind of financial burden." The frustration was clear in her voice. "That's as much as I'm prepared to tell you. If you're still interested in hearing more of the sorry details, take it up with him."

Check your facts, she'd said. Usually he knew every nuance, every possible angle of any deal he was interested in. Today he was acting only on Melody's say-so. And although Melody was genuinely worried, she could sometimes be too quick to react. He didn't want to doubt his sister, but he wanted to believe this woman with the fire in her eyes too. Wanted to with a need that went deeper than it should. He ignored that need. He had to, at least until he knew the truth. "Rest assured I will. In the meantime, stop calling him."

"I will call my business partner whenever I deem it necessary. You have no power over me. If Jason doesn't answer my calls during the day, then I'll try him at night."

Her defiance shouldn't have surprised him. He'd do the same were their positions reversed. Nick opened his mouth to speak, but she cut him off. "Your sister may be happy for you to interfere in her life, but rest assured, Mr. Brunicadi, I won't tolerate interference in mine." She stood up and pulled a set of car keys from her pocket. "I'm going out now. I figure that's the only way I can guarantee to free myself from your company. But I hope for both our sakes you catch your flight, because I never want to lay eyes on you again."

If he challenged that assertion, if he stood and curved his hand around her neck, touched his lips to hers, how would she react? He shouldn't even want to know.

She may not want to tolerate what she called his interference, but he did what he needed to protect those he loved. He stayed seated while she stalked away, all long legs and bouncing ponytail. At the top of the steps she paused, then turned back. "How much do you have to do with Cypress Rise wines?"

"Very little. Usually. It's Melody's baby."

Relief flashed in those liquid eyes. "Thank goodness for that."

"I'm flattered." If she'd felt something for him once, he'd surely killed it. He shouldn't feel the cold sense of loss.

"You've got to admit it would be extremely uncomfortable."

He shrugged. "It could be. For as long as you're a part of Ivy Cottage, or for as long as your firm has Cypress Rise's business."

She walked back toward him with slow, deliberate footsteps, studying his face. "Is that a threat? Will you move the account because of what happened between us or because of baseless accusations?"

"We make business decisions based on sound reasoning." He didn't tell her that any decision would be made by Melody alone, and Melody wanted only the best for Cypress Rise. That was why she'd chosen Ivy Cottage PR in the first place, and she'd been more than happy with that choice. "It was merely an observation. The PR industry is notoriously fickle."

"Actually, I've found my clients to be incredibly loyal."

"Then you're very lucky."

"Or very good, Mr. Brunicadi. I believe you're aware of the award I won recently."

He almost smiled. That was the second time she'd called him Mr. Brunicadi, as though belated formality could somehow erase the intimacy of what they'd shared. "Given our past, I think you can call me Nick. And I'm well aware of how good you are."

He saw by the widening of her eyes and the heightening of her color that she'd caught the double entendre. "Leave the paper behind." She did an admirable job of speaking through clenched teeth. "Don't do the crossword. And shut the gate behind you when you go out." Chin high and back ramrod straight, she stalked off again and disappeared around the side of the house. A minute later, an engine roared into life and a silver Triumph MG, old but in good condition, sped down the driveway, kicking up a cloud of dust in its wake.

A little over a week later, Callie swung her car into the Ivy Cottage parking lot. As always, she felt a swelling of pride at the sight of her business. Everything from the gardens to the sign-written exterior was both professional and welcoming.

She'd been nineteen when she first resolved never to be dependent on someone else for her livelihood. Her PR firm was the end result of that promise to herself. Over the years the business had had its ups and downs, but she'd hung in there and weathered the storms.

The last twelve months with Jason's leaving hadn't been easy—his departure had made several clients edgy, but they were pulling through. And last week's award had already proved good for business. There had been a marked increase in calls from prospective clients. That type of acknowledgment was also reassuring for existing clients. She knew they were happy with her work, because she got results, but independent validation never hurt.

Swinging her satchel, she pushed open the front door and surveyed the reception area—the comfortable leather couches, the apricot roses in a vase on the coffee table. Shannon looked up from her computer screen, her dark hair spiky and with a hint of—was that blue?—in it. "How was your weekend?" Callie asked. Shannon's weekends were invariably more interesting than Callie's, sometimes scarily so.

"Great. But don't worry. I didn't do anything you wouldn't do." Shannon grinned, an impish smile that made her look so very young. Given that Shannon could have no idea what Callie had done at Jason's wedding, she oughtn't to be worried by that reassurance. "What about you?" Shannon asked. "Any hot dates?"

"You know I don't do hot dates." The wedding incident couldn't even be classed as a date. Were there no bounds to her shame?

"You should, and when you were late I thought maybe finally…"

Callie laughed, the sound forced to her ears. "I overslept. And not," she forestalled Shannon, "because I'd been out on a hot date. It happens sometimes."

"Yeah. But not to you."

"I'm human too."

"No." Shannon threw up her hands in mock horror, then dropped them to her desk to give herself a shove and send her chair coasting backward. "I'll get you some coffee. And I bet you didn't have breakfast, either, if you overslept."

It felt odd being mothered by someone ten years her junior. "You're right. I didn't. I'll get something from Dan the Sandwich Man when he calls in. And maybe tea rather than coffee." Coffee hadn't been sitting all that well with her the last few days. "I'll leave a couple of dollars with you and you can get me a muffin from Dan. He always seems to give you a particularly good deal."

Shannon smiled. "He likes my bad-girl looks. The nerdy ones have always been attracted to me."

The phone rang and Shannon picked it up. She held up her hand in a stop gesture as Callie was about to head into her office. "I'll check for you, sir, but her schedule is quite full today."

She hit the hold button and looked at Callie. "A man called Nick. He seems to think you'll make time to see him. Sounds like the guy who was looking for you the day of the awards dinner. Not bad-looking, either. For an old guy."

Tension seized Callie at the very mention of his name. What did he want this time? Whatever it was, she wasn't ready to see him. It was that very reluctance that made her realize she'd best get this over and done with. Besides, he'd already demonstrated he didn't take no for an answer. "I can give him ten minutes at ten o'clock, otherwise it'll have to be tomorrow." She ignored the surprised lift of Shannon's dark eyebrow and pushed through her office door and away from her scrutiny.

A few minutes later Shannon brought in a cup of tea and confirmation of her ten o'clock appointment. Her watchful silence was curious. Callie ignored it.

If only it was as easy to ignore the threat of an impending meeting with Nick Brunicadi. She was supposed to be working on a point-of-sale brochure for a farm machinery company, but her progress was almost nonexistent.

When Shannon tapped on her open office door Callie jumped, then quickly regained her composure. "Send him in," she said coolly.

"Dan?"

"Dan?" she repeated, uncomprehending at first. "Oh." She got to her feet, glad of the distraction.

Marc, her graphic designer, made an appearance in the reception area at the same time as Callie, and together they pondered what suddenly felt like a vital decision. An apricot Danish or a date scone?

Opting for one of each, Callie was standing with her hands full when the front door swung open and Nick, radiating purpose, strode in. For a second, the four of them already in reception, froze.

Shannon was the first to recover, discreetly placing her cinnamon bun out of sight on her desk. "Good morning. You must be Nick."

He nodded, then looked at Callie, making her feel guilty with the lift of one dark eyebrow and a glance at her full hands. "I can see why you could only spare ten minutes."

She refused to be cowed. Transferring the scone to the Danish hand, she held her chin high and her right hand out. Nick's gaze raked over her, taking in her dark pants and jacket. If only she'd worn higher shoes, that way she might at least be able to look him in the eye. With a smile she didn't trust for a minute, he stepped closer to enfold her hand in his. He held on for several beats too long, heat infusing what she'd intended to be a cool, professional handshake. His expression was far too complacent and far too unsettling because of it.

Callie broke the contact. "I'm surprised to see you again so soon."

"Not a pleasant surprise?" One corner of his lips tugged upward.

"Not at all," she agreed.

The wolfish smile grew. The dimple dimpled.

Damn him. He would make beautiful babies.

The thought ricocheted through her, accompanied by the knowledge that her next period was now a couple of days late. But it had been late before. She wasn't letting it mean anything.

Callie pushed the thoughts aside and strove for calm indifference. "I thought we'd said all we had to say to each other."

"We're only just beginning."

Those four words blew any hope of calmness or indifference right out of the water and froze her to the spot. Silence stretched between them.

"I can say what I need to out here if you like." Nick looked around the reception, took in the unabashedly curious faces of Shannon, Dan and Marc. "I thought, however, you'd prefer to have this conversation in private."

Callie considered her options—it didn't take long.

She gestured to her open door. "Come through to my office." The invitation was made grudgingly, but she had to get him away from Shannon.

More than once, Callie had lectured Shannon on the beauty of a committed relationship. She didn't want the girl knowing that Callie hadn't been able to live up to her own standards.

"Coffee?" Shannon asked, her gaze keen.

"That won't be necessary. I'm sure whatever Mr. Brunicadi wishes to discuss won't take long." It went against the grain to be deliberately inhospitable to a client, but Nick was the exception to the rule. She needed him gone. His mere presence caused such a complicated slew of emotions that she scarcely knew how to react—anger, defensiveness, guilt and below it all a charged sensual awareness. She couldn't help noting the strength in the clean line of his jaw, the breadth of his shoulders. She could still almost feel the clasp of his hand around hers.

With a quiet click, she shut the door behind them, enclosing them both in the suddenly too-small space of her office. Needing the physical barrier, she moved to stand behind her desk and folded her arms across her chest. "What do you want?"

He turned from his perusal of the awards and certificates hanging on her wall, his expression unreadable. It had been bad enough a week ago, when he'd been on her veranda; this was worse. Was it really as easy as it seemed for him to put thoughts of what they'd shared out of his mind? Finally, he sat in one of the leather armchairs opposite her desk, crossing his long legs at the ankles, a picture of ease.

The only thing that bolstered her confidence was

that, apart from that one error of judgment, a too hasty dance floor decision, she had done nothing wrong. Callie's hands went to her hips. "I take it you're here to apologize for your groundless accusations." She faked a nonchalance that she had yet to feel in his presence. "You must know by now that I'm not trying to keep Jason in my life. In fact, I'll be dancing on my desk for joy when I don't have to deal with him anymore." Nick raised his eyebrows, but the silence stretched, and no apology was forthcoming, so Callie continued. "If it's not that, and you're not here to tell me Jason is ready to sell, which he would have told me himself, I need to ask you to leave."

His gaze steady on her, Nick nodded his head slowly, as though in agreement, but he made no move to stand.

Callie reached for her phone. "Regardless of your threats last weekend, I *will* call security. Tell the press whatever you like. I'll deal with the consequences. Negating bad publicity is one of my strengths."

Finally, he unfolded himself from the chair and stood. But instead of heading for the door, one effortless stride had him standing right in front of her desk. He rested his fists on the top of it and leaned forward, making it suddenly hard to breathe. He was so close she could see gold flecks in his green eyes. "I have good news and bad news for you." He leaned even closer. Callie wanted to move away, but stood frozen, her heart thudding in her chest. "Do you have a preference?" he asked quietly.

"My preference is for you to leave." She reached for her phone. "Will you go, or shall I make that call?"

Unhurriedly, Nick straightened. He picked up the peace lily from her desk, shifted it to the top of her filing cabinet, nudging aside the asymmetrical award she'd won a little over a week ago to accommodate the plant.

"What are you doing?" Her hand tightened on the phone, but she watched in a kind of morbid fascination.

"Clearing your desk for you."

"Why?"

Finally he turned, riveting his attention on her. "The good news is Jason has agreed to sell his share of Ivy Cottage."

Callie let go of the phone. She should have felt a surge of elation and relief; her business would be fully back under her control, her contact with Jason would be over, but there was something about the way Nick continued to study her, like a jungle cat toying with its prey. "And the bad news is?"

He smiled. "He's sold it to me." He held out his hand, palm up. "Shall I help you onto the desk?"

Four

"No." Callie dropped into her chair and then stood again, thinking for an awful moment that she was going to be sick. She glanced at the door that would take her to the bathroom, but through sheer determination she stayed in place and the nausea subsided. The sense of shock remained. "That's not possible," she said quietly. This couldn't be happening. Not with Nick, the man who was supposed to be one night of passion and nothing more. Her guilty secret.

He said nothing as his green eyes assessed her, their calmness a counterpoint to her turmoil.

"Jason wouldn't be able to sell without my knowledge." Her voice rose and she fought to keep it under control, to keep *herself* under control. "We had an agreement. A contract." She studied the face of the man shaking the foundations of her world.

Finally, expression showed as a disapproving frown creased Nick's brow. "The agreement you had with Jason was lamentably sloppy. Though I've seen it before," he said thoughtfully. "Agreements set up between two people who trust each other, no checks and balances, no provision for a change in the relationship. Very naive. You should have kept more control."

"No." The denial sprang again from her lips. Not a denial of her naïveté, or her trusting in Jason, but another gut-level denial that this could be happening at all.

Nick didn't contradict her with words, just that steady gaze that told her he wasn't joking and that he was utterly confident of his position.

Legs weak, Callie lowered herself to her chair. The awful realization churned in her stomach. He was right, of course. Jason had been responsible for drawing up their agreements, had used a lawyer friend of his who'd given them a great price. She hadn't foreseen a time when one of them might want to sell. They had, as Nick said, trusted each other. Or she at least had trusted him. "But Jason wouldn't do that without telling me. It's my business."

"Correction, it's ours." Nick sat down again and gestured to the phone. "But please, call him for verification if you like. However, it would seem that pleasing his new brother-in-law, in whose company he now has a lucrative position, was more important than pleasing his ex-girlfriend." Even though it had gotten him what he wanted, Nick spoke the words with a hint of distaste.

Callie's heart sank. Wasn't that just like Jason, always one eye on the main chance? He was principled, but only to a point. And that point usually involved money. "You bribed him."

Nick showed no reaction. "I gave him options. The

choice was his. It didn't seem a particularly difficult one for him."

She hadn't thought Jason still had the power to hurt her, but this final betrayal proved how wrong she'd been. The years they'd shared meant that little to him. Callie looked at Nick, shaking her head in disbelief. "Why have you done this?" She could understand why Jason had sold out, but what did Nick want?

He leaned back and gave a disinterested shrug. "Control, leverage. I don't like my family being threatened."

"No one was threatening your family. Didn't you talk to Jason? Didn't he tell you that what little remained of our relationship was friendship?"

"I talked to him. And he was quite convincing. But then he would be, wouldn't he? I'm his new brother-in-law. And his boss. We come back to the fact that rightly or wrongly, Melody feels threatened."

"Wrongly." Callie thumped a fist on her desk.

The gaze that had followed her fist came back to her face. "All the same," Nick's voice was quiet, reasoned, "I thought an element of control would help ensure that things run smoothly."

"They were running smoothly."

"And long may they continue to do so."

It was probably a good thing that he'd cleared the top of her desk, because otherwise she'd surely have thrown something at him by now. "I know that you buy and sell companies all the time. But this is my business. It means everything to me. My staff are like family." She held his gaze before adding, "I can't work with you."

"I understand what you're saying. Anticipated it even, and the solution is simple."

Callie held her head in her hands, foreboding crashing down on her. He was going to force her out. She would lose everything she'd worked so hard for. She looked up, met that implacable gaze. "Will you pay me what you paid him?"

He shook his head. "That's not how it's going to work."

And she wasn't even going to get properly compensated. "You expect me to just walk away. I have responsibilities, people and their businesses depending on me."

His eyes widened slightly in surprise. "I'm not a monster, Callie. I did do some research. It didn't take long to realize you were right about being the driving force behind this business. It's clear how hard you've worked at it. I also have an inkling of what it means to you."

She let her expression speak her disbelief.

"I don't want anything to do with the day-to-day running of the business. I do expect a reasonable rate of return, as with any venture I buy into, but as long you ensure that, and have no further contact with Jason or Melody, then I'll stay out of your hair."

"Cypress Rise is a client, remember. Contact with Melody is necessary. Unless you're taking the account away?"

"I have no problems with you keeping the account, so long as someone else does the liaison."

How she'd love to throw the account back in his face. But she couldn't. It meant too much to her business. "The Jazz and Art festival is on in less than a month," she reminded him. If she left now it would throw it into chaos. The biggest loser would be its charitable recipient, the Mary Ruth Home, a shelter for runaway teenagers.

"Do what needs to be done, but have someone else liaise with the winery." He made it sound so simple.

"Is your sister really that insecure? She always struck me as confident and capable." On the surface, Melody appeared to have it all: a background of privilege, looks and a career she seemed passionate about.

Nick sat straighter, his gaze cool. "She is confident and capable. In business. In her personal life she isn't always so confident. She has her reasons. If it's in my power to protect her, then I will."

"I don't want you breathing down my neck."

His gaze dropped to her throat, then flicked back to her eyes.

He remembered. He might not want to any more than she did, but he recalled their fleeting intimacy. She wasn't sure whether that was a good thing or a bad thing.

"It's a relative term. I have, because circumstances warranted it, bought into this business—" he looked critically about her office "—with rather less information than I would usually insist on." His gaze came back to her face. "I've had to take Jason's assurances and publicly available information as fact."

"You're expecting sympathy?"

He almost smiled. Amusement flickered in his eyes, then was gone. "There are two ways of doing anything, Callie, the easy way and the hard way."

"Meaning do it your way, or you'll make it difficult, if not impossible, for me?"

"I have a half share in your business. Either one of us can make this difficult for the other. But I don't see why we should. You get the backing of a silent partner and I get—"

"Control. Leverage."

"Precisely. All I want from you at this point is information. Once I'm satisfied I know all that I should, I'll back off and leave you to it."

Would he let it be that simple? "What is it you want to know?"

"It's a little late for due diligence, but I'd like some more detail on what I've bought into. How about we start by you showing me the financial records?"

Callie stood and considered her options as she watched that impassive face, that deceptively calm gaze. She'd been on the dance floor with him, but she could see no sign of that man. *Freedom, he'd said. Hah!* Now she felt like she was in the boxing ring with him.

She could refuse, but it would serve no purpose. Reeling and tight-lipped, she strode past him to her credenza, pulled out a bound booklet and held it out to him. If she gave him this, then maybe they could both retreat to their corners and she'd have time to figure out what was happening, and more importantly, what she was going to do about it.

He took the book from her and tapped it thoughtfully. "May as well give me the last five years." He spoke casually, as though asking for nothing more than a second cup of coffee.

"We've only been going five years." Callie couldn't quite keep the exasperation from her voice.

"Even better."

Wordlessly, she turned back to the credenza and found the reports he was asking for, holding on to the thought that as soon as he was gone, she could call her lawyer and find a way out of this mess.

"So, I can work here?"

Was he baiting her? She glared at him, but could

read nothing in his green eyes. "Of course you can't. I have meetings in here."

He kept that disconcerting gaze on her. "We could enjoy working together, Callie."

She took a deep breath, but this time couldn't help rising to the bait. "We won't be working together. And we won't be enjoying anything. Take those reports and go."

"You're not going to introduce me to *our* staff?"

She couldn't conceal her horror at the prospect. "Not today."

"I'll have questions." He tapped the reports. "We should make a time for another meeting."

The phone on her desk rang with the tone for an internal call and she snatched it up. "Mr. Keane from the rafting company," came Shannon's voice.

"I'll be with him in a minute." She turned to Nick. "Now, if you wouldn't mind leaving." She pointed, stiff-armed, to the door. "Call me if you have questions."

"Perhaps you should give me your home number?"

"Like you don't already have it?"

And this time, despite how quickly he repressed it, there was no doubting the amusement that creased the corners of his eyes. She wouldn't be surprised if he'd had an entire dossier compiled. He probably knew what she ate for breakfast and the color of her underwear. Correction, he already knew that. And she only had herself to blame.

He nodded. "You'll be hearing from me." He headed toward the door.

Callie stepped out from behind her desk, took a few steps after him. "But so long as I continue to run the business well, you'll stay out of it?" She needed that as-surance. She wasn't worried about having nothing further to do with Jason or Melody; she could manage that side of things. She was, however, worried about having to confront Nick on any regular basis. Having to pretend what had happened between them hadn't, constantly feeling the pull of an attraction that was as unwanted as it was undeniable, would be torture.

He paused, turned back to her. "It's a promise."

"And I'm supposed to accept you at your word?"

"You haven't got a lot else to go on."

"There's not much reassurance in that." She shook her head. The enormity of what was happening, to her business and therefore her life, was slowly sinking in.

Something softened in his expression. "I'm as good as my word, Callie."

"Like you said, I'll have to take that."

"Believe it or not, I have a business of my own to run. A corporation that's far more important to me than this." He nodded at the financial reports in his hands, as though that was all her business boiled down to.

He was almost close enough that she could grab the lapels of his expensive suit and shake him. "You're acting like this is no big deal."

Understanding passed through his eyes. "It doesn't have to be a big deal. My stake in Ivy Cottage is an insurance policy for my sister's peace of mind. And just like with my insurances, once I know exactly what I'm getting for my money, I'm happy to pay the premiums and forget about them." He reached for the door handle, and with a nod in her direction, turned and left.

Callie stared at the door as he closed it gently behind him. If only it would be as easy for her to forget about *him*.

Five

By Sunday afternoon, through grimly determined effort, several ruined canvases and a month's worth of painting supplies, Callie had succeeded in blocking thoughts of Nick from her mind. So much so that the insistent knocking on her door startled her. Horrified, she glanced at her watch. He was early, but only by five minutes. She had no time to change, no time to mentally prepare herself. With care born of a desire to delay the inevitable, she put down her brush and wiped suddenly clammy hands on her stained shirt. Taking a deep breath, she headed resolutely for the door.

Nick had wanted to meet again, and this afternoon had been the only time that worked for both of them. Usually, she refused to let work intrude on her Sundays, but in this case it suited her well enough. She hadn't yet told Shannon and Marc that there was a new stakeholder in the business. If Nick came to Ivy Cottage again there would be no avoiding that revelation, he'd make sure of it. As it was, Shannon's pointed questions had already been hard for Callie to deflect.

As Callie opened the door, Nick, who had been looking in the direction of the neighbor's property, turned toward her. The sight of him momentarily took her breath away. His suave masculinity would be at home in an ad for European cars. His own European car, parked beyond him on the driveway, gleamed in the sunlight.

He lifted his sunglasses and his gaze found hers, his eyes green and calm. He nodded. "Callie."

"Nick." She tried to hide a reaction to his presence that was almost physical, a leaping to alert of all her senses.

This was the first time she'd seen him dressed casually. A black knit shirt stretched across his contoured chest, a heavy silver watch encircled his tanned wrist. He wore dark pants and leather shoes.

His gaze swept over her, took in her unruly hair, her oversize, paint-smeared shirt, her bare feet, before coming to rest back on her face. The contrast between them couldn't be greater. A faint smile tugged a corner of his mouth up and one eyebrow lifted. She stood back from the door, resisting the urge to respond to that smile and to explain her appearance. "Come in."

He stepped over the threshold. "So, no joy wriggling out of the agreement." It was a statement of fact.

"Trust me, it wasn't for lack of trying." She'd spent the best part of the intervening week in ultimately fruitless meetings and phone calls with her lawyer.

"I expected nothing less from you."

Surely she was mistaken in thinking the glint in his eyes might be admiration.

"But when I do something, I do it properly."

And suddenly she was remembering how thoroughly and well he had loved—no, not loved, *pleasured*—her the night of Melody's wedding.

Callie glanced at the clutch of reports in his hands. "Let's get this over with." Stepping away from his latent intensity, she led the way to the villa's cool kitchen, acutely aware of his presence behind her, of his scrutiny.

"Nice place."

"I rent it." She'd been here nearly a year, and loved the villa's spacious Old-World charm. It was far enough out of the city that visitors didn't often call. She liked that about it too.

"Who from?" The interest in his voice, in his eyes, seemed genuine, and she had to guard against it.

"A neighbor. Who, sadly, wants to sell it in six months." She glanced back, saw that Nick had stopped in front of a painting. It was one of her own, abstract, completed entirely in varying shades of blue and green.

"It reminds me of the sea."

Callie paused, then told herself it was no big deal. Art spoke to different people in different ways.

"Of the water at Cathedral Cove," he added thoughtfully as he studied it. "I visited an American colleague holidaying in that area last month."

A shiver passed through her.

"What's wrong?" he asked.

She shook her head and started walking again. "Nothing."

"Did you do it?" His voice was nonchalant.

"Yes." Given the state of her shirt, there was no point trying to hide the fact that she painted. But her art was personal, not something she liked to share. It was her version of therapy, colors expressing her moods and emotions. Six months ago she'd had a ceremonial burning of the awful, somber ones she had painted after her breakup with Jason. Today, fiery oranges and reds had dominated.

She pulled open the refrigerator. "Can I get you a drink?"

When he didn't answer she looked around the fridge door, to see him studying another of her paintings. Slowly, he turned toward her. "No, thanks."

And if she was going to be polite he could jolly well do the same. She pulled a jug of water from the fridge. "If you're going to be my business partner then we at least need to be amicable in each other's company."

"This is amicable." He dropped the reports onto the breakfast bar.

Resisting the urge to snort, she tilted her head to the side and regarded him. "All the veiled threats were amicable?"

A faint smile lifted his lips. "It's all in the interpretation. Solitude or loneliness, threat or opportunity."

Solitude or loneliness. She knew only too well where that had come from, and she didn't want him going down that track. "Please don't remind me of that night. I try never to think of it." She wasn't particularly successful, but she really did try.

He regarded her thoughtfully. "Whereas I take great pleasure in remembering it."

Callie's throat ran dry. Just looking at him, the green of his eyes, the smile that lurked there, the small V of skin revealed by the few undone buttons.... "You shouldn't. We're business partners."

"Don't you sometimes remember it? Perhaps when you're supposed to be thinking of something else entirely, you find yourself instead remembering how we—"

"No. Never." She had to cut him off, because there was something about him, something enthralling, that slipped through her self-possession, her determination. He was more relaxed today, and that made him all the more dangerous.

He met her gaze and knew she was lying.

She looked away and poured ice water into two tall glasses. "Thank you," he said with a hint of irony.

She gritted her teeth. "I need to change my shirt. You might like to wait on the veranda." She had planned on them sitting at her dining table, but she suddenly didn't want to be in a confined space with him.

He shook his head. "I'm fine here."

"And it might be construed as ill-mannered to stay in someone's kitchen when quite clearly they don't want you there."

"The veranda you say?" The small smile stretched, revealing the satisfaction he got from unsettling her.

"It's shaded and cool."

"And presumably I should take my drink?"

"Yes."

Still smiling, he gathered up the reports and strolled back the way they'd come. Stalling for time, Callie washed her hands and changed her shirt, vacillating over her decision. The clothes and makeup she wore during the week were her armor, and if ever she'd needed armor it was now. But on the other hand, she didn't want Nick reading insecurity or a desire to impress him into her choice. In the end she opted for a T-shirt and her favorite jeans.

All the while her thoughts were on Nick, outside, waiting. And his smile. Did he know how it weakened her?

She shook her head. This was a simple business meeting; nothing she couldn't handle. It was on her territory, it was about her business, and she would be able to answer any questions he had. Though it would help if she had some idea what those questions might be.

And it would help even more if she didn't still have that other worry—the one about her now undeniably late period—hanging over her head. She'd gone so far as to buy a pregnancy test kit. It sat unopened in her bathroom cabinet. But as long as it remained unopened she could believe—hope—she was safe.

Nick stood on the veranda and surveyed the rolling hills that surrounded Callie's place, so much greener than those back in Australia. He saw again the neighboring vineyard, the grass around the vines still too long. The only sound was the rustling of leaves in a nearby stand of poplar trees. Some of the tension he hadn't realized he was carrying seeped from his shoulders. He could see why she liked it here.

At the sound of the door opening he turned. Clutching her glass of water as tightly as she had her champagne the night of the wedding, Callie stepped onto the veranda. Her dark curls were loose about her face, jeans, faded with washing, molded to the flare of her hips, a white T-shirt skimmed oh so gently over her curves, its neckline at the base of her throat.

He'd never before met anyone who could make demure look so utterly sexy.

Business. This was about business, he reminded himself forcefully. He was good at compartmentalizing.

Usually.

She met his gaze calmly, but her throat betrayed her with small, nervous swallows. Nick smiled. Complacent. If the business at hand happened to give him a little advantage over Calypso Jamieson, helped her see that he wasn't someone to be trifled with, then so much the better.

Yet so much about her resonated with him. The work she'd done on the Cypress Rise account had captured the essence of the winery. What he had been able to glean about the way she ran her business struck a chord of familiarity, the paintings that hung in her home spoke to him, the depths in her chocolate-colored eyes haunted him. Even that smudge of red she'd missed beneath her jaw affected him, made him want to reach out and touch it. Touch her. As though it was his right.

He couldn't shake the feeling that stirred whenever he saw her, a feeling of connection.

Acting on that feeling had caused this mess in the first place.

He could make her regret walking out on him, but knew that the distance she wanted to keep between them was for the best. She wasn't the type of woman he got involved with. Contrary to what he'd thought the night of the wedding, she was long-term, the sort who made deep and permanent connections. Many of her clients had been with her from day one. And she was a nester. It was obvious in the way she'd used personal touches to turn this rented villa into more of a home than the designer apartment he'd owned for six years.

Nick had believed both Jason's and Callie's assurances that there was nothing left between them. But he didn't quite trust his own need to believe. That was one of the reasons he'd bought the share of her business. There was logic in having that insurance policy, even though the part of him that insisted on honesty told him there was more than just that to his decision.

For the moment though, things were back under his control. And he liked to have control—of the beginnings, the middles and the ends.

Callie set her water down carefully, then frowning, looked beneath the table to see the folded paper he had wedged beneath one of the legs to minimize the wobble. She glanced quickly toward him. "It's not perfect and it's only temporary," he said.

"I've been meaning to fix that," she said, then took a deep breath. "Thank you." He suppressed the urge to smile at how much the words seemed to cost her. They would get this meeting over and done with and that would be it. It needed to be, because he liked just being with her far too much.

He pulled out a chair for her, caught a faint trace of her perfume as she passed close by him to sit.

"So what are these questions?" She looked at the reports that lay between them, touched a slender finger, stained a faded red, to the brightly colored markers protruding from beneath the covers.

"How about you give me a little background on the business to start with. The personal side."

"It's not all there in the numbers?"

"The numbers tell a story. But I'd like to know what's behind them. How did you start up? How long have Shannon and Marc been with you? What's your style of doing business?"

"You don't want much, do you?" Gentle sarcasm laced her words.

He ignored it as he ignored the other wants that were always present when she was near.

"How much time have you got?"

Nick leaned back in his chair and stretched his legs out. "As long as it takes."

She sighed, her gaze flicked to him and then away, and she started telling him about the business, her story hesitant and factual at first. But as he asked questions she seemed to forget who she was talking to. He listened to her mistakes and her successes with equal attention. He could understand how tough it had been in the early days and admired the way she had hung in there.

He teased out the details and stories of Ivy Cottage's history. His opinion should only matter because, the more confidence he had in her, the easier it would be to leave her alone. She was careful also to give credit to Jason. He didn't mind the sense that it was begrudgingly given. Her ex-partner had done her no favors. Nick liked his new brother-in-law a little less for that fact.

Somewhere in the telling of her story, her stance shifted from defensive to conspiratorial.

Nick forgot the passage of time. Could just be with her, listening to her, laughing with her. Watching her.

He didn't realize how long they had sat talking till she looked up, and he followed her glance, to see the orange glow of sunset coloring the horizon. She touched her fingers to her lips in surprise. "I'm sorry. I didn't mean to talk for so long, and we haven't even got to the reports."

He shook his head, leaned forward in his seat. "Don't worry about the time on my account." He captured her wide brown gaze with his own. "I'm only going back to my hotel room. But what about you? You have your painting to do."

Her lips parted, but it wasn't until she broke the contact of their gaze that words came out. "It hardly matters now. I've lost the light."

He knew he disconcerted her, that beneath her efficient facade shimmered an awareness she wanted to deny. He wasn't going to let her, not completely. But he needed to retain the upper hand, and talk of darkness and hotel rooms could too easily lead his thoughts down dangerous paths. Time to redirect them. "Have you always painted?"

"For as long as I can remember. I even started a fine arts degree."

There was something wistful in her tone. "Started?"

She frowned. "I changed to commerce." And suddenly her tone was as businesslike as her degree.

"Why?"

"Because there's a livelihood in it." Again the serious tone. Her hands had gone to her hips.

"Who are you quoting?"

Her eyes widened.

"Weren't you quoting someone just then?"

She tipped her head to one side and studied him. A rueful smile touched her lips as she nodded once. "My mother's partner at the time."

"You changed your degree to please someone else?"

She shrugged. "Not exactly. But he'd been made redundant, and he helped me see that I needed something solid to rely on, something I had control over. It made sense to study commerce."

"Not if it wasn't what you really wanted to do." He suddenly laughed, surprising himself as much as her.

"What's so funny?"

"That advice coming from me. I chose the university I attended because of someone else."

"What do you mean?"

He looked out over the hills. "My girlfriend at the time wanted to study at Adelaide, so I went there too. To be with her." This was a definite foray into the personal, a shifting of the ground.

"If you were choosing universities together, you must have been practically childhood sweethearts."

"Something like that."

"What happened to her?" Callie's tone was teasing.

"She left me for an affair with her English professor." It was the last, the only time, he'd been the one to be left.

"Bad trade."

Nick looked sharply at her, expecting to discern sarcasm. But her gaze was serious. He allowed himself a smile. "I like to think so." But he regretted the confidence he'd shared. Why Callie? Why had he told this woman what he never talked about? The past was past, and certainly had no place here. His uncharacteristic loss of focus could only have been caused by the woman opposite him, by the way her softly parted lips made him long to cover them with his own.

He pulled the top report off the small stack. "This shouldn't take long. Clarify a couple of anomalies I've found, and then you needn't see me again. We can both get on with what we do best." He'd found enough in his reading of the reports, and from talking to her and others in the industry, to know the business was in capable hands.

"That's a promise?"

She wanted to end the contact too. The fleeting closeness of this afternoon had been an illusion. "You won't even have to see me in person—phone and e-mail should be all we need." Impersonal. Freedom for both of them.

Callie studied him. It was strange to think of him

hurting. He seemed so strong, so impervious. The warmth she'd felt only minutes earlier in his presence had cooled. But over the last couple of hours, she had come to realize that he didn't have to be an adversary, could in fact be an ally. Through talking they'd reached a tenuous understanding. She could trust him and his word. She would be able to run her business how she wanted, and she wouldn't have Nick's constant presence to remind her of that one mistake.

That one night of magic.

He turned back the cover on the first report and she leaned forward, resting her elbows on the table so that she could read the small print better. The table wobbled slightly. She straightened in remembered reflex, and her arm collided with her glass, sending it flying. It crashed onto the wooden boards, shattering on impact.

Callie dropped to the floor, began picking up the larger pieces. Nick crouched opposite her. "Leave it," she instructed him. "I'll fix it."

He ignored her and picked up another shard.

They reached for the same piece at the same time and his fingers brushed hers. She glanced up to see if he, too, had felt that jolt of heat. His gaze was steady on her. Pulse pounding, Callie scooted back. Her heel caught on an uneven board and she started to fall. Her hands flew out to break her backward tumble and glass sliced into her palm.

Sitting on the wooden boards, she cradled her hand in her lap to examine it. The cut was clean, but long and deep.

Nick stepped closer. "What have you done?"

"Nothing." She let him help her to her feet. "I just need a Band-Aid." Nursing her hand and her throbbing wrist, she headed inside, dripping blood. Her T-shirt was already a mess, so, as best she could, she wadded up the fabric and held it against the cut to stanch the flow. In the bathroom, she pulled open the door of the cabinet. Grabbing a tissue, she swabbed away the blood, then found the box of Band-Aids and awkwardly extracted one and stripped the covering paper from it.

"Are you okay?" The deep voice, softened with concern, sounded close behind her.

The Band-Aid folded in on itself, sticking irretrievably. She threw it into the trash and reached for another one. "It's nothing serious."

"Do you need a hand?"

"No. Not even a finger." She pressed a tissue to the cut that still oozed blood.

Ignoring her feeble joke, Nick stepped closer, crowding her in the small bathroom. That proximity, that faint scent, overrode the pain and did straightaway what she'd earlier denied—sent her thoughts back to their first encounter, and the thrumming sensuality of it. He reached for her hand again, and this time she let him see the cut. She was beginning to think she might need more than a Band-Aid. "I've kind of hurt my wrist too."

Gently, he wiped the blood away, then, still cradling her hand in his, he looked up and met her gaze. "I'm taking you to the emergency room."

The threat of his suggestion quashed her awareness of his proximity, of the gentleness of his touch, the caring in his eyes. "I don't like doctors. Or needles."

His grip on her hand tightened. Green eyes met and held hers. "Deal with it." The sympathy stayed in his gaze. "Where's your first-aid kit? We'll do what we can here. But then you *are* going to see a doctor."

She looked at the cut again. Maybe he was right. Reluctantly, she nodded at the bathroom cabinet. "The cupboard beneath the sink. Red box. White cross on it."

Nick's half smile softened his features. He crouched down and reached into the cabinet. For a second his movements stilled, and sudden fear clenched in her chest. He stood with the first-aid kit in his hands. She couldn't see his face as he bent over her hand and deftly applied a couple of Steri-strips.

The twenty-minute trip, with her wrist iced and her hand bandaged, was made in silence. Callie knew what was in her bathroom cabinet beside the first-aid kit, could too easily picture the pristine box. She'd spent long enough staring at it over the past few days. She just didn't know whether Nick had seen it, whether he had time to read what it was.

And she wasn't about to ask him.

The A&E clinic was mercifully quiet. She filled in a form on a clipboard, and after waiting a short while a nurse approached. "If you'd like to come with me," she said, sounding far too cheery. Callie wanted to turn and run. She glanced at the door, then at Nick.

"Do you want me to come with you?" There was a tightness in his expression and a frown marred his brow. But still, he seemed the lesser of two evils. She nodded and they followed together as the nurse, her right shoe squeaking quietly with each step, led them to a room with a white-sheeted bed, a desk and a couple of chairs. The smell of disinfectant permeated the air. Callie felt the nausea rising.

"Take a seat. The doctor will be with you in a moment." The squeaks faded away down the corridor.

"How much don't you like doctors or needles?"

She didn't look at him. "It's nothing I can't handle."

Before he could question her further, the doctor appeared. He scanned the form on the clipboard, then turned to Callie. "Let's take a look at you. Why don't you sit up on the bed?"

She eased herself onto the bed, legs dangling vulnerably over the edge. The doctor carefully examined her hand and then her wrist.

"You'll need stitches, and you've sprained your wrist, but it's nothing serious," he said cheerfully, apparently having been to classes with the nurse.

Didn't they know there was nothing remotely cheery about being here, about the prospect of stitches? Callie hesitated. She looked up and saw the gaze of both the doctor and Nick on her. "Perhaps it'll be best if you lie down," the doctor suggested, a sudden wariness creeping into his expression.

Did that mean she'd gone as white as she felt? Callie was happy to oblige. She lay back on the bed and screwed her eyes shut.

"And sir," the young doctor said, "you might like to hold her other hand."

Callie opened her eyes to see both of them still watching her. She gave her head a small and apparently unconvincing shake. In two steps, Nick was at her side and took hold of her good hand. She didn't want to need anyone, and especially not him. As she was about to pull her hand from his clasp she looked across at the doctor, saw the syringe he held and felt as though she was falling. She turned her head, and her eyes found Nick's, saw strength and comfort offered in the depthless green. He was here with her for now, and this would be all right. He told her so without speaking. She closed her eyes and tightened her fingers around his hand. His thumb stroked gently across the back of her hand, warm and sure. A calmness stole through her.

That calmness had fled by the time Nick stopped his car in front of her house. "Thanks for helping me out." It was over, and now she needed to get rid of him. "You don't need to come in, I'm fine now."

He turned off the lights and cut the engine.

The silence pressed down on her. "I know I was a sissy back there, but honestly, I'm fine." Using only her left hand, she unbuckled her seat belt and opened her door. "Thanks again."

Nick opened his door and got out as she did. He looked at her across the roof of the car, his face illuminated by the sensor lighting that had come on. He did not look happy. "We haven't finished talking."

She remembered the financial reports still stacked on her outdoor table, hoped against hope that it was those reports he was referring to. Not the box in her bathroom cabinet. "The reports can wait. It's late, you must be tired. I am." She faked a yawn.

"I don't want to talk about the reports," he said quietly. He shut his car door and climbed the steps to the veranda, then stood waiting at her front door.

Callie took slow, dread-filled steps toward him. He made no move to help her as she fumbled with her key, finally slipping it into the lock and pushing the door open.

"Can I make you a drink? Tea, coffee, something stronger?"

He shook his head, lips pressed ominously together. But at least he didn't mention the box.

She didn't want a drink, either, but playing for time,

Callie filled the kettle, set it to boil. Even in the distorted reflection of the kettle's curving stainless steel she could see that he watched her. Avoiding facing him, she pulled a mug from an overhead cupboard, dropped a tea bag into it. Nick sat on a bar stool on the far side of the breakfast bar. She turned back and watched the kettle. The only sound in the room was the low whisper of the water heating and the occasional quiet drum of his fingertips on the countertop. The feeling of vertigo that had assailed her at the clinic threatened to return. Her heart thundered in her chest.

A chair leg scraped across the floor, footsteps sounded down her hallway. Perhaps he just needed to use her bathroom. Callie poured boiling water into her cup, prodded the teabag with a spoon. As the footsteps returned she dropped the sodden bag into the bin and added a dash of milk to her drink.

Finally, she could delay it no longer. Cup in her good hand, she faced the breakfast bar. Nick was seated again, watching her. On the counter in front of him sat a rectangular blue-and-white box. She dragged her gaze from the box to the man. The Nick who'd held her hand at the clinic was gone. This one's icy glare chilled her to the marrow.

"When did you buy this?"

Callie opened her mouth to answer, but no words came out. She'd only bought it a few days ago, when she could no longer ignore the lateness of her period. She quailed under his scrutiny. Could she lie, tell him that the box wasn't hers or that she'd bought it a year ago, but then never had to use it?

Tension radiated from him. "What aren't you telling me?" The question was harsh, more like an accusation.

She looked at the box. Guilt and fear rose within her. "This wasn't supposed to happen."

"What wasn't supposed to happen? Are you pregnant?"

"I don't know," she said quietly, not meeting his gaze. "That's why I bought that." She nodded at the innocuous-looking box, a cardboard grenade with the potential to explode throughout her life.

"You told me you'd had your period."

"I did." Finally she looked up. Confusion and distrust were etched on his face.

"So, how is it we're now looking at this?"

"It was a little late and very light. And I've since learned that can sometimes happen when you're pregnant, but I was hoping it wasn't the case, that it was light because of stress. But now the second period is late."

"How late?" The bluish outline of a vein pulsed in his temple.

"Two weeks."

"Why haven't you told me?"

"Because I don't know yet. Because you were celebrating your freedom. Because you don't need the worry."

"And you do?"

"I don't have a choice. And I don't have your obvious fear of commitment."

He shook his head, his expression scathing. "You don't know anything about me."

"I know enough."

He wasn't to be sidetracked. "Were you going to tell me?"

"Yes. If it turned out that I was pregnant, I would have told you."

He gave an almost imperceptible shake of his head. As though he doubted even that. His doubt cut her more than she'd thought it would. Maybe because it was at least partially deserved, or had she started liking him again, liking that respect and recognition she'd discerned in his gaze?

She had to be stronger, more insular. "It doesn't really matter now whether you believe me or not. This whole argument could be pointless. I may not even be pregnant. This is exactly what I was hoping to avoid."

"When are you planning on taking the test?"

"I thought I'd wait a few more days. Maybe a week." Keep waiting and keep hoping. As if hope alone would make her period come.

He studied her for long seconds. "Take it now."

She looked at him horrified, took a step back. "I can't."

Nick's chair scraped across the floor as he stood and strode into the kitchen. "Why not?"

Callie backed up against the counter. "I'm not ready."

"What do you have to do to be ready?"

"Nothing. I meant that I'm not ready to be a mother. To deal with that news."

He took a step closer. "And you think I'm ready to be a father?"

She looked up at him. "But you wouldn't have to—"

"Wouldn't have to what?" The sudden edge to his voice sent a chill along her spine.

"To deal with anything for a good few months yet. Everything would change for me from the moment I found out. *If* I was pregnant."

"Let's find out then."

"But—"

"You're not ready?"

Callie, usually eloquent, fell silent.

"I'll tell you what. You take the test. I'll look at the

results, and I won't tell you what they are. That way you won't have to deal with anything. When you are ready to know, you'll only need to ask."

"You know I'm not going to do that."

"That's just it, Callie. I don't know anything of the sort. I don't know you. I mean, here I am assuming that if you're pregnant then I'm the father. Is that a valid assumption? Has there been someone else before or since me?"

Her temper rose. "How dare you? If you want to deny paternity go right ahead. I won't fight you."

"But I *will* fight you if you try to deny me what is mine."

"A child is not a possession."

"I didn't suggest that. I'm talking about a child's right to a relationship with both its parents. And a parent's right to a relationship with that child. And you still haven't answered my question."

"What's the point? You clearly have trouble believing anything I say."

"Tell me, Callie. This is no time for playing games."

She met and held his gaze. "You're the only man I've slept with since I broke up with Jason. In fact, you're the only man other than Jason I've *ever* slept with. If I'm pregnant, then you are the father."

The accusation in his eyes eased. "Thank you." He said it so quietly she almost didn't hear the words. He dropped his gaze and turned the box over in his hands. In the stretching silence she heard the quiet crackle of the cellophane wrapper. Finally he spoke. "You need to take this test." He looked up. Held her gaze.

Callie swallowed. "I passed every test I ever took in school. I think this one's going to be a positive result, as well."

"You've had other symptoms?" His anger had been replaced by a kind of resignation.

"No. At least no morning sickness or weird cravings, and I don't even think my breasts have changed size." They both looked at her chest, then looked up again. "Although I have gone off coffee, and I'm sleeping more than usual."

"You're procrastinating."

She nodded. "Wouldn't you?"

"No. I want to know, so that we can deal with whatever we need to deal with. I like to face my… I like to face things head-on."

He'd been going to say "problems," she knew it. But he wouldn't be so very wrong, a pregnancy would definitely create problems. In business she told herself that problems also always presented opportunities, and if the big "if" was true, she knew in time she'd see the opportunities, that there would be a definite plus side to all this.

Nick picked up her good hand and surprisingly gently pressed the angular package into it. For a few seconds his hands, large and warm, cradled hers as she held the box. Then he released her and stepped back. "Take the test."

Six

It felt like a lifetime later when Callie stepped onto the veranda where Nick waited. The night air, warm but cooling rapidly, closed around her. A half moon hung low in the sky, only a handful of stars able to compete with its glow. She was reminded forcefully of that other night not so very long ago when it had been just the two of them on a darkened balcony.

New beginnings, new lives. They'd certainly achieved that, though not in the way either of them had imagined.

Nick stood with his back to her, staring out into the night. At first glance his stance, as he leaned against the railing, appeared relaxed. A closer look revealed tension in the muscles of his shoulders. She waited for him to turn. The beat of her heart was a slow, heavy thump.

He remained immobile.

Numb, she walked to stand beside him, followed his

gaze into the blue-black night. The song of nearby cicadas filled the air. "When I was little," she said, "I used to lie in bed at night listening to the cicadas, pretending I was Pocahontas. I thought if I listened hard enough I would hear secrets they were trying to tell me."

He turned at last and studied her. "You're pregnant."

She nodded. That blue line still seemed imprinted on her retina.

"Could it be wrong?"

She shook her head. "Not three times." She turned away as tears suddenly welled. Weren't children supposed to be a joy? All she felt was overwhelmed and more than a little frightened. She didn't know how to do this alone, to be a mother, to raise a child. Especially when her relationship with its father was so fragile.

She glanced over her shoulder at Nick, saw him still studying her. She could read nothing in his gaze, no anger, none of the fear and uncertainty she felt. She wanted to say something, but no words came. For the second time he took her hand in his, interlacing their fingers. His touch again gentle, warmth seeped into her, a physical manifestation of that unseen connection they now shared. Slowly he led her to the cane couch on the veranda. They sat down wordlessly, shoulders touching, and looked out into the night.

Drifting clouds had obscured the moon when he finally spoke. "I want what's best for our baby." His voice revealed no emotion, gave no clue as to what he thought or felt for himself.

"So do I. But I'm frightened that I don't know what that is or how to give it." In an instant her life had been turned upside down, and being pregnant felt so…huge, that it put everything she'd done before into a new perspective.

It was a long time before Nick responded. "Do you want me to take the child?"

Callie shot up from the couch and whirled to face him. "Of course not."

"I don't expect to be that bad a parent. And I can get help. A nanny?" He was still too calm.

"How can you think for one minute—"

"I was just asking." The facade cracked and frustration seeped out. "I need to know how things stand, what you want."

"I want this baby." Callie held her hands protectively over her abdomen.

In one fluid motion he was standing too. "The one mere minutes ago you didn't even want to know existed?"

"Yes, that one. Because now I do know it exists and the only thing at all I'm certain about is that I want it."

He held her gaze. "At least we're clear on that."

She turned and leaned on the veranda railing, gripped its rough solidity. Thoughts whirled in her head. "We've only known for a few minutes. It's too early to have it all sorted out. There's too much to take in, to think about." She was pregnant. There was a life growing inside her, separate from her and yet a part of her. She could barely even wrap her head around that concept.

Nick came to stand beside her, his presence solid and imposing. She'd seen the way he protected his family. No matter what her relationship with this man, she didn't doubt that their child would at least always have that fierce protection. But how would it affect her? Would he see her as an obstacle to be outmaneuvered, as he had with her business?

"So, you're willing to work things out with me on this?"

Was she being paranoid, or was that a veiled threat?

Would he be calling his lawyers first thing in the morning? "Of course I am." His offer to have the child had spooked her. Perhaps she should be the one to call her lawyer in the morning. He already had proved he was capable of taking drastic precautionary measures.

"There's no of course about it." She heard a shadow of her own uncertainty in his voice. "We don't know each other well."

"And yet here we are, partners in a business and about to have a baby."

He said nothing.

Callie filled the gaping silence. "I don't know what you expect from me, what rights you want or think you have."

"This isn't a promising start," he growled. "Do we need to talk about custody and visitation, about financial arrangements?"

"Don't, Nick." She turned to face him. "It's too soon. Can't you just…"

"Just what?"

A moth fluttered past the porch light and then out into the night. "Just leave. I need time to think." It was either ask him to leave or ask him to hold her, but she couldn't let herself need him.

He studied her. "How much time?"

She shook her head. "I don't know."

"All right," he agreed slowly. "I'll see you tomorrow then."

"Tomorrow?" What was he thinking? "No. This isn't *sleep on it and I'll have it all figured out by morning* type of news."

"I want to get this sorted out."

"So do I. But tomorrow's not enough time. Not nearly enough."

"What's more important than this?" He gestured to her stomach.

"Nothing." She fought for calm. Why wouldn't he understand? "I need time, and that's the one thing we at least have a little bit of. We don't have to have anything sorted out by tomorrow, or even the next day. It can wait. Give me…a week." She watched that impassive face. "Please?"

The frown creasing his brow advertised his reluctance to give her even that much time. He was the sort who tackled life head-on, who, if he had a problem, worked at it till he found the solution. But his way wasn't right for her. "I still have work to attend to. And unlike you, I don't have an endless stream of minions I can delegate to." Right now work was the least of her concerns, but perhaps Nick would find that excuse easier to accept.

"Will you be able to make time to go to the doctor next week? Can you fit that into your hectic schedule?"

She ignored the undertone of scorn. "I'll go to the doctor."

"I'll come with you."

"To make sure I go, or to offer support?" She thought she knew which.

A rueful smile touched his lips. "Perhaps both." The smile vanished. "I fly to San Francisco tomorrow morning for a series of meetings. If I reschedule some things I can be back by next week. Make the appointment for then."

He glanced at her stomach. Callie looked down, hadn't realized that, as they'd been speaking, she'd placed her hand over her abdomen.

When she looked up again Nick's gaze hadn't shifted, and he was reaching slowly toward her. He touched her hand with his fingertips.

He looked up and for a moment their gazes met. Did she see an echo of her own awe and wonder in his eyes? Beneath their hands lay new life.

Nick's hand dropped back to his side. "Is there anything you want me to do?"

"Like what?"

"I don't know." The words, the lack of certainty they revealed, seemed to pain him.

Callie felt a strange stirring of sympathy. She resisted the urge to step closer, to take hold of his hand once again. To give or take comfort? She wasn't sure which. So instead she stepped back, wrapped her arms about herself. "There's nothing you can do now," she spoke softly. "Except give me some space. Please."

He nodded slowly and then turned and strode away, his footsteps echoing in the night. She heard his car purr into life and watched as red taillights disappeared down her driveway.

Callie sat in her car, staring at the red brick building in front of her. She should go in. Just get out of the car, walk up the three gray concrete steps to the front door and go in. She only wished she didn't feel quite so alone, but there were no friends she wanted to share the knowledge of her situation with yet. Nor was she ready to tell her mother. She wasn't even entirely sure where her mother was right now. Her last postcard from her had been of Inca ruins in Peru.

Slowly, she unbuckled her seat belt. As she touched her fingers to the door handle her phone rang and she snatched it up gratefully. "Hello." Her greeting was quick and eager. Perhaps they needed her at work and she'd have to go.

There was a pause. "How are you?" The question earnest, seeking an honest response. The voice deep and warm. "Did you sleep last night?"

Implying that he hadn't?

She hadn't thought she wanted to hear from Nick again, and certainly not so soon. But apparently she was wrong. Her spinelessness was great enough to make his call welcome. "Better than I expected. At least the uncertainty is gone now." No more lying in bed wondering whether or not she was pregnant. Just lying in bed wondering what happens next.

"Where are you?"

The one question she hadn't wanted him to ask. Callie took a deep breath. "Outside my doctor's office. Working up the courage to go in." She glanced at the wooden front door and then at her watch.

She grimaced as she counted the seconds of the pause. Finally he spoke. "You were going to wait till I came back."

She hadn't actually agreed to that, but now probably wasn't the time to argue her point. "I'm taking a leaf out of your book. Although I'm not so sure that I like it. But now at least you won't have to cut short your trip." She glanced again at the suddenly ominous building and remembered the other proactive call she'd made. The one setting up an appointment with her lawyer. Nick sounded conciliatory now, caring even, but she'd learned her lesson—and she was going to protect herself and get good legal advice.

"I'm in the country still. Give me the doctor's address." In the background she heard a flight departure announcement.

"You're at the airport?"

"Yes, but I'll change my flight."

The offer seemed to give her strength. "Don't, but thanks," she said quietly. "It'll be okay. I'll be okay. I just have to get to the front door. And I should really do it now. My appointment's in a few minutes."

"Okay."

But neither of them hung up.

"Thanks for calling."

"Get out of the car, Callie." This time she definitely heard a smile in his voice and felt an answering tug at her lips.

"I am," she said as she opened her door and got out. "My doctor's lovely." She walked across the car park. "A gentle, older woman. She's known me for years."

"How long?" He encouraged her to talk.

"She delivered me, so she knows what she's doing." Feeling like he was at her side, Callie climbed the steps and pushed open the door. "I'll call you afterward, if there's anything I think you'd want to know."

"Call me anyway."

She called, Nick thought, as he slipped into the auditorium and stood in the shadows at the back of the crowded room. He'd give her that much. But her call had come while he'd been on the plane. She'd left a message, her voice soft and awestruck, assuring him that everything had gone well.

Soon after that she'd left a second message, professional, though vaguely defensive and full of excuses, as she listed far too many reasons why they should delay meeting again for another two weeks. He wasn't having it, so he'd flown back to Sydney where she was presenting at this conference.

And so here he was, watching as she stood in the center of the stage, exuding passion and expertise. A microphone the size of a pinot noir grape was attached to the lapel of her tailored jacket. Her dark hair was pulled sleekly back from her face. Her fitting skirt skimmed her knees. Ostensibly, there was nothing provocative about her. A pair of ankles and a shapely calf should not make his thoughts go where they were heading. Back into the land of fantasy. But he knew how soft her skin was, knew the throaty sound of her laugh. And he wanted her. The reaction was instinctive. The logical side of him could and would deny it, but it was there.

He could scarcely reconcile this polished professional with the woman with paint smears on her face, or the woman standing frightened and uncertain in the moonlight. He had ached to wrap his arms around her then, too, and just hold her, but he couldn't trust himself, he was too willing to overlook logic and reason where she was concerned.

It was almost ironic. He was usually the one who stopped people from getting too close. He knew the hurt that led to. And now Callie was trying to keep him at arm's length. She had given him no idea of whether she would want too much or not enough.

From the front of the room she glanced his way and paused a beat, but he was confident she couldn't see him. She stood in the full glare of the lights, while he was in shadow.

He hadn't missed her assertion the other night, that aside from Jason, her then partner, he was the only other man she'd slept with. It didn't seem possible. A woman this vibrant, this attractive? But the implications of that fact ran deep. She took her relationships seriously.

He frowned as he noticed the bandage on her hand, realized also that she was wielding her pointer with her left hand with a hint of slowness. Her right hand passed in front of her abdomen, still flat.

She was carrying his baby.

Regardless of what she did or didn't want, he *would* be a part—an integral part—of his child's life.

As the door to her hotel room swung shut behind her, Callie slipped out of her shoes and wriggled her toes on the carpet. She shrugged out of her jacket and tossed it onto the first of the two beds. As she was peeling off the panty hose from beneath her skirt, the phone on her bedside table rang. Still pulling the last leg of the hose off, she hopped over to the phone and dropped onto the bed as she picked up the handset. "Callie speaking."

"You made it to your room at last."

She knew that deep voice too well. "Nick?" Her pulse quickened, as it always did around him.

"You were expecting someone else?"

She stood as though that could give her the strength she needed to deal with this man. "I wasn't expecting anyone." She'd known she'd hear from him again sooner or later—she'd valiantly hoped for later.

"Even though we agreed we'd talk this week?" His voice sounded almost pleasant. Callie didn't trust it for a moment. He'd be annoyed that she'd put him off, knew that his gentleness when she'd spoken to him outside the doctor's had been a passing illusion. Not something she could, or would, want to rely on.

"I called and left you a message explaining."

"It was a cop-out, Callie. We both know that."

"It wasn't a cop-out. I didn't have my personal organizer when we agreed on this week, and you'll appreciate my thoughts were in turmoil that evening. I have it with me now—give me a second and I'll get it from my briefcase." She dropped the phone on the bed and retrieved her organizer, then switched it on as she was picking up the phone again. "I've got it in front of me, and next week is looking more flexible. Name your day."

"I don't want to leave it till next week to talk to you."

She knew better than to think that meant he wanted to see her for her own sake. "I can't see you any sooner than that. I'm tied up at a conference this week and I won't be back in the office till next week."

"You didn't mention in the message you left where the conference was."

She hesitated. The omission had been deliberate. And given that she was now on the phone to him, he obviously knew where she was. "Sydney," she said on a sigh. Sydney, where the head office of Brunicadi Investments was located.

"Then I think we should meet sooner than next week."

"Nick, I don't—" A knock sounded on her door. "Hang on a second, someone's here."

"I'll talk to you soon then." The dial tone sounded in her ear.

As she crossed to the door Callie knew he'd gone too easily. *Duh.* The unexpected knock suddenly made depressing sense. She looked through the peephole, saw him waiting in the corridor. And even through the distortion of the glass she saw that mix of careless elegance and intensity that was Nick's alone. His dark jacket hung open, revealing the white shirt beneath. She opened the door and for a second they looked at each other. Again, Callie felt the awareness that invariably rolled through her like a deep tremor whenever she saw him. Green eyes searched her face. Then, breaking that contact, he strolled in.

"I have a sponsor's dinner to go to shortly." She spoke to the back of his dark head and broad shoulders.

Nick surveyed the room. Too late, she remembered the clothes scattered around and the panty hose discarded on the floor by the phone. She also remembered that one other time she'd been in a hotel room with him. Clothes discarded then with even less thought. Her face heating, she strode past him, picked up the scattered items and dropped them into her suitcase, pushing down the lid that stood open.

"If there's such a rush, why weren't you up here earlier?" He turned and suddenly his river-green gaze held hers—dark, unreadable.

Her heart quickened, and again memories surged of that other hotel room, the penthouse suite. A gaze darkened with desire then. Callie spoke slowly, tried to make her voice sound even. "I was in the salon trying to get a hair appointment." The parameters had been set— they were business partners and accidental parents to be, nothing more. She reached behind her head and removed the clasp that held her hair in place. Unruly curls cascaded around her face. "But there's a celebrity auction for breast cancer here tonight, and they can't fit me in. And neither can any of the other nearby salons." She ran her fingers through her hair. "It needs a wash and I can't do it because I can't get this stupid hand wet." She lifted her right arm. "For which, rightly or wrongly, I hold you in part responsible."

"Why is it still like that? The stitches should have been out by now." The concern in his voice surprised her.

"It got infected." She shrugged. "It should be okay in a few more days."

His gaze shifted from her hand back to her face. "I saw your presentation this afternoon."

"That was you standing at the back of the room?"

He nodded.

She'd had a feeling that he was there, had looked for him in the audience once it was over, then decided she'd been imagining things.

Idly, he picked up her organizer from the bedside table, flipped it over to look at the back, and then replaced it before Callie could protest. He turned the full force of his attention on her. "We need to talk about your pregnancy, about our child. About what we're going to do."

Our child.

Hearing the words out loud made it so very real. She was pregnant by her client's brother, her ex-boyfriend's brother-in-law and her new business partner. She couldn't have made this any messier if she'd tried.

Callie crossed to the small sink and poured herself a glass of water. She spoke to the tap. "I've hardly been able to think about anything else. Anytime I have a moment to myself, that's where my thoughts go. But once there, they circle around and around." The words tumbled from her. "I haven't got any answers. I don't know how to make this work. How you and I can be the parents we each want to be? How to run a business and be a mother at the same time?" It felt so good to let the words and her confusion out. No one else knew she was pregnant. She wasn't ready to share the news, but that also meant she had no one to talk to. She turned to find Nick standing inches in front of her, looking down at her, his brow furrowed.

Any further words died on her lips. She had no idea what he was thinking, wasn't sure she wanted to know, because whatever it was, it looked ominous. Perhaps talking about it wasn't such a great idea. Callie lifted her glass. "Do you want a drink?" He shook his head and she took a sip herself. The water did nothing to ease the sudden dryness in her throat.

He studied her face, his own a mask of grim determination. "Marry me."

Seven

Callie almost choked as she swallowed. She took a deep, gasping breath and put down her glass. "I think you misheard me. I said, 'do you want a drink,' not, 'I love you and want to spend my life with you.'"

One side of his mouth twitched upward. "I heard you." The half smile disappeared. He shoved his fists into the pockets of his black pants.

"Then maybe I misheard *you*."

He shook his head. "I didn't mention love or wanting to spend a lifetime together, either. I presented the obvious solution to your dilemma, which is for us to get married. Surely you expected no less."

Her words from their first meeting came back to her as she met Nick's gaze: "If you're choosing between bad company and loneliness, choose the latter." His eyes widened and she pushed on. "So, flattering as your heartfelt proposal is, I don't think the best solution for my dilemma is to create an entirely new set of problems. I compromised once before. I won't do it again. My expectations don't include having any more to do with you than I have to. And given that we're business partners as well as parents-to-be, I'm confident I'll have more than my fill."

Some of the tension eased from his stance, but the lines across his forehead deepened. "You're saying no?"

She almost smiled. Had he really thought she might say yes? "Absolutely, I'm saying no. When—if—I get married, I have certain requirements."

His eyebrows lifted. "I don't meet them?"

"For starters, men who bulldoze their way to getting what they want have never really done it for me."

"Bulldoze?" He looked as though he might argue with that.

She held his gaze. "Bulldoze, steamroll, take your pick. Like you did with my business."

"I try to find the most efficient way of tackling my problems," he said quietly.

"Regardless of who's in your way?"

Something shifted in the green depths of his eyes. "I always take into account who's in my way."

Right now they were very much in each other's way, standing inches apart. Callie's pulse leapt traitorously. There were some things that she didn't doubt would be good between them, at least in the short term.

She took a step back. "I really need to get ready for this dinner."

"Go ahead," he said easily.

"But—"

"I'll wait for you." He picked up the hotel's complimentary newspaper from the table.

She looked into his eyes, saw the implacability, and for a moment thought she saw something else too, something like—not vulnerability—but perhaps need, as though this really was important to him.

Sighing, Callie found her clothes for the evening and took them into the bathroom. She showered, keeping her cut hand outside the curtain, and did her very best to shut out thoughts of Nick; but that was easier said than done when she was standing naked under a stream of hot water and far too aware that he was on the other side of the door. Even if he was engrossed in the paper.

She had just finished drying herself when his deep voice carried through the door. "You don't think marriage and a stable family life is the best way to raise a child?"

So much for reading the paper. "I definitely think that." She reached for her underwear and stepped quickly into it. "If the marriage is happy."

"It puts in place the best structure for raising a child." His voice through the door was calm and measured.

Callie was anything but. "Best in the right circumstances." She slipped her dress over her head, smoothed it over her hips. "These aren't them."

"A child needs two parents."

Callie turned and rested her forehead on the door. "Who love each other." This was hurting. As if he could read her thoughts he was raising all the arguments and insecurities that circled as she tried to sleep at night. She straightened and opened the door. He was close, his forearm raised above his head as he leaned against the door frame. His jacket hung open and her gaze caught on the small V of masculine skin revealed by the undone top button of his shirt.

She dragged her gaze upward. "Supposedly, it takes a whole village to raise a child. That doesn't mean it's a good idea to marry the baker, and the blacksmith and the woman who takes in laundry."

"People can grow to love each other." He said thoughtfully, as though considering the concept.

Callie couldn't fathom anything in those deep green eyes, and yet they held her, slowed the beating of her heart. "What are you saying?"

He shook his head, breaking the contact of his gaze. "I'm saying marry me. I want the child to have my name."

The hollowness swelled within her and she took a step back, turned to the counter and busied herself looking in her makeup bag. "No."

"Think about it."

"I just did."

Nick sighed. "Then think some more. But regardless of when or…if you marry me, I'll provide whatever you need." He spoke to her back. "But in return I want to know that you're not going to try to shut me out. That you'll let me be the best father to our child that I can."

She set her mascara and lipstick on the counter and turned back to him. She wasn't going to be drawn in on the marriage issue, but she could assure him on some points at least.

"Three things. First—" she held up one finger "—I wouldn't try to shut you out. I wouldn't do that to our child. He'll need and want contact with his father. I know that."

"He? What did the doctor tell you?" The question was sharp and very interested.

"Not that. I'm only ten weeks, and they won't be able to tell the sex till I have a scan around twenty. But I can't keep calling it, 'it.'" She smoothed a hand over her still-almost-flat stomach. "Sometimes I think *she*."

"She," he said abruptly. "She's a girl." He looked as though he regretted the words as soon as they were out of his mouth. His gaze slid away from her.

"Why do you say that?"

He lifted one shoulder. "Devil's advocate," he said lightly, then nodded, the movement abrupt. "Go on."

"Second," she said as she cleared a circle on the steam-dampened mirror with a hand towel. "I play fair." Even in the mirror she could read the skepticism in his eyes. "Ask Jason." She leaned toward the glass and brushed smoky eye shadow over her eyelids.

"I'd rather not ask Jason about you."

It was small consolation that, if this was messy for her, it was at least as messy for him. "Do he and Melody know?"

"No."

She swept on her mascara. "Why not?"

"I haven't seen much of them lately. Besides, I didn't think they needed to know. Not yet anyway."

Callie put the mascara back in her bag. "How will Melody take the news?" This was the woman who thought she'd been trying to cling to Jason. And now Callie was having her brother's baby.

"Mel's swept up with her own pregnancy. Her first thought will probably be, great, a cousin for my child."

"Extended, divided families. It promises to be so much fun." Callie paused. "Is she still worried about me and Jason?" She stretched her lips and carefully applied plum-colored lipstick.

"No."

She turned away from the mirror and met his gaze directly, tried to read his thoughts. "Are you?"

His gaze lingered for a moment on her lips. "It was never about what I thought. And the third thing?"

He hadn't answered her question, but Callie let it pass. She wasn't sure she wanted to know his answer. "The third thing," she tried to remember what it had been as she packed her cosmetics back into her bag and closed it. "You own half of my business. Something to do with control and leverage, if I remember correctly." He had the power to do her a lot of damage.

The light in Nick's eyes changed. "I'd forgotten."

It was reassuring that he had. He wasn't already looking at this as a battle and assessing potential weapons.

Callie opened the bathroom door wider and stepped past him, doing her best to ignore the gaze that swept her from head to toe. She reached into the closet for her shoes—too high, but gorgeous black patent leather evening sandals. She was about to slip them onto her feet when she remembered her toenails. She glanced at the bedside clock. There was still time.

Sitting on her bed, she shook a bottle of nail polish and watched as Nick paced the room. He picked up a menu for the hotel restaurant, glanced over it before dropping it back down and turning to her. "You claimed at the awards dinner that a rumor of pregnancy would be bad for your business. How will the reality affect it?"

She shook the small bottle more vigorously. "I'll manage it."

"How?"

"I don't know yet." The questions put her on the

spot. He was doing it again, getting way ahead of her and what she was ready to deal with. "Whatever it is, I'll manage. It's what I do."

"I'll help."

That she was so ready to believe him should probably worry her. It was his business too, she reminded herself. He was only protecting his investment. But she didn't doubt that, for some things at least, he would be in her corner. The even more worrying thought was that he would be a good man to have there. "Thanks," she said, and meant it.

Silence settled over them. Callie loosened the lid of the bottle and looked at her toes. Nick's dark shoes appeared in her line of sight. "If you really want to help, you could do this for me." She held up the nail polish.

Showing neither surprise nor reluctance, Nick took the bottle from her and sat on the opposite bed. "Give me your foot." She should have known better than to hope that her request might scare him off.

Callie was suddenly the reluctant one. "Do you know what you're doing?"

He smiled. "It's been a while, but Mel used to get me to help her when she was younger." He shrugged. "I have steady hands." Callie watched those steady hands unscrew the lid. "How will your family take the news?" he asked, holding out a hand for her foot.

She placed her heel into the cradle of his palm and watched, fascinated, as, holding the delicate brush in large fingers, he brushed on an even stroke of glistening plum polish.

"You do have family?" He glanced up before applying another stroke.

She nodded. "A mother."

"That's all?" He moved to her next toe.

"Obviously I have or had a father, but I've never met him." She'd had a good childhood, but knew she didn't want that same vague sense of something missing, of abandonment, for her child.

It seemed a long time before he spoke again. "You've told your mother?"

"Not yet."

"It might be easier to break it to her along with the news of our engagement."

She met his gaze. "Or not."

He nodded, but somehow it didn't seem to mean agreement.

"How will she take it?"

"She has no grounds for criticism, if that's what you mean." In fact, Callie, who'd tried so hard to be different from her free-spirited mother, had instead followed right along in her careless footsteps in accidentally getting pregnant.

Nick finished another toe and looked up again. Concern softened his gaze. "I meant, will you get support from her?"

"Yes. If I ask." And it was the asking that would be the hard part. Asking, that Callie saw as a sign of not being able to cope on her own. A sign that she'd failed. Stupid really, because Gypsy would only want to help, would delight in a grandchild—one she could lavish her affection on when she breezed into the country. "What about your family?"

He shrugged as though he hadn't given it any thought. And yet he'd wondered about her family's reaction. "So long as they're allowed to feel the child is part of the family, they'll be happy."

He made it sound so simple.

Callie withdrew her finished foot from his clasp and paused before she lifted her other one, settled it into the hand that rested, waiting, on his thigh. He met her gaze over her leg, his green eyes soft. For a few moments it was as though everything would be all right, that between them they could make it so.

"And you?" That gaze assessed her closely. "Are you okay with being a single mother?"

Callie took a deep breath. "I think life is trying to tell me that I can't plan it all out. I wanted to do things the right way—stable relationship, love, marriage, then kids."

For long seconds neither of them spoke. Nick of the steady hands painted her toenails. "Love, marriage and kids. That's what you thought you were getting with Jason?" He finished a toe and looked up, intent.

"Yes. I'd thought, hoped, that was where we were going. But I guess I was projecting my fantasy ideals onto him. And he was comfortable with the situation— till a better offer came along."

Nick's fingers stilled. "Are you suggesting he married Melody for—"

"I'm not suggesting anything. Jason loves her in a way he never loved me." He'd kindly told her that himself. "I just didn't realize how much more was possible than what we had." She paused, felt the hollowness inside. "I won't settle for less a second time."

Nick replaced the cap on the bottle and his hand came to rest on the top of her foot, warm and strong, fingers curving around it. "And marrying me would be settling for less?"

"You know it would. I want the real thing, and I don't want to deny either of us the chance of finding it."

He lifted her foot, blew gently on the nails before lowering it back to his leg. "What if there is no real thing?"

The warm breath, the gesture, disconcerted her, she scrambled for thought. "There is." There had to be.

"You may never find it."

Callie pulled her foot from his hand, placed it firmly on the floor. "I know that's a possibility." And at almost thirty the possibility seemed very real. "But it's better than the certainty that if we tie each other up in a marriage we'll never find it. Or it'll be really messy if one of us does. Besides, you're not in the market for any kind of commitment."

"I can commit."

She held his gaze. "Professionally and financially, sure. But not personally or emotionally. I did some research. You've been romantically linked to numerous beautiful women. Nothing has stuck. And you're forgetting I know about Angelina, I remember you celebrating the end of a relationship that was looking like too much commitment."

Nick was silent for a long time. He was looking at her, but not really seeing her.

"That was different."

With that nonargument, a weight settled in the air. Callie glanced at her toes, wiggled them a little. "Good job on the nail polish. I could probably get you some regular clients."

"Don't you dare tell a soul," he growled, but he was smiling and she remembered how and why she'd been so attracted to him that first night. His smile did something wonderful to his face. "I hope our baby gets your smile." The words slipped out.

His gaze sharpened on her, then softened and lingered. "And your eyes."

He liked her eyes? Startled by the warmth that simple statement generated, Callie stood. She needed to remain neutral toward him, needed to retain her independence from him. "I should get going." She slid her feet carefully into her open-toe sandals.

Nick stood too. "I'll walk you down."

As they passed the still open wardrobe door, Callie glanced critically at her reflection in the full-length mirror. She lifted a hand to her hair. She'd left it out, curling softly around her face. If she'd been able to get an appointment—

"It looks beautiful. *You* look beautiful." Nick fingered one of the curls, his knuckle brushing against her neck igniting her skin.

She met his gaze in the mirror. "What if I say yes?"

"Then we'll get married."

"And make each other miserable."

A hint of a smile touched his face. "Perhaps." He paused, the smile faded and his mouth turned serious. He shifted his hand to her shoulder, turned her toward him. "You deserve to be happy. I would find ways to not to make you miserable."

"That would have sounded good in the marriage vows. I'll find ways to not make you miserable." Callie tried to make light of the situation, but still neither of them moved. A connection shimmered in the air between them, slowing her heartbeat to a heavy, anticipatory thump.

Her phone rang in her evening bag, shrill and abrupt. Once then twice. Blinking, Callie found it and glanced at the caller ID. "Marc, how's it going?"

As Marc spoke, she exhaled heavily, her thoughts firmly back in reality. "Of course you have to go home. Don't worry about the festival, I'll sort it out." She listened a little longer, then cut in. "I meant it when I said don't worry. Just get yourself home as quickly as you can."

She shut off her phone and looked at Nick, who'd moved away, but was watching her. "Marc's your side-kick at Ivy Cottage?"

She nodded, still processing the news he'd delivered. "He's been at Cypress Rise. I had him organizing the Jazz and Art festival."

"And?" Nick probed gently.

"His sister's been in a car crash. She's in a coma." The woman Callie had met only a few times had been so vivacious it was impossible to imagine her lying still and injured in a hospital bed.

"Does he need help getting home?" Nick's concern was immediate. "Brunicadi Investments has a jet that's available."

Callie shook her head and started toward her hotel room door. "He's booked on the next flight out, and is already on his way to the airport."

Nick opened the door for her. "Good."

She waited for him in the corridor. "It does leave a problem with the festival."

His gaze sharpened. "Who'll cover it now?"

They walked toward the elevators. "That's the problem. Aside from me there isn't anyone else. Before he left, Jason used to do a lot of these sorts of things. If he's available to help, I guess he could step in. But he would still have to liaise with me."

Nick shook his head.

So he still doubted her. And it hurt. "Don't you think the festival is more important than these insecurities? Heck, we can have a third person present during all contact if that makes it any easier."

He shook his head again. "Jason's out of the country."

"Oh." It hadn't been concern over her and Jason. At least not entirely. "Then I'm the only other person who can take over." She watched him closely as they waited for an elevator to arrive. She'd put Marc in charge of the day in an effort to minimize her contact with the winery and Melody. But she really was the only one who could step in now, the only other person who'd had involvement with the caterers, artists, performers and security.

He saw her dilemma. Knew it, because he'd created it.

"I know it goes against what we agreed—what you demanded I agree to—but that really wasn't necessary in the first place. For the winery's sake, and for the sake of the teenage shelter, we need to do it right and do it well."

The elevator arrived and they stepped in. "I'll drive you." There was no hesitation, no reluctance in his calm response.

Did that mean he trusted her? And should she want that trust as much as she did? "I don't want to put you to any trouble." She matched his calmness, but already her thoughts were torn between cataloging what still needed to be done in the run-up to the weekend, and how she would juggle the work on her desk back home; and underneath all that ran a ripple of anxiety about what it would be like to be on his territory.

"It's no trouble. I promised Mel I'd be around this week."

The ripple increased. "You're helping out at the festival?"

"You sound surprised."

"I hadn't realized, that's all. Doing what?"

"General drudge work, as far as I can tell. She's making all the family come and help." One side of his mouth kicked up in a grin as the elevator came to a halt. "So when do you want to go?"

This was happening too fast, but she knew it had to. "Early tomorrow morning I guess," she said hesitantly. "I'd like to get there in time to put in a full day."

"You're not needed here?"

She shook her head. "This dinner is the last thing I have to be here for."

"I'll pick you up at six then."

Suddenly, the trip in the car with him, spending days on his territory seemed like a very bad idea. He confused her, and confused her senses.

They stepped into the foyer. In a bar area off the far side of the marbled room, several of the people she was meeting for dinner stood clustered together, sipping cocktails.

The adjacent elevator doors opened, and Len Joseph, whose company was one of the principal conference sponsors, stepped out. A smile spread across his lined face as he saw Callie and Nick. "Wonderful that you could join us for dinner." He clapped Nick on the shoulder.

Callie's heart sank. Yet another opportunity for Nick to intrude in her life, a further confusing of the lines. And she couldn't even accuse him of bulldozing when the opportunity was handed to him on a plate.

"Thanks, Len." Nick glanced at Callie. "But I can't tonight."

"Sorry to hear that. Some other time." Len headed for the group of dinner guests.

She looked at Nick. "Thanks."

"For not bulldozing?"

"Something like that."

He smiled and Callie dragged her gaze away to look at the group Len had joined. Their presence anchored her and reminded her what she was doing here and who she was, Callie Jamieson, PR professional. She knew how to be that woman. All she had to do was focus on that and do her job. The rest, the confusing stuff—her pregnancy and more specifically her relationship with Nick—she could deal with later.

"The pregnancy changes everything, Callie." He spoke close to her ear. "You're having my baby," he said as though he'd read her thoughts. "Whether you like it or not, and even before you agree to marry me that makes you a part of my family. The two can't be separated."

Eight

Still mulling over his parting words, Callie stood under the hotel's portico the next morning, watching the Sydney street come to life. From his cool non-offer of marriage, she'd been catapulted into the prospect of days spent in Nick's company, with all the things they'd said—and done—hanging between them.

Five minutes ahead of time, a black Range Rover eased to a stop in front of her. Nick nodded a greeting as he got out and opened her door. Wearing snug jeans that were faded just a little, and a black polo shirt, he looked more casual than she'd yet seen him. Casual, yet no less potent. She had to pass close to him to get into the car, and remembered of all things, the warm caress of his breath on her bare toes. She caught his scent, clean and masculine, as she climbed into the deep beige seat. He shut her door, leaving her with a feeling similar to what she got when she strapped herself into the seat of a rollercoaster. Suddenly, when it was too late to back out, there was an overwhelming uncertainty as to whether this wasn't a very bad idea.

He stowed her bag in the back, climbed in beside her then pulled smoothly away. Definitely too late now. "You've been in touch with Marc this morning? How's his sister?" he asked as he passed her a paper bakery bag. All business, she noted, though his concern was genuine.

"Yes. He got home all right, but there's no change in his sister's condition." And she was almost equally surprised when she looked inside the bag and saw a cream cheese bagel and a date scone. Beside her, in the cup holders, sat two bottles of mineral water.

"And nothing else we can do for him or his family?"

"Not at this stage. I've told him to take as much time as he needs off work." She watched to gauge his response, but if she was expecting any protest at the likely effect on her bottom line, she didn't get it. Nick nodded his agreement. "Is this for me?" She lifted up the bag.

"I didn't know if you'd have had time for breakfast. We can stop somewhere along the way, once we get out of the city, but that's—" he pointed at the bag "—just in case."

Did he know that she was almost constantly hungry? The pregnancy book she had bought informed her that the baby, at just under three months, was only a couple of inches long. How did something that size have such a profound affect on her appetite? "Thank you." She broke a corner off the scone, light and buttery and still warm from the oven, and popped it into her mouth.

"How was your dinner?"

"Good." She paused. "You could have come if you'd wanted to."

His laughter was the last thing she expected, filling the interior of the car with its warmth and surprising a laugh out of her too. "All right," she admitted, "I was relieved when you turned the invitation down."

They lapsed into silence. Callie sought for something to say. She glanced across at him. Her gaze caught on his hands, strong and capable on the steering wheel, took in the light covering of hair on tanned forearms. The urge to touch her fingertips to those arms to see how the play of muscle would feel caught her by surprise. She swallowed and looked resolutely out the windshield.

Uncomfortable in the confined space, hyperaware of his presence and Nick's nearness, Callie made phone calls to keep herself occupied, following up on Marc's arrangements, satisfying herself that everything was under control.

Nick remained silent, keeping any feelings on her impending presence at Cypress Rise to himself. Outside, the vast summer-browned countryside slid by.

She finished a phone call with the caterers and looked across at him. "Does Melody know I'm coming?"

He nodded.

"And she's okay with it?"

"She understands why you need to come." After a pause, he added. "She never knew I'd told you to cut the contact. She had asked me to check you out, so to speak. After which, all I told her was that she didn't have anything to worry about."

"I don't understand how someone like Melody, who would appear to have it all, gets to be so insecure."

"A woman like you wouldn't."

"What's that supposed to mean?" Callie bristled.

Nick flicked a glance in her direction. "It's a compliment. You're strong."

"Oh." He thought she was strong? He had no inkling of her uncertainties, her fears of being inadequate for the things ahead of her.

"Have you always protected her?"

He shot her another glance, took his time answering. "I guess so. Because of the gap in our ages, in some ways I was more like a father to her. Our own father wasn't around that much."

"Where was he?"

"He was heavily involved in his work."

"And your mother?"

Nick paused, this one even longer than the last. "Died when Melody was three."

Callie hid her shock at the thought. Nick could only have been thirteen. Her heart ached for the boy he'd been, and for Melody too.

"Rosa, my grandmother, stepped into the breech," he continued. "We never wanted for anything."

Callie studied his profile as he pulled out and passed a tractor towing hay-baling equipment. He looked so strong, and he was strong—not letting himself need anyone—but it had come at a price.

"Not wanting for anything didn't mean you weren't hurting."

He gave a slight shake of his head. "We were okay. It made us closer at the time."

"And you're still close?"

"We're family." He said it as though that simple statement answered everything. And last night he'd said she was now a part of that family. "Mel's been better the last few years. Along with the success of the winery, her self-confidence has grown. She's intelligent and savvy. But those days cast a long shadow, and she's always been a little insecure."

And how had those days affected Nick? Clearly, they'd made him protective of his sister; but were they, combined with his girlfriend's betrayal, behind his reluctance to commit emotionally? Was that how he was able to keep marriage as a solution to a problem, without offering anything of himself?

"Mel's okay now. She's partially blaming hormones for her concerns over you."

There were two of them dealing with that particular issue. Callie was aware of the exaggerated peaks and troughs of her moods and emotional responses to things that wouldn't usually bother her, like sappy television commercials, like the times when a perceived gentleness in Nick could make her want to throw away her principles as she threw herself into his arms. "When does Jason get back?" And how would that affect the mix?

"Do you want him to be there?" Nick's gaze stayed trained on the road, but she knew his attention was on her.

Callie considered the question. "I haven't spoken to him since he sold out to you. So there are some things I'd like to say to him." She grinned. "But it's probably for the best if I don't."

"He's in California. He's due back in just over a week."

The subject sat uneasily between them. She wanted Nick at least to think better of her than his sister did, but he revealed so little of what he really thought. Maybe that was for the best, because if someone knew him and grew to care for him too much, that person would ultimately be the one who got hurt.

She had thought that she would be stronger after

what had happened with Jason, that she would develop a tougher outer shell. But Nick had already shown her the cracks in that shell. She would lean on him, if he let her, like at the hospital. And she couldn't afford to lean.

They drove through vine-covered land rich with the greens and browns of late summer. "It's beautiful here." Nonchalant, uninvolved. She could do it.

"Do you want to go to the house first, or straight to the winery?"

"The winery, thanks. I have a feeling it's going to be a big day."

A few miles farther along, Nick swung the car off the road and drove through an imposing gateway set in a low, stone wall, and lettered with the flowing logo for Cypress Rise Wines. They followed a side road that took them behind the public reception area used for wine tastings, and then around the back. She undid her seat belt as they eased to a stop, and they got out.

Nick led the way to a simple office building. Off to one side, stainless steel vats and stairways rose from the ground. He pushed open a door and stepped back for her to precede him inside.

Melody sat at a desk, computer monitor in front of her, neat piles of paper stacked on her left. This was the woman who'd thought Callie was trying to sabotage her marriage. Callie wasn't sure whether she should still feel angry about that, or just sorry for her. Melody looked up, and at the sight of Callie a slight flush rose up her face. She stood and came around to meet them. "I'm so glad you could make it. How's Marc's sister?" There was a wariness in her eyes. Eyes that Callie saw now were the same green as Nick's.

"She's stable, but other than that there's no change."

"We were so sorry to hear about her accident. We don't know her, of course, but all the staff were enjoying working with Marc. He had such a great sense of humor. We've sent her some flowers. Irises and daisies…" She trailed off.

Melody was definitely babbling, and she'd never struck Callie as a babbler before; so that meant Callie, and whatever lay between them, was making her nervous. A quagmire spread before her: did she mention the wedding, the honeymoon, ask after Jason? Questions that, with another client, would have been no more than polite. "I imagine things are really heating up here. Is there anything pressing we need to address?"

"Yes." Mel's face relaxed. Getting straight to business obviously suited her fine. "There's an interview scheduled with a local radio station in half an hour. It was supposed to be tomorrow, but they brought it forward. I hate that sort of thing, and Marc was going to do it."

"Did he get any notes on the questions they plan on asking?"

"Yes." Mel rummaged on her desk, picked up a sheet of printed paper and held it out gratefully to Callie. Marc's neat handwriting lined the margins and the spaces between the questions. "Have you got time to run through this with me?"

"I'll do anything you want, if it means I don't have to do that interview."

They started going through the questions together, both thoroughly professional, even if the interaction lacked ease or warmth. At the sound of Nick clearing his throat they looked up. He stood at the door. "I'll see you both later."

Callie nodded. Melody uttered a small "Oh". Then recovered. "Okay."

The door swung shut behind him, his absence leaving a strange vacuum. Had Melody wanted to call him back too?

But any doubts Callie had about the potential for uneasiness between them turned out to be unnecessary. There was so much to do that there was no time for awkwardness. Jason had always been the main contact between Ivy Cottage and the vineyard, and then Marc; but Callie had kept herself up-to-date and had occasionally dealt with Melody, and they'd always worked well together. It was no different today, professionally speaking. Occasionally Callie caught Melody looking at her, her glance quick and curious.

It was several rushed hours later before Nick came back through the door. "Lunch? Rosa's waiting."

"You go ahead," Melody said, "I brought lunch to have here. I've got a phone call to make."

"You're sure?" Nick asked.

Melody's glance darted between Nick and Callie. "Positive." Callie figured she planned to phone Jason.

Nick shrugged and held the door open. She passed by him and they walked toward his vehicle. "How did it go this morning?" he asked.

"Well. Everything's on target. We got a lot done. Though the big stuff was already sorted. It's really only tying up the details over the next couple of days. But there are more than enough of them."

He nodded as he helped her into the car. "You're not too tired?"

She turned in her seat and met his gaze, didn't want the closeness she felt at his concern, didn't want special treatment. "I'm not an invalid."

"Just busy," he said calmly, "and pregnant. And you

had a late night and an early start. It wasn't an unreasonable question." He shut her door gently, crossed in front of the car to get in behind the wheel.

"Sorry. I'm fine." Callie backed down. "Thanks for asking." She had to make this work, had to stop herself reacting—correction, overreacting—to him.

His knowing eyes didn't conceal the flash of humor as he glanced at her.

He pulled away from the winery and back onto the main road, then turned off again a few miles farther along.

A couple of minutes later he slowed and turned again, this time into a cypress-lined driveway. As the road wound its way up a hill, the trees gave way to reveal a sprawling Mediterranean-style villa.

"This is home?"

"I divide my time between here and my apartment in Sydney. I prefer it here, but the business dictates I spend a fair amount of time where I'm accessible for meetings and close to the airport." He looked out the window, scanning the surrounding countryside. "My family has lived in this area for three generations." He glanced at her, his green eyes enigmatic. "Four soon, I guess."

She supposed he could call it that. Though how much time their child got to spend here remained to be seen. Or perhaps he was referring only to Jason and Melody's child.

He slowed to a halt and got out. Before she'd even finished unbuckling her belt he had opened her door. A wave of heat washed into the cool interior. Nick's face was level with hers. Her gaze lighted on his lips. And the heat intensified. She remembered too well kissing those full lips. For a moment she thought of kissing them once again, of tasting him. Quickly averting her gaze, she blamed errant hormones for the passing temptation.

"I'm glad Melody won't be here," he said as he held out his hand.

Unresisting, Callie placed her hand in his. "Why?" she stepped down from the car. Nick didn't move, didn't release his clasp. They stood mere inches apart. Could he feel the way he made her pulse race?

He looked toward the house. "It's best we meet Rosa on our own."

Did he even know he was still holding her hand, his clasp warm and sure, gently possessive? "You're making her sound scary. Does she bite?" Callie extricated her hand. She needed to think straight.

"No. And she's not scary." He turned back. "But I should warn you about her."

Her gaze was caught by the dark lashes fringing those deep green eyes. He was still so close, so captivating. She need only lift her hand to touch him again. "Warn me?" She tried to keep her voice light. But it obviously wasn't only his grandmother someone needed to warn her away from, because she didn't seem able to heed her own warnings not to let herself feel anything for him.

Nick searched her gaze before speaking. "Sometimes she *knows* things, or thinks she does." The words seemed drawn reluctantly from him.

Callie tried to read in his eyes the meaning of the emphasis he'd placed on the word *know.* "What sort of things?"

"Usually, only things to do with family." A slight frown creased his brow.

She wanted to touch her fingertips to his forehead, to smooth away the lines. She swallowed. "Like what?"

"Like, who's calling when the phone rings. Or she'll suddenly decide to make extra cannelloni for dinner, and then friends drop in on the spur of the moment. Coincidental things, but uncanny all the same." His gaze held hers—a hint of apology in it—and he took a deep breath. "Pregnancy—the expansion of the Brunicadi clan—is her specialty."

They both looked toward the house just as the enormous front door swung open. "Dominic." A plump, gray-haired woman dressed in head-to-toe black, her face creasing into a smile, bustled toward them.

"Rosa," he greeted her.

She kissed Nick on both cheeks before enfolding him in an embrace. Then she turned to Callie, and before Nick had even finished introducing them had kissed her twice too. Still holding Callie's shoulders, she stepped back and surveyed her. Her eyes narrowed for a moment. "Come inside. Lunch is ready. I've made gnocchi."

As they walked into the house she glanced twice more at Callie.

They were in the cool, spacious kitchen, filled with the aromas of cooking, when Rosa looked again at Callie then turned to Nick. "Why didn't you tell me?"

Surely she couldn't have guessed already. Callie glanced at Nick, who had tilted his head inquiringly, as though he didn't know what his grandmother was asking. But Callie was suddenly certain that everybody knew what was being asked.

"The *bambina*."

He glanced at Callie, gave a resigned shrug. "We haven't told anyone, Rosa. You're the first to know." He almost made it sound like they were a couple who planned on sharing their news with friends and family.

The old woman rounded on Callie, a smile crinkling her already well-wrinkled face. "When is the *bambina* due? You need to eat more, you're too skinny." She grabbed Callie's hand, her grip surprisingly firm, and pulled her toward an expansive table.

She had Callie sitting with an enormous bowl of gnocchi in an aromatic sauce in front of her before she'd had time to gather her breath. "I bought pink wool last week. Now I know why." Another Brunicadi certain she was having a girl. Callie glanced at Nick.

But he was looking at his grandmother. "It's early days, Rosa," he cautioned.

"Paah! You think these things can change halfway through," she said scathingly. "It's a girl. I'll start knitting this afternoon." Rosa scarcely paused. "When is the wedding? I'm not having Melody tell me I need another new dress. She's too wasteful, that one."

Nick looked at her, giving her a chance to change her mind before he gave Rosa the bad news. Callie shook her head.

"We're not getting married," he said, and she was grateful for the certainty of that statement, at least in front of his family.

Rosa sat up straighter. "No grandson of mine will live in sin."

"We're not going to live together." His tone was firm but resigned. He obviously knew what was coming.

Rosa's chair scraped across the terra-cotta floor tiles as she pushed it back from the table and stood. "Come," she barked the order at Nick. Then she nodded sympathetically at Callie. "I will talk to him. *Un momento, per favore.*"

"But—"

Nick touched a hand to Callie's shoulder and shook his head to silence her protest, then stood and followed his grandmother to a door leading off the kitchen. Just before he passed through it, he turned back. "Her bark is worse than her bite," he said in a low voice, "but it's loud all the same."

"You told me she didn't bite at all."

He was smiling as he closed the door behind him. The slab of solid wood did little to disguise the tirade of angry Italian coming from the other side of it. Callie wasn't sure whether to feel sorry for him or to laugh.

But her conscience would only let her sit there for so long while he took all the blame for the fact that there would be no wedding. She stood and followed them, pushed open the door to see Rosa, who scarcely came up to Nick's shoulders, with a finger in his chest. They both looked at her, and Rosa's diatribe halted.

"Mrs. Brunicadi—"

"Rosa," the older woman quickly interrupted.

"Nick asked me to marry him." A strong hand came to rest on her shoulder. She looked across at Nick, who'd come to stand beside her, caught the small shake of his head and ignored it. "It's not what I want," she said as she looked back at Rosa.

"Of course it is."

"No. It's not," she said quietly, aware of two pairs of surprised eyes on her.

Rosa harrumphed, glared for a while longer at Nick, then, with an air of injured dignity, went back into the kitchen.

Nick stood in front of her, his head tilted to one side, his green eyes curious. "I don't think anyone's ever done that before. Tried to defend me to Rosa." A half smile tilted his lips. "You didn't have to."

"It seemed only fair. Besides, I get to leave after the end of the festival. Escape any more fallout."

The smile turned rueful. "She'll come around. But she needed to rant, to get it off her chest."

With one reassuring hand at the small of her back, he guided her back to the table, and unperturbed, waited for her to sit. They ate in relative companionability, though every now and then Rosa muttered to herself in Italian, and either frowned at Nick or looked pityingly at Callie. And Callie knew that she still thought it was Nick's fault there would be no wedding, that no woman in her right mind would turn down his offer of marriage. It was easy to see why she thought that way.

Nick watched Callie swallow the last of her gnocchi and edge her bowl away. "I'll show you the guest cottage." As seductive as watching her eat was, he needed to get her away from Rosa, who couldn't be counted on to forbear on the subject of marriage much longer. And while he wanted Callie to come to accept that marrying him was the best option, she needed space to do that, not badgering.

She paused as they rounded a bend in the path. "Cottage?" she challenged with a grin and a glint in her eyes. That grin was its own version of sunshine and temptation. Shaking her head, she kept walking toward the house that was a smaller version of the family home.

Nick held open the door that led into a spacious and light-filled interior furnished in creams and neutrals.

She trailed behind him as he showed her the bedroom, its broad, high bed piled with pillows, and the marble bathroom with its deep spa bath.

Back in the living room a ceiling fan spun lazily above them, barely moving the warm air. Nick leaned against a door frame, watching her and waiting for her reaction as she crossed to the wide windows and looked out over distant rows of green vines stretching across the hillsides. She turned. "It's beautiful here," she said, her expression enchanting.

She turned back to the window. "It's so peaceful. It quiets something inside. Gives a perspective that makes you believe everything will be okay."

That was how he'd always felt coming here. Cypress Rise was good for his soul. And she felt it too. That thought troubled him almost as much as it pleased him. He needed her to like it here. He didn't need to feel that she belonged. That she, too, might be good for his soul. Because his soul was just fine without her.

He stepped back. "Whenever you're ready I'll take you back to the vineyard office."

"I'm ready now."

In his car again, she looked at him. "I can't see that Melody's going to be thrilled at the prospect of me having your baby."

He reached across, touched his hand to her shoulder. "It's our business, Callie. Not anyone else's." He put his hand back on the wheel. "Though they'll definitely try to make it so. Still, you don't need to worry at the moment. Rosa won't tell anyone about the pregnancy yet, although we won't be able to stop her from knitting."

"When will you tell Melody?"

"Maybe after the festival, when she doesn't have so much on her mind. She'll know you better by then. You two will like each other."

"Is that another Brunicadi prediction?"

"No. This is a knowledge of people. Of Melody and of you."

"You don't really know me."

"I know you better than you think, better than you want to believe."

Nine

Melody was on the phone as Callie walked into the office. The remnants of a salad-filled sandwich and an apple core lay on a plate in front of her. A second phone on her desk was ringing. Callie gestured toward it and Melody nodded for her to pick it up. Odds were it would be about the festival.

"Cypress Rise."

"Darling. I forgot to say—"

"Jason?" Funny, a part of her observed, how the sound of his voice did nothing to her. She was still annoyed at him. But it was an unemotional kind of annoyed.

"Callie." The pause was long. "I've been meaning to get in touch with you to explain—"

There were no explanations she needed or wanted from him. "I assume you want Melody." She lowered the phone and held it out.

As Melody finished the call she was on, Callie passed over the phone, busied herself in paperwork, humming quietly to drown out whatever Melody was saying. And when Melody hung up they picked up where they had left off before Callie had gone for lunch.

The afternoon was just as busy as the morning. They spent time with the vineyard staff, as well as with artists and musicians arranging and rearranging details of the weekend. There were the usual last-minute hitches and panics, but by six o'clock Callie was confident everything was under control. The to-do list for the rest of the week was full but manageable.

Melody sat back in her chair and breathed a heavy sigh. "We should go up to the house. Rosa expects everyone to eat dinner together." She patted her faintly rounded stomach. "And I'm finding I have to eat really regularly anyway. This little boy is doing terrible things to my appetite. I'm going to be the size of a house by the time he comes." Melody's jaw dropped and the hand that had rested on her stomach suddenly clapped over her mouth.

Did Melody think Callie didn't know about the baby? "I heard a whisper at the wedding. It's wonderful news." Callie tried to put her at ease. "I haven't congratulated you and Jason yet—" *because your brother forbade me to talk to either of you* "—but I wish you all the best with your pregnancy. I'm sure you'll be wonderful parents." She meant every word, didn't feel any of that sense of inadequacy she had when she'd first heard about their pregnancy.

She really had moved on. And that was due in part to Nick. For better or worse, he'd presented her with enough issues in her own life that she didn't have the time or energy to spare to be anxious about anyone else's life.

Melody's smile was a mix of relief and pride. "I didn't know whether… How you'd… If…" She tripped over her words, her eyes wide in her delicate face. Callie could suddenly see why Jason had fallen for her. Not only was she beautiful and sweet, but there was a fragility about her that Jason would want to protect. She would let him be the big, strong man he pictured himself as. Callie had never let him be that for her.

She didn't want that in a man. She wanted a partner. She thought of Nick, who was a partner in the commercial sense. She mentally exchanged the word "partner" for "equal," and realized he was that too.

"I'm thrilled for you," said Callie, dragging her thoughts back to safe ground. "Just be careful you don't let the stress of the festival get to you. Take all the rest you need to. Pass whatever you don't want to deal with over to me." Heck, Melody was even bringing out Callie's protective instincts. She almost laughed at the concept—had forgotten for a while that she was pregnant too.

"Thank you." Mel picked up a glass paperweight and turned it in her fingers. The gesture reminded Callie of Nick. "There's something else I wanted to discuss with you."

Callie thought she knew what was coming, and if, as she suspected, it was anything to do with Jason, or Melody's doubt, she'd really rather not have this conversation. At the sound of a tap on the door they looked around—Callie with relief—to see Nick.

His gaze went to Callie, assessing, then flicked to his sister. Apparently satisfied with what he saw, he spoke. "Rosa's waiting for you both."

He held the door open for them. Melody went out first,

Callie followed. As she passed him he caught her eye, touched a gentle hand to her elbow. "Did it go all right?"

His concern was for her. She didn't want to like him in this stupid, melting kind of way; she didn't want to be as aware of the simplest of touches as she was. She had to fight both those urges.

As if sensing something of her battle, Nick smiled, warmth in his eyes, and against her will she melted a little bit further. At that moment, Melody looked back over her shoulder, and just as quickly looked away again. But she had seen Nick's hand on her arm, his smile, and a small puzzled frown had drawn her brows together.

The family sat outside for dinner, grouped around a long, rustic dinning table. Candles on twisting, wax-covered, wrought-iron holders lined the center. A vine-covered pergola partially screened the dusky sky. Two men Callie recognized from Melody's bridal party joined them. Nick, who was seated opposite her, introduced them as his cousins, Michael, their head winemaker, who Callie had met earlier in the day, charming and urbane, and Ricardo, the vineyard manager, quiet, with what looked to be burn scars on the left side of his face.

And as for Nick's claim to have little to do with the winery and vineyard, it was obvious that the others had enormous respect for him, asking his opinion on matters both professional and personal.

Rosa supervised the bringing out of course after course, and dusk gave way to evening as the family ate and talked. Another cousin, Lisa, carrying a small baby girl, joined them partway through the meal, squeezing herself into a seat next to Nick. Callie had to make an effort not to stare in fascination at the baby cradled in its mother's arms. Sometimes it still didn't seem real that she, too, was going to be a mother.

She had anticipated the meal being strained. Nothing could have been further from reality. People talked over one another, argued and laughed. When Michael offered to pour Callie's wine and she declined, Melody sent her an odd glance. And twice Callie noticed Melody looking between her and Nick. But apart from the occasional searching glance, Nick paid her no special attention. He gave no hint that anything lay between them, showed no visible reaction when Michael flirted with her, though Callie knew he was aware of it. He joined in the conversation and was more relaxed than she'd seen him before. His dark eyes sparkled when he laughed. And he laughed often.

Callie felt included in a circle of warmth and friendship that she'd never experienced in her own family. It had the feeling of something deep and old and certain. Even when she had lived at home, she and her mother had seldom sat at the table. And there had definitely been none of this lingering and laughing and teasing.

She didn't want to like Nick, didn't want to see him as warm and caring, because it only highlighted what she couldn't have. And worse than that was the awful thought that this would be a wonderful environment for a child to grow up in. Much better than she, a single woman living on her own, could provide. This family, in itself, seemed *the village* that it supposedly took to raise a child.

As dessert was served, the baby became fractious and Lisa decided to leave. She passed the child to Nick so she could get out of her chair. Callie watched those big, competent hands take the baby, clearly comfortable with the infant. She saw the tears that had threatened vanish, to be replaced by a smile and then a small gurgling laugh.

Michael laughed and looked at Callie. "Nick's charm with the ladies is legendary." The hint of Italian in his accent was pronounced, because of the time he'd recently spent in Tuscany. "But you can see it is not ill-founded. It works even with babies."

Callie looked from Michael to the baby to Nick, confident and at ease.

And watching her.

His gaze challenged her, seeming to say that this would be them one day. The child he held would be their own. As she met and held his gaze in wordless communication, a sense of wonder and connection settled over her. How could the concept of raising their child together be so very foreign, and yet seem almost right at the same time?

Something changed in his gaze—emotion surfaced from the still, green depths, flickered and then was gone. Frowning, Nick turned and handed the baby up to its mother, releasing Callie from the enthrallment of that gaze. Lisa stood, jiggling the child as she made her goodbyes, and passed on and accepted last-minute messages from and to her absent husband. She turned to Melody as she tucked a shawl around the baby. "How's the nursery coming along?"

A collective sigh rose up from the men at the table, and Melody scowled theatrically at them before turning back to Lisa, her chin high. "Good."

"But…" Ricardo prompted.

"The paint color," several voices whined in unison.

"Philistines." Melody turned to Callie. "You'll help

me with the paint color, won't you? You have such a good eye for color. And an understanding of the importance of getting the right shade." She shot another glare around the unsympathetic table.

Callie remembered how long they'd taken over the brochures for Cypress Rise. But in the end they had something they were both thrilled with. "Of course. I'd love to."

But it was two days later before they had the chance. As the two women climbed the stairs after another leisurely and loud family dinner, Callie noted Mel's hand come to rest on her stomach. "Is everything all right?"

Melody smiled widely, her gaze softening. "Perfect."

"It's not too much for you? The festival and everything?"

"No. Today for a change, I have boundless energy. I think this evening I'll even get some more work done in the nursery."

"What do you need to do?" Callie had no idea about nurseries, or what sort of equipment and preparations she'd need for a baby. Helping Melody was a good pretext for getting her own thinking in order. She wanted to do things right, wanted to show Nick that she could.

"I've picked out the furniture, but I still need the curtains, and I can't do that till I've chosen the paint color. And I've seen some borders that I really like too." Melody talked nonstop about her plans as she led Callie up the stairs. They stepped into a bright, cozy room that would get lovely morning sun. No curtains hung at the wide windows that gave a view of dark silhouettes of rolling hills. An ornate wooden cot occupied one corner of the room.

"I've narrowed it down to a choice between those two

yellows." Melody pointed out two squares among the dozen rough-edged patches of color painted onto the cream walls. "Which do you prefer?"

Callie studied them for a moment. Her thoughts wandered. She didn't even know where she'd be living when her child was born, let alone know what color she was going to paint the nursery.

Her gaze caught Melody's and she pulled her attention back to the paint. "The one on the left, the more buttery one. It has a warmer feel."

Melody crossed to the wall and touched the paint. "I was leaning toward this one too." She was still facing the wall when she next spoke. "I'm sorry for what I thought about you and Jason." She turned quickly, pinned Callie with her gaze. "For doubting you and thinking you were trying to hang on to him."

Honey, you're welcome to him, would have been the wrong answer. "I guess the late-night phone calls could have looked a little odd."

"They weren't that late, and it's not like you hung up or anything when I answered. I just got insecure."

Callie shrugged. "You didn't need to. Jason really loves you."

Melody turned and looked out the window. "I do know that. I was tired and hormonal and feeling a bit vulnerable about the pregnancy and everything."

"For what it's worth, Jason's a good man. And he loves you in a way he never cared for me." And lately Callie had come to realize that she, too, was capable of much stronger feelings than the unthreatening comfort of those she'd had for Jason. Just how much stronger she didn't want to analyze.

"Having him seemed too good to be true." Melody

ran her fingers along the windowsill. "And I thought that, if it seemed that good, then I was probably missing something."

"Life kicked you in the teeth a few times?"

Melody laughed. "Once or twice. My own fault, usually. That's why I tend to be overcautious."

"It's not your fault if someone treats you badly."

The smile vanished from Melody's lips. "I guess not. But sometimes you also have to take responsibility for the situation you find yourself in. And if need be, do the right thing to get yourself out of it. I didn't always do that soon enough."

"You don't have to explain."

"But I do need to apologize. Especially if we're going to be seeing a lot more of you."

"I'll be gone in a few days."

"But you and Nick?"

"Nick and I?" Callie asked, unsure what Melody suspected.

"He's never brought a girlfriend here before. I thought it must be serious."

"I'm only here for the festival, because of Marc. He hasn't told you there's anything between us?"

"No. But he never tells anyone anything. We all figure it out by watching. I was wondering already, and then this morning, when he took you on the tour of the winery and vineyard himself, instead of letting Michael do it."

The supposedly quick tour that had stretched to three hours without either of them realizing the passing of the time, because Callie had had so many questions and they had been talking and laughing. She had forgotten everything but the pleasure of being with him.

"And he seems to care about you," Melody added. "He watches you with a different kind of look in his eyes."

Callie shook her head. "The only reason I'm here is because of the festival." And the child she was carrying, who would be a part of this family. Nick had said that much. So, although the demarcation lines were blurred, they were still there.

"You watch him too."

She'd tried to disguise the fascination he held for her, tried to stop the fanciful daydreams that sometimes caught her unawares. Obviously, she'd have to try harder. She shrugged. "He's not hard to look at. None of the Brunicadi men are."

"No. But Michael's even better-looking, and you don't watch him."

If she argued that particular assertion, it would work against her, so Callie said nothing. But while Michael might be technically more perfect, he didn't have the intensity that was so intriguing in Nick, didn't have the depths in his eyes.

"All the same. It's not what you're thinking."

"Oh. Sorry." Melody headed for the door. "I guess it's for the best. Nick's relationships never last long. He always ends them before they get serious."

Callie stifled a yawn as she held up a skirt and top. She met her gaze in the mirror and sternly repeated Melody's words: "His relationships never last long." She'd do well to heed that warning, a repetition of what she already knew, but was in danger of dismissing.

Keep her mind on the job, that was all she had to do, not on thoughts of Nick, on his rare smile, on the hidden depths in his eyes.

She could want far more than she should from the Nick she'd come to know. Far more than he would be prepared to give.

The festival was the day after tomorrow. And the day after that she would be leaving. She only had to shore up her battered defenses for that long.

She was a professional. She could do it.

She surveyed her reflection. The skirt and blouse would be good for tomorrow, but—she lifted her hand to her scalp—she really needed to wash her hair. *Soon,* she thought as she laid the clothes on her bed. She'd wash her hair soon. She'd managed it one-handed a couple of times. It was awkward and tiring, but not impossible.

In the living room she sat on the couch and opened her laptop. But instead of rechecking the schedule for tomorrow as she'd intended, she called up one of the Internet sites she'd found on pregnancy, looked at the image of a fetus cocooned in a womb and tried to concentrate on the information swimming in front of her. Leaning back, she closed her eyes.

"Callie." The softly spoken word, the hand on her shoulder, startled her.

She spun to see Nick beside her on the couch. "Where did you come from?"

His eyes were narrowed with concern. "I knocked."

"I must have dozed off."

"You think?" His face softened, humor lit his eyes.

"It's been a long day."

The amusement vanished. "That's why I wanted to check on you. You looked a little tired at dinner and my family doesn't exactly let a person get a word in edgewise. From my office, I can see some of the comings and goings at the winery. You didn't stop all day. And then Melody dragged you up to the nursery. You need to take it easier. Learn to say no."

"Nick, I'm fine." He'd been watching her? Even as she thought about him and wondered where he was and what he was doing?

"So fine that you're falling asleep while you're still trying to work." He gestured to her laptop on the coffee table, the screen saver meandering across the screen. "Go to bed, Callie," he said gently.

"I will. As soon as I wash my hair." She speared her fingers through her curls. "And actually," she admitted, "I wasn't working. I meant to, but…" She leaned forward to touch the mouse pad and the screen came to life in front of them. The picture of the baby was still there.

Nick was quiet for a moment. "I've been looking at these sites, as well. There's so much to learn."

"I know." She kept her gaze trained on the screen, focused her thoughts on the image there. And not on the man sitting a whisper away from her. "Sometimes I can hardly believe it's all real. That it's happening to me. Maybe once I feel her kicking. But they say—" she scrolled down a couple of pages "—that that won't happen till around sixteen weeks."

In wordless agreement, they looked through the sites each of them had found, exclaiming, and a little awe-struck at what was happening. Callie only wished she wasn't equally captivated by Nick's hands on the keyboard, the dexterous fingers, the tanned forearms exposed by the rolled-up sleeves of his shirt. And if only she was as good as Nick at ignoring their inadvertent touches—a brush of shoulder or knee. The touches that sent heat coiling through her.

If they didn't have a guaranteed future together that

needed to be negotiated, she could want so much from this man. *For now,* she told herself. *Only for now.*

As he navigated the sites she stole glances at his profile, the faint shadow of beard on his jaw, the seriousness of his expression. She liked, a little too much, that he'd been doing his own research.

He turned, caught her watching him. She looked quickly back at the screen.

"What's it like? For you." His voice was quiet, earnest.

She met the gaze that was now intent on her. It was several seconds before she could gather her thoughts to answer. "It's like…magic. I can't believe it's real. And yet it is." She placed her hand over her stomach. "And I guess it's kind of scary too. There's so much I don't know."

"Are you worried about the birth, about the hospital?"

"No. Not yet."

"But you will be?"

"Probably."

"I'll be there." His eyes scanned her face.

"You will be?"

"Yes." There was no hesitation in his response, and still that green gaze was trained on her. Waiting.

"But do *you* want me there?"

Callie turned back to the computer screen. "Yes." She couldn't think of anyone she'd rather have there than Nick, with his quiet strength. She just didn't want him to see quite how much she wanted it.

They looked at a few more sites, but when Callie stifled a yawn Nick stood.

"You need to go to bed. Now."

Callie stood too. "As soon as I've washed my hair."

"I'll help you."

"It's okay. I'll manage."

"I'll help you." He strode to the bathroom, and soon the sound of the shower running reached her.

Callie followed him. Steam billowed from the shower and splashes of water dampened his pale shirt.

"You wet it. I'll do the shampoo."

"Nick."

"What?" he asked, as though he really couldn't see why she'd have a problem with him washing her hair. And maybe he was right. She was pregnant with his child. Having his hands in her hair could do no further harm.

"Nothing. Just turn away for a second, would you?"

He turned his back. "I have seen you naked before."

Callie ignored his words as she peeled off her clothes and stepped into the shower, grateful that, from knee to chin height, the glass was smoky and opaque. "This is different."

He turned back and leaned against the far wall, arms folded across his chest as she sluiced water over her hair. "Pass me a towel please?" she asked once it was thoroughly wet.

Nick held one of the thick, cream towels out to her. Callie shut off the water and reached a hand through the door, took the towel and wrapped it around herself before stepping out of the shower. She pushed her shampoo bottle into his hand, folded her arms across her chest, anchoring the towel under her armpits, and closed her eyes.

And waited.

She opened one eye. Nick stood close. He wasn't smiling, but she could see the dimple in his left cheek as he studied her.

"It's not going to hurt."

She closed her eye again. "Just get on with it, would you," she snapped.

And now she was sure he was smiling. Her own lips twitched. And then those strong, capable hands were on her head, massaging shampoo through her hair. And suddenly there was nothing remotely funny about her situation. He surrounded her, his arms either side of her face. And if she opened her eyes, she'd see his chest inches in front of her. She closed her eyes tighter. Beneath the fragrance of her shampoo she caught the faintest trace of his cologne.

"Rinse." He turned her back to face the shower.

Callie dropped the towel and stepped in.

Please let him not know how hard her heart was pounding when, a few minutes later, she reached a second time for the towel and passed him her conditioner. His hands were slower this time, fingertips sliding across her scalp. The strength threatened to flee from her knees. His hands moved to the back of her head, massaging, the pressure of his touch exquisite. Callie kept her eyes closed as a desire that she couldn't let him see built low within her. Her breath grew shallower, and suddenly his hands paused as they cupped her head.

Her eyes flew open in time to see him hesitate before he lowered his head. And then he was kissing her, his mouth hard and hungry. And she was most definitely kissing him back. Greedily. Her towel forgotten, her arms slid around him, even as a part of her brain whispered feebly, *don't do this*. That part of her brain was effortlessly overpowered and ignored by the demands of her body. The need for his touch, for this closeness. It was everything she feared because it was everything she wanted.

Strong hands held her head as he deepened the kiss. His tongue swept her mouth, learning anew her taste.

Joining them. In primal response, she pressed her hips into his and felt the evidence of his need. His hands slid over dampened skin to grip her shoulders. He kissed her jaw, her neck, inflaming her. He was all she remembered. And more. Being with him, she could forget everything.

Just as she had that night.

That night that had gotten her pregnant.

Callie broke the kiss. "Nick," she gasped his name, shaking her head. "No." She wanted him fiercely, desperately, but also she wanted more than just this.

He stepped back, regret etched into his face. "Rinse." He turned and left.

Nick came out of the winery building, where he'd been talking with Michael about this year's vintage and the likely effect of the summer's weather patterns. With only one day till the festival, the grounds were alive with hurrying people and shouted communications, as marquees were set up, tables and chairs delivered and a myriad of other jobs commenced or finished. He scanned the activity, found what he sought as he caught sight of Callie in a summery skirt and sleeveless blouse, looking as fresh as new leaves on the vines in springtime.

She'd kept her distance from him today. Undoubtedly a good thing. She had sensed the driving need that had slammed into him last night. He had wanted her. Wanted to back her up against the bathroom cabinet and claim her.

But she wasn't his.

She had her own life, her own dreams. Dreams of love and happy families. She'd told him that when she'd explained why she wouldn't want to marry him.

And he had his life too.

If only he could stop the desire that ambushed him every time he saw her.

They shared a baby; and because of that child they had to have a relationship that worked and that lasted. Sex, as desperately tempting as it was, would only confuse matters and quite probably destroy that something else, that tentative bond—the one that should terrify him but didn't—that was building between them.

He liked knowing she was near, it had a sense of rightness. And at mealtimes, when everyone gathered around the outdoor table, she blended in—a natural part, giving as good as she got from his cousins. His family liked her.

And she liked them.

An idea was beginning to percolate, a plan that capitalized on her emotions and that would meet both of their needs. He would tell her tomorrow, after the festival.

She looked his way, then quickly looked away again. She was in professional mode, elegant, efficient, but a little repressed. Her secrets and dreams hidden. And she was still working too hard, accepting the demands placed on her from all directions.

He wanted to take her away from all this, he wanted to make her laugh, he wanted to see her again in that enormous paint-splattered shirt. That was the Callie who fascinated him; that was the Callie who for one night had danced in his arms and who had trusted herself. And him.

And look where that had got them.

She stood talking to Noah, the glass artist whose blue heron in flight hung suspended in a window alcove of the winery's reception area. An artist, just as she was at heart. Did his devil-may-care appearance, his carved jade necklace, appeal to her? It was hard to tell from this distance whether or not Noah was standing too close. Callie pointed to her left, describing something with her hands.

Nick would make her his. He didn't want anyone else to know the scent of her hair. *He* knew it. It had enveloped him in the steamy bathroom. It had lingered on his fingers through the night. And he would never catch that scent again without thinking of her. The sun shone on her dark curls now. They would capture and hold that heat. If he plunged his fingers—

Snap out of it.

The turning away got harder each time, but he managed it again. It would be too easy to be swept up in her. To think of nothing and no one else. The battle within was constant.

His previous relationships had been easy, possibly superficial. That was how he liked them. There was nothing easy about what he felt for Callie. He'd seen the mirror of wanting in her eyes. But she was the one who'd had the strength to end their kiss. She was looking for happiness, for forever. He couldn't give her those things, but he could and would provide for and protect her.

One of the catering staff hurried out of a marquee, heading for Callie. Nick strode to intercept him. The least he could do was lighten a workload that she would deny needed lightening.

Ten

Callie surveyed the crowd of festival goers, almost ready to breathe a sigh of relief. The morning had opened with a line of people waiting at the gates, and had got steadily busier. The weather was being kind, a gentle breeze taking the edge off the oppressive heat. Still, nearly all the guests wore sun hats and made the most of the shade covers and marquees set up around the public areas. The headline jazz band had started up, and beneath the sultry strains of the saxophone came the sounds of laughter, conversation and the clink of glasses. So far, so good. To the casual observer, the day was running with effortless efficiency.

"Ms. Jamieson." Robert, a young vineyard worker, appeared in front of Callie, his breathing heavy.

She nodded for him to continue. What new crisis, imagined or real, needed to be dealt with? Efficiency was never effortless.

"There's a problem with the sculpture of the jazz trio. Something to do with the bass player."

Callie sighed and started walking between two rows of vines, heading for the gleaming stainless-steel assemblage of nuts and bolts and old machinery parts that comprised the strangely animated sculpture. She only had to hang in there for a few more hours. Then the guests would be gone, and the cleanup and moving crews could start. And then she could take a break.

Nick had found her an hour ago and suggested she take a break then. He didn't understand that she needed to be on hand to deal with issues just like this one. His eyes had told her he thought she was making excuses. He also didn't seem to understand that she needed to be busy—so she didn't think about him, that kiss, the way she wanted him to hold her. So yes, maybe it had been partly an excuse.

As she passed the end of a row, a hand snaked out and grasped her wrist, tugging her off balance and against a warm, hard body.

Callie recognized his scent and the solid feel of Nick behind her. Her back pressed into his broad chest. His fingers encircled her wrists. And for a second she stood there letting him support her, cradle her, letting his strength seep into her. She allowed herself the brief luxury, then tried to pull away. "I need to get to The Jazz Players."

He held firm to her wrists and she felt the movement of him shaking his head behind her. "There's nothing wrong with The Jazz Players." His deep voice was warm in her ear.

"Robert just told me there was a problem."

Nick's hands skimmed up her bare arms, his touch like the dance of a firefly. His hands rested on her shoulders and he turned her to face him, to put a little more distance between them. Not nearly enough for her comfort. "The only problem is you not taking a break all day long. You brushed me off when I suggested it earlier. Now I'm making it happen. I know the perfect spot."

She studied his face, the deep green of his eyes. She should argue, but some time alone with Nick—in the safety of daylight—tempted her powerfully. She nodded. She was leaving tomorrow, she would take what moments she could.

The handheld radio buzzed at her waist. She reached for it, but Nick was quicker, whisking it out of her reach and turning it off. "It's nothing that can't wait."

"But—"

He sighed and grasped her hand, his touch warm and sure. "There are plenty of people here to help out. They'll deal with whatever it is." He tugged her up a gentle slope, away from the jazz and the art and the crowds, to a secluded spot on a hill beneath a spreading oak tree. A picnic rug lay on the ground, a wicker basket resting in its center, a golden baguette poking temptingly out from beneath the lid.

"Sit."

He'd done this. For her? Callie lowered herself down gratefully.

"A glass of water? Or would you prefer something stronger? I've packed soda and orange juice."

Callie smiled. "Water, thanks." She watched his hands and the play of muscle in his forearms as he unscrewed the cap from a bottle of mineral water and poured the liquid into two elegant wineglasses. "You don't have to drink water just because I am." He didn't answer, just passed a glass to her and raised his own in a silent toast. Callie took a sip.

Nick started pulling food from the basket. "I've discovered that pregnant woman are exceedingly difficult to pack a picnic for. Apparently, you're supposed to be wary of cold meats, and soft cheeses and pâtés."

"Everything that makes for a good picnic." She tried not to let it show how touched she was that he'd taken the trouble to find out what she should and shouldn't eat. He was just being Nick. Whatever he did, he did well.

"Not everything." He sliced the baguette into chunks, and his heavy silver watch glinted in the sun as he produced an array of plastic tubs containing everything from butter and mayonnaise to cheddar cheese and artichoke hearts—and of course grapes, as well as pineapple and mangoes. She couldn't stop the strange softening within her.

"What about Melody?"

"Melody has other family looking out for her." Nick filled a plate with food. "It's you I'm concerned about. Now eat," he said, as he passed her the plate. Callie suddenly discovered she was not only tired but ravenous, and a picnic lunch seemed like the best idea in the world. Nick filled his own plate, and they ate to the distant strains of jazz drifting through the vines.

"How did you know this is exactly what I needed?" she asked a little later as she bit into a strawberry, the last thing on her plate.

Nick watched as, with her other hand, she brushed crumbs from her front. "It was fairly obvious."

Callie lay back on the blanket and watched the sky through the filter of the leaves above her. She closed her eyes, resting her hands on her stomach. Nick stretched out beside her.

The silence lengthened, and the awareness that he

was watching her grew. She chanced a glance at him from beneath her lashes, saw his eyes fixed not on her face but on her abdomen. His gaze flicked upward and caught her scrutiny. She saw a movement, felt his touch as he picked her hand up and shifted it to rest on her ribs. His palm, broad and flat, settled over her stomach. Just that. No more. He held it there absolutely still. Her thoughts went to the child inside her, her first hello from her father. Ever since Rosa's pronouncement, she'd thought of the baby as a girl. A three-way connection, baby and both its parents.

It felt so very right.

She remembered how, back in her hotel room, Nick had also said the baby was a girl. "The other night, why did you say the baby was a girl?"

His fingers spanned wider across her abdomen. "Did I say that?"

"Yes. Just like Rosa did."

"Huh." The sound was noncommittal and vaguely disbelieving. "There's a fifty-fifty chance."

"You sounded certain."

His hand shifted, picked up hers and placed it back where his had rested. She missed the gentle weight of his touch.

"No. How could I be?" His fingers skimmed up and back down her arm, trailing warmth.

"Are you like Rosa? Do you know things?"

The hand stilled. "No."

"I've heard that in the financial markets they call you The Profit, but that it's a play on words. That you do seem to be unusually lucky."

"People like to call skill and hard work 'luck.' It makes them feel better. I've had my share of losses too.

They forget about those when it suits them. And Rosa, she gets lucky sometimes, but she's wrong sometimes too. I wouldn't paint the nursery pink on her say-so."

"Melody thinks Rosa's right about her baby being a boy."

"Like I say, there's a fifty-fifty chance she is right. Melody's happy to buy into it."

Callie was silent for a while. "Do you remember the painting at my home? The one you said reminded you of Cathedral Cove?"

"Yes." There was hesitation in the way he drew out the word.

"I painted it there."

He paused a beat. "You did a good job. You have talent."

"It was only the water. No landmarks, not the hole in the rocks."

"The water there has a certain quality, don't you think? It must have, otherwise you wouldn't have painted it."

"Maybe." It was her turn to be noncommittal. His refusal to share that something of himself she sensed, hurt.

As she studied him she was hit with a knowledge herself. She could want this man. No. Not could. Did. Certainly, she wanted more of him than he was willing to give. She knew his touch, his kiss, and wanted it again. It was dangerous territory to let her thoughts wander to. "The turnout is fantastic."

"Mmm."

"Right in line with our most optimistic predictions." *Come on, Nick, help me out. Give me something to stop me thinking about the shadow of beard on your jaw.*

"Mmm."

Stop me thinking about lacing my fingers between

yours. "If gate sales keep up at the rate they have been we may have to restrict numbers."

"Callie."

"Yes."

"I brought you here to have a break."

She lapsed into silence, but unable to stop looking, she continued to study Nick, stretched out on his back, hands clasped behind his head, biceps curving against the sleeves of his polo shirt. A smudge of grease streaked above his elbow. His eyes were closed and his dark lashes rested lightly on tanned cheeks. It would be too easy to just lie there drinking in details of his appearance.

"Close your eyes."

How did he know? Quickly, she shut her eyes and tried to relax; but lying so close to him made her too conscious of his nearness. Awareness vibrated through her. If she didn't talk business she'd think about him, maybe do something stupid like reach out and touch him. "Almost half the artwork has sold already."

He expelled a sigh of exasperation.

Callie pushed on, warming to the topic. "And I think there's someone interested in the copper dragon. That's our most expensive piece."

He gave a sudden low growl and she heard the rustle of movement. The light that had dappled her face gave way to shadow. She opened her eyes. Nick loomed over her. For a second their gazes locked. Then with another softer, shorter growl, he lowered his head and his lips claimed hers.

Callie's mouth parted beneath his. He tasted of sunshine—heat and light. Sensation bloomed and overwhelmed her. Her hands went to his shoulders, the muscles hard and contoured beneath her touch. Kissing him was like stepping into a fantasy. Her senses swam. Reality threatened to slip away beneath the magic of his touch. His fingers slid up her jawline, threading into her hair, cupping her head, drawing her closer yet for the demands of his mouth.

Her hands found their way to the dark warmth of his hair, the strong column of his neck, the silken steel of his shoulders. He held her to him, his body pressed along the length of hers. Against her will, forgetting all the reasons she shouldn't be doing this, she arched into him, pressed her hips to his, driven by a compulsion to get closer still. A hint of beard gently abraded the sensitized skin of her jaw. His hand cupped her breast through the fabric of her blouse. Just that, an exquisite, almost unbearable touch, and a small moan of pleasure escaped her.

"Callie."

She loved the sound of her name on his lips. "Yes."

"A bed."

"Yes." The single syllable was all she was capable of. It threatened to turn into a mantra and a plea.

In the privacy of the guest cottage, the strong hands she loved to look at, loved the feel of, slid up her arms, over the curve of her shoulders till they cupped her face. Long fingers slid into her hair as he lowered his head.

He kissed her for the longest time. Holding her close against the masculine warmth and solidity of his body, savoring her. And greedily she drank in the taste and feel of him, clung to the power and vitality of him.

Standing here, kissing this man, Callie felt more at one with him than she'd ever felt with another human. She carried his child. She knew him. He knew and understood her. She'd never had that before.

The ceiling fan spun lazily above them as his mouth moved over hers, and they made their way slowly across the room till the bed pressed against the backs of her legs. And still they kissed. His lips explored and pleasured. He savored her like he savored a fine wine. Sipping gently, searching for every nuance with tongue and lips and seeking hands.

Those hands shifted, found the hem of her blouse, slid underneath till warm palms skimmed over the sensitized skin, trailing fire in their wake. His fingers traced the contours of her body as his tongue learned her mouth with slow, sweet seduction. Palms cupped the weight of her breasts, his thumbs grazed over lace-covered nipples, spearing need through her.

She had wanted to give, but that wanting threatened to be overpowered by the consuming need to take. Nick lifted his head and studied her. She saw the need and desire in his darkened eyes. He reached again for her. Slowly, he slipped each of her buttons undone till he could brush apart the sides of her blouse. Lowering his head, he closed his mouth over the thin lace, dampening the fabric and the tight aching nipple beneath it. Compulsion arched her against him, into him, her hands slid through the dark, sun-warmed silk of his hair, pulling his head closer yet.

His fingers slipped under the thin lace strap on her shoulder, grazed it across and down her arm. He lifted his mouth only long enough to ease the fabric aside and expose already dampened flesh to the air before his mouth again closed over her, hot and seeking. The faint stubble of his jaw grazed her flushed skin. His tongue flicked and her body jerked in reflex as a desperate gasp escaped her.

Reaching for his shirt, she sought access to the warmth of his smooth skin and the muscles beneath. Layer by layer, seeking hands knocking and tangling, they peeled away each other's clothes—her blouse, his shirt, her skirt, his pants—until there were no barriers between them.

The stillness of awe and wonder settled over her at the sheer male beauty of him. Stark planes and contours. Like a creature of a fantasy world. Her fantasy world.

And in return, the heat of his gaze, the hunger and raw need in his eyes swept through her, inflamed her. "Calypso." Her name was husky, strangled, on his lips. And that one simple word, spoken that way by him, threatened to buckle her knees.

Then he was moving, touching her again, guiding her till they lay down together on the softness of his bed. They touched. Fingertips to skin, lips to lips. The touch grew fevered as desire burned brighter. She hadn't known wanting the like of it before. This fierce desperation. She wanted to take and she wanted to give. But she needed this moment too. The exploration, the appreciation, the slowness, gentleness and oneness.

Her palm grazed over a small, hardened nipple, settled over the strong beat of his heart. And in her mind she claimed his heart with that gesture. Claimed it for herself. For always.

He groaned, and she reveled in the contradictions of that sound, powerlessness and fierceness in one. An echo of her own paradox. How was it possible to feel the strength of a warrior and utter languidness at the same time? To be flying and falling? Demanding and surrendering?

She was his if he only knew it. This man who cared so deeply, loved so thoroughly.

She'd known his body before and yet everything was different, everything had changed between them. Sensation dizzied her, carried her like Dorothy's tornado out of a world she knew and into a realm more vivid than she could have imagined.

Her skin was alive to his touch. In the warm glow of sunlight her eyes saw only him, the half-lowered eyelids, the line of his jaw, the curve of his throat and shoulder. Her hands felt only him, curving muscle, heated silken skin.

Desire grew fiercer, exquisitely unbearable till it became a clawing, clamoring need, overpowering everything.

He raised himself over her and she opened to him, guided him into her. She met him, clung to him. Her hands slid from shoulders, to hips, to taut muscle, needing him closer yet.

With a ripple of powerful hips he thrust deeper, and she rose to meet him so that he filled her completely.

He bent his head and kissed her. So gentle, so fiercely erotic.

The moved together, two bodies with one entwining purpose. Slowly. Exquisitely. And then inexorably faster, desire flaming and obliterating restraint or even thought until only dizzying sensations and desperate need remained. And love.

She called his name as release pulsed through them.

The laughter and the camaraderie of dinner washed around and over Callie, and filled her with an aching sense of loneliness. She couldn't let herself be seduced by this world. A world she couldn't have. A world she almost desperately wished she belonged to. This was the family life she imagined when she allowed herself to dream.

The prospect of going home tomorrow and carrying on with her life felt unbelievably hollow.

She should be happy. The festival had been an unqualified success, and that was what she'd come here for. Nothing more. The money that would now go to the teenage shelter was at the top end of their most optimistic predictions. A good thing. Professionally.

Personally, she was a mess.

She had made love with Nick. Worse than that, she *loved* Nick. And she had no idea how he felt.

She would be flying out of Sydney tomorrow. And she didn't want to go. So much had changed. For the short time she'd been here she'd been happy. And the biggest part of that happiness had been Nick. Knowing he was there for support, for help, to talk with, to laugh with, to sit quietly with in the evening. Part of her was conscious of his whereabouts if he was near, and alert for his return if he wasn't. Things felt right this way. Yet it wasn't going to be.

He didn't do commitment.

She, however, did, and her commitment at the moment had to be to her business—her clients and staff back home. And in looking after them, she would be providing a future for herself and her child.

The family was lingering over coffee when she looked up to find Nick watching her. He stood, came around to Callie and held a hand out for her. "Come with me, there's something I want to show you."

With just that gesture and those words she suddenly felt that everything would be all right.

Half a dozen pairs of curious eyes followed them as they left. She sat with him in the Range Rover as he drove a few miles down the road, pointing out places of interest, pointing out other vineyards. He was Nick the tour guide. It was as though their lovemaking had never happened. He took a turn onto a smaller road, following it as it wound up into the hills.

After several minutes driving, they rounded a corner and he pulled over on the crest of a hill almost facing back the way they had come. The valley spread out below them, bathed in the golden glow of the sunset.

"What do you think?"

"It's beautiful. I've always loved the light and shadows of sunset. Look at the way the clouds are lit up." So beautiful it made her ache. Like being with him made her ache.

He smiled and that ache deepened. "So, you like it here?"

There was so much she liked here. The place cast a spell over her that was an extension of the one the man himself seemed to cast. Something about it, about him, threatened to make her forget herself. "What's not to like? The valley, the hills."

He pulled back. "Not the view, which I'll admit is beautiful, but the bungalow."

She followed the direction of his gaze. A little way ahead and to their right, partially screened by tall poplars, stood a spreading white bungalow, encircled by a deep wisteria-covered veranda. Callie could picture an easel set up on the veranda, imagine herself painting the valley through the seasons and the changing of the light.

She looked back at Nick. "It's gorgeous."

"It's one of ours. Lisa lived here when she first came to work for us a year ago as a lab technician. Then she met and married Gregory."

"She seems like she's been part of your family for years."

"She fitted in from the very start. You do too," he added quietly.

"They're easy to be with."

"They can be overwhelming. Lisa maintained that this place—" he pointed to the bungalow "—was the perfect distance. Close to the family and the winery. But not too close. It gets good light too. For your painting."

Callie watched him, uncertain. "Could we back this conversation up a little? Why would I be painting here?"

"Not just painting. Living."

A flare of hope ignited within her. She didn't dare trust it. "You're suggesting what?"

"That you move here."

Just that? That she uproot her life and shift here. She waited, but he added nothing further. The hope withered. It took several seconds before she found her voice. "I'm not going to live here. I have a home back in New Zealand. A business. Clients."

"You can work from here, or Sydney if you need to. The flights back to New Zealand are quick and regular. And you said yourself that your lease on your place is about to expire. Think about it." His voice was calm, patient. "You like it here. You've said as much."

He'd thought about everything. Made it sound so rational. But there had been no mention of those things that weren't rational, like feelings, like love. Nick the tour guide was suggesting she move here, not Nick the lover. The man she wanted to…love.

"And of course, you're having my baby."

She laid a protective hand over her stomach. "That's not the issue."

His gaze followed the movement, then he looked back up at her. "It's very much the issue. It's the beginning and end of the issue."

Meaning, if there was no baby he wouldn't care where she lived. Her head was spinning. "You're serious, aren't you? You actually think I'm going to move to the Hunter Valley to suit your convenience." The sad thing was that a part of her, the vulnerable part, desperately wanted to at least consider it.

"Think about it, Callie. It could work. We like each other well enough. I'd be able to see you and our baby regularly."

"You like me well enough." She couldn't keep the incredulity from her voice. She'd thought she hadn't needed Melody's warning, thought she was in no danger from Nick. But the danger had crept up nonetheless. And she was vulnerable to him. More than vulnerable, she realized. She'd gone right ahead and fallen in love with him. A man who didn't have the word *love* in his vocabulary. Not the type of love she wanted to give him and to have from him. She felt like she was about to crumple in on the sudden emptiness within herself.

"So, let me get this straight." She kept her voice level, didn't want to betray the fragility of her emotions. "Because I'm having your child, and there's a house free on one of your vineyards, and because it would be convenient for you, and we 'like' each other well enough— I should uproot my life and come and live here? For what, Nick?"

Nick didn't say anything.

"What about sex? You forgot that. Maybe you could come over sometimes for sex too. I mean, we know that's good between us."

"You're taking this all wrong. Getting worked up about something simple. I'm trying to make this easy for you."

"You're trying to make it easy for yourself. You get all the benefits without having to make any changes. Without even having to open your heart a little."

His gaze narrowed. "You refused marriage." Finally that reasonable tone cracked and exasperation crept in. "This is the perfect compromise, a stepping stone."

She had no response.

"What do you want from me?"

That was the crux of the matter. She looked out her window. She couldn't say "love." It wouldn't be fair to him, when, at least in that regard, he'd been honest. She was like all those other foolish, blind women who'd fallen for him. But what about the possibility of it? "Nothing," she said slowly. "I don't want anything from you."

"This is the obvious solution." He tried again. Reasonable, logical, as though he hadn't heard her. "It could work really well for us all."

She shook her head. "This is so not the obvious solution. I have a business to run and it's based in New Zealand." It was Ivy Cottage that gave her independence. She was thinking, belatedly, of protecting her heart. And for that she needed to be away from this man who was offering her nothing of himself.

"You wouldn't even have to keep working, unless you wanted to." He countered. "I'm happy to support you for as long as you want. You could sell Ivy Cottage to Marc, I'll finance him."

He'd tried to think of everything, but he'd missed the one thing she wanted most of all, the one thing he couldn't or wouldn't give: something of himself. "You have all the answers, don't you."

"I'm trying to be logical."

"It can't always be about logic."

"What is it about, then?" His gaze searched her face. She didn't answer, couldn't tell him.

"All right then, put it this way, I'm trying to do the right thing. I thought we were both going to try to do what was best for the baby."

"Best for the baby or best for you?" she snapped. "What about this 'obvious' solution? I can find a place for *you* to move to, near where *I* live."

"Whoa." He held up his hands in a gesture of surrender. "How about we forget I said anything?"

But he said it, not in a *maybe I was wrong and I'm sorry* kind of voice, but in an *obviously you're not rational at the moment and you need to calm down* voice.

"Gladly." But what she wouldn't forget was that all his reasons had been practical. An ache swelled in her heart. There had been no mention of him feeling anything at all for her beyond the pale *like*. He would fit her into a corner of his life, and she was supposed to be content with that, be grateful for the crumbs he offered her.

It wasn't going to happen. She closed her eyes and made that promise to herself. She'd compromised before and she wouldn't do it again. Not when she was the only one doing the compromising.

Nick started the Range Rover, pulled slowly back out into the road, swinging around to head back the way they had come.

They drove in cold silence. He stopped at the guest cottage. Neither of them spoke as she got out.

Eleven

Callie sat in the Range Rover, Melody at her side driving. "I appreciate you taking me back to Sydney." The lump was still there in her throat, where it had lodged last night, a smaller version of the one in her chest.

"It works out really well." Melody smiled, oblivious. "I want to see my obstetrician anyway. I've been getting some odd twinges. I'll stay at Nick's apartment tonight and meet Jason off the plane tomorrow. Then we're going to go and look at nursery furniture."

Callie felt a pang of envy. Shopping for nursery furniture with the father of her baby was not going to happen for her.

"Besides, it's the least I could do, after all the work you did for the festival. It felt so good to be able to help out the shelter, and as a bonus, the vineyard's profile has gone right up. The publicity you got for us was fantastic." Melody started talking about the vineyard and her plans for it. Callie tried to keep up. Tried to stop her thoughts going back to last night.

She had dreaded going down to breakfast almost as much as she had wanted to see Nick. The dread and the wanting were wasted. He hadn't been there. That was enough of a signal that he didn't care about what she said. The loss threatened to swamp her.

She had to take just one day at a time. Today was the day to go home and regroup, to figure out what was happening to her, which of her feelings were real and which were a by-product of the situation she was in and of capricious pregnancy hormones. Because she knew one thing for certain—her feelings for Nick were completely out of the realm of her experience. She knew now the love that could be so much more than the pale imitation she'd had before. But the pain increased in proportion.

Focus on the here and now. That was all she could do.

"Are you still expecting me to believe there's nothing between you and Nick?"

Callie glanced at Melody. If anything, there was even less between them than when Melody had last asked. "Nick and I have some things to sort out," Callie conceded. "But it's not what you're thinking."

"I was thinking you're pregnant."

Callie stiffened. "Why do you say that?" Was the whole family psychic?

"You haven't drunk any wine the whole time you've been here. And the only other person doing that is me. Rosa's knitting a pink cardigan, which I know isn't for Junior. And sometimes you touch your stomach and look the way I feel. Awed."

Melody's reasons at least were sound. Callie took a deep breath and answered. "Yes."

"And Nick's the father."

Not a question. A statement.

"Yes."

"So, what—"

"It's complicated." And it wasn't anything she felt like talking about.

For a moment, Mel's expression didn't change, and then a delighted smile lit her face. "I don't care what you say. That's wonderful."

Obviously, to her the complications meant nothing. Callie, on the other hand, had to fight the threat of another wave of tears.

"When are you due?"

At least that was a question she could answer. "Mid-September."

"Two months after me. Junior will have a cousin almost the same age."

This so wasn't where Callie wanted to go, talking of the future and family relationships. But she needn't have worried. Melody wasn't looking for any answers from her. "Have you had morning sickness? Mine was awful at first. Not just mornings, but all day long."

They drove, Melody's conversation darting from pregnancy symptoms to birthing options, and the best stores to buy nursery equipment. Callie got the feeling Melody probably even had plans for where her child would go to college. She envied her that certainty.

Melody's hand dropped to her abdomen, pressed against it, and for an instant her mouth tightened. "Nick's a good man." Another sudden conversational switch.

"I know. But his relationships never last." Melody's own words.

She was silent for several seconds. "I know I said that. And it's true. But they haven't lasted before because he hasn't wanted them to. He doesn't let people get close. Sometimes he'll even push them away. Deliberately distance himself."

Wasn't that the truth?

Melody patted her stomach, but her palm closed into a fist against it and she winced.

"Are you all right?"

"It was a cramp. I've had a few today. I don't know what they are. It's too early for Braxton Hicks contractions." The color had drained from her face.

"Shall I drive?" Callie offered.

"That might be a good idea. I'm sure I'm fine. The first trimester is the riskiest period, and I'm into my second now. But I am a little tired."

Melody guided the car to the shoulder of the road and they swapped places. Once in the passenger seat, Melody reclined it and closed her eyes, but a frown pleated her brow and she kept her hands clasped over her abdomen. Concern tightened Callie's grip on the wheel, and she drove as fast as she legally and safely could.

As they came into the city, Melody directed Callie to her obstetrician's offices. By now, Mel was white and tears were swimming in her eyes.

Callie went around to her side of the car and opened the door. Mel got out and doubled over. That was when Callie saw the blood.

Callie was sitting at the side of Mel's hospital bed, holding her hand, when the door swung open. Nick strode into the room and halted. His gaze darted between them, fear and questions in his eyes, then settled on Melody. "How are you?" His voice gentle, hurting.

Mel opened her mouth to speak but no words came out, instead her tears started all over again. Callie didn't feel that she had the right to hers, but they fell anyway, as they had throughout the afternoon, for Mel, for Jason, for the baby who would never be.

Nick crossed slowly to his sister, hugged her. Melody's arms snaked around his shoulders, and she clung to him, still crying. Feeling like she was intruding, Callie stood to go. Nick looked at her and mouthed the word, *stay*.

Her heart breaking a hundred different ways, Callie shook her head and left. Nothing had changed for them.

Nick leaned against a corner post of the veranda, his fists in his pockets in a parody of nonchalance that he was light years from feeling. When Callie had turned and walked away a week ago, he'd told himself that he could let her go. That through grim determination, he could make himself not need her. But even before she'd gone from his sight, he knew with blinding clarity that wasn't ever going to happen. He no longer wanted to live the shutdown existence of his past. He would do whatever he had to to get her back into his life.

Permanently.

Melody had lost her baby. He was not going to lose Callie or their child. Because he—who hadn't thought he needed anyone—needed Calypso Jamieson with every breath he took. He needed her spirit and her laughter. And her love. In denying that, in letting her go, he'd made a colossal mistake. But now he was back to fix it.

It had taken all of the intervening days to set his plans in motion. And each and every one of those hollow days that had dragged by had only reinforced how vital she was to his existence.

He watched now as barefoot, she stepped through the open French doors of her villa. The first rays of sunlight caught her pale face and she stilled. Her gaze swung unerringly toward him, her brown eyes wide.

Like a thirsting man, he drank in the sight of her, and for long seconds the world stopped.

He shouldered off from the post and she looked away, breaking their tenuous contact, and glanced instead at the bright yellow mug cradled in her hands. Lifting her chin, she walked to the edge of the veranda. She set her mug down carefully and looked out over the rolling green countryside. White-knuckled fingers gripped the railing.

He studied her profile, her dark curls loose about her face, as she stood there aloof and alone as he'd seen her once before. Her oversize shirt, smudged in black and fresh, bloodred paint shrouded her body.

He took a step closer. "Is this loneliness or solitude?" His future hinged on her answer. He knew with painful certainty which of those the last aching, empty week had been for him.

"Loneliness." She spoke so quietly he almost didn't hear. That single word gave him hope. Gave him courage. If she'd been even half as lonely as he had…

Nick closed the distance between them, his steps on the wooden boards loud in the enshrining silence. He looked at her slender hands on the railing and at his own, larger and gripping almost as fiercely. The faint scent of her shampoo reached him and he closed his eyes as though that could help him fight its visceral impact.

He'd analyzed everything. Everything they'd said and done. But all the careful analysis in the world couldn't give him the answers he needed. They lay with her alone. He could hope—desperately—but he couldn't be certain.

He looked out over the distant rows of vines. "I've bought your neighbor's vineyard."

He sensed rather than saw her head jerk up. "What? Why?"

"Because you didn't want the bungalow. You wouldn't come to me." He looked at her, noted the dark smudges beneath her eyes. "You never really explained why you didn't want the bungalow."

Color leached from her already pale face. "Leave it, Nick." The words were angry and the gaping chasm at his feet widened. "It hurts too much."

He knew too well that crippling hurt. Just as he knew the terror of failure—possibly for the first time ever. His hand closed around the small box in his pocket. No other outcome had ever mattered this much. "I can't leave it. I have to know."

She turned to him then, met him with a fierce glare. "Because I won't be tucked conveniently away. I won't compromise."

"Neither will I." He wouldn't, couldn't, be relegated to a corner of her life. Alternate weekends as the father of their child. Perhaps not even seeing *her.* "I signed my share of Ivy Cottage back to you."

"I know. The documents came yesterday. Good for you. One less commitment. What I don't understand is why, with that out of the way, you're here now?" She turned away. "Shouldn't you get going? Don't you have a plane to catch? A life to live?" She bit down on her lips as she stared straight ahead, as though the existence of the world beyond depended on her not breaking her gaze.

"That's not why I did it." How had she got that so wrong? How had he? "I did it because I wanted you to have freedom."

"I know. Freedom. You were always honest about that. So—great. I've got it. Thanks." She started to turn away, to head back into the house.

"Not freedom from commitments but freedom to choose."

She paused, her back to him. "To choose what?"

"To choose your commitments."

She half turned, looked at him askance. Hurt and hope warred in her expression. He had to do it. It was the only way. All or nothing. He crossed to stand in front of her. He needed to see her eyes. Needed her to see everything that was in his. In every other facet of his life he maintained absolute control. But somehow he'd ceded control over his happiness, his future, to the woman standing in front of him. He pulled the small velvet-covered box from his pocket, held it open toward her. The diamond solitaire caught the light. "I'm asking you to marry me."

Her arms stayed by her sides. Her fists clenched. "No."

His throat tightened as he gently closed the box, slid it back into his pocket. "No?" With his thumb he wiped away the tear that slid down her cheek. It was not a happy tear. And this wasn't going at all how he wanted—needed—it to.

She took a step back, away from his touch. "I can't marry without love. Don't ask me to. Don't do that to either of us."

"I'm not asking you to. I could love enough for both of us. For all three of us."

"I...don't understand." Confusion clouded her eyes.

"You asked once if I sometimes *knew* things and I said no. But I do. I know our baby is a girl. And the first time I saw you I knew you would change my life. Irrevocably. For the better. But I denied, even to myself, that knowledge. And I've been so busy denying my feelings for you that I never stopped to take a measure of their depth. Fathomless." He reached for her hands. "I love you, Calypso. I need you. Life is too short to throw away happiness when it's there for the taking. I'm not asking you to compromise. I'm offering you everything. All I can give." He tugged her a little closer and his heart leapt as she yielded to that pull. "I want to go to bed with you every night and to wake up with you every morning."

He turned her hands over, studied the neat, straight scar at the base of her thumb. That day seemed so long ago. "Callie." Her name came out as a whisper. He looked back up, tried to read her thoughts in her eyes. A myriad of emotions flickered there, none he could be sure of.

He tucked a strand of hair behind her ear, just for the excuse of touching her further. "We talked about freedom. But real freedom comes with having choice. And I choose you. I just need you to choose me back. I love you. I want to marry you, to live with you always. You're already in my heart, already a part of me, hopelessly entangled." He waited. Watched. "Say yes, Callie." His whole being focused on that one plea.

Her silence lasted an eternity. Her eyes brimmed with tears. Please let them be happy tears. And suddenly he was terrified of her response.

She nodded, and a tear spilled from her lashes and down her cheek toward the smile that trembled on her lips. "I love you."

"Is that a yes?" He hardly dared hope.

"That's a yes." She smiled as she stepped into his arms, tilted her head up and silenced his questions the very best way possible—by taking his breath away completely.

Epilogue

Callie sat at the table beneath the vine-covered pergola and let the laughter and conversation of the Brunicadi clan wash over her. She looked at Nick, her husband, and the man of her dreams, sitting opposite her, and her attention was captured and held by the fathomless love in his river-green eyes.

"It's my turn now." Her mother, heedless of interrupting their silent communication, appeared at Nick's shoulder, her arms held out expectantly, silver bangles tinkling.

Nick gazed at Emma, two months old, cradled in his arms and still wearing the lacy antique gown each of the Brunicadi children had worn for their christenings for the last three generations. He touched a knuckle to her cheek.

Once he'd recovered from the awe of their daughter's perfection, he had taken to fatherhood with the confidence and competence with which he did everything. And with the fierce love and protectiveness Callie had predicted. He held Emma a little closer. "But she's asleep."

"It's a grandmother's right. Besides, you know she won't wake. She sleeps like…a baby." Callie's free-spirited mother could be surprisingly adamant when it came to her only grandchild. And she took sly delight in pushing any advantage she could over her new son-in-law. It was a subtle interplay they both seemed to enjoy.

Smiling down at his daughter, Nick reluctantly relinquished her, then took the opportunity to come and sit beside Callie. Beneath the table, he laced his fingers through hers and they watched as Gypsy sashayed around the gathering showing off her granddaughter to renewed *oohs* and *ahhs*. She paused beside Michael, who was flirting shamelessly—but to no visible effect—with Shannon.

Callie leaned in to Nick. "I'm so glad Shannon could come over for this. She's loving running the New Zealand office."

"You knew she would."

"And with the new designer they've taken on, they may not even need me to come back."

"We'll all always need you. Just remember, the freedom to choose is yours."

"I know." Callie turned to Melody seated beside her, before the love in Nick's eyes had her taking his hand to leave the celebration early. "How are you doing?" she asked, looking at where Mel's fingers rested over her gently pregnant belly.

"We're doing good." Mel was under the close watch of her obstetrician and had so far breezed through the pregnancy. But they were taking no chances. "Everything's progressing as it should." She leaned in a little closer. "I felt the first movements yesterday." Her smile proclaimed her joy. Mel turned that smile on Jason, as he came to stand behind her, resting his hands possessively on her shoulders, massaging gently. He bent his head between Callie and Mel. "Rosa's knitting again," he whispered as though revealing an addict's relapse. "More booties."

Nick laughed. "Rosa," he called down the table, "you have to stop knitting. There are only so many booties a baby needs."

Rosa smiled, a knowing twinkle in her dark eyes, and spoke into a lull in the conversation. "But twins need so much more."

A sudden hush fell over the table. Melody and Jason looked at one another, eyes wide and smiles even wider. "Guess that saves us deciding when to share that particular news." Mel reached up to cover Jason's hand with one of her own.

That night, as Nick and Callie stood looking down at their daughter sleeping in her crib, Callie turned to him. "Are there any more Brunicadi predictions I should know about?"

Nick touched a finger to her cheek, and his eyes darkened, even as his dimple appeared. Callie couldn't stop the bone-deep reaction that was as swift as it was powerful.

"Yes," he said as he reached for her hand. "I have a feeling it's going to be a very good night."

* * * * *

 *Desire*™

 **2** *in* **1**
GREAT
VALUE

HIGH-POWERED, HOT-BLOODED by Susan Mallery

CEO Duncan needs an image change. His solution: a sweet kindergarten teacher who will make him look like an angel…

WESTMORELAND'S WAY by Brenda Jackson

After a mind-blowing night of passion with the raven-haired beauty, this Westmoreland has decided he's the man destined to satisfy *all* her needs…

MILLIONAIRE UNDER THE MISTLETOE by Tessa Radley

After unexpectedly sleeping with her enemy and secret benefactor, Miranda's taken by surprise when he proposes a more permanent arrangement!

HIS HIGH-STAKES HOLIDAY SEDUCTION by Emilie Rose

Forced to pretend a past relationship he never had for the sake of his twin, this CEO finds himself caught in the middle of a passionate affair based on mistaken identity.

THE TYCOON'S SECRET AFFAIR by Maya Banks

Impending fatherhood is not what Piers Anetakis wanted from one blistering night of passion. Still, he insists on marrying his lover… but a paternity test changes everything!

DEFIANT MISTRESS, RUTHLESS MILLIONAIRE by Yvonne Lindsay

Bent on ruining his father's company, Josh lures his assistant away. But the one thing he never expects is a double-cross! Will Callie stick to her plan?

**On sale from 15th October 2010
Don't miss out!**

*Available at WHSmith, Tesco, ASDA, Eason
and all good bookshops*

www.millsandboon.co.uk

MILLS & BOON®

are proud to present our...

Book of the Month

Proud Rancher, Precious Bundle
by Donna Alward
from Mills & Boon® Cherish™

Wyatt and Elli have already had a run-in. But when a
baby is left on his doorstep, Wyatt needs help.
Will romance between them flare as they
care for baby Darcy?

Mills & Boon® Cherish™
Available 1st October

Something to say about our
Book of the Month?
Tell us what you think!

millsandboon.co.uk/community
facebook.com/romancehq
twitter.com/millsandboonuk

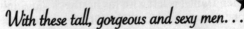

THEIR PRECIOUS LITTLE GIFTS

These sexy men will do anything to bring their families together for Christmas

Santa Baby by Laura Marie Altom

The Christmas Twins by Tina Leonard

Available 15th October 2010

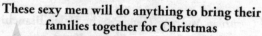

Two sparkling
Regency delights

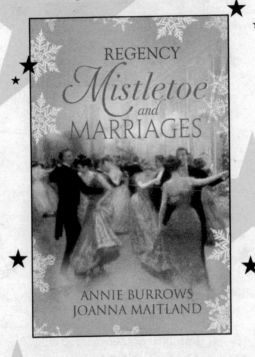

REGENCY
Mistletoe
and
MARRIAGES

ANNIE BURROWS
JOANNA MAITLAND

A Countess by Christmas by Annie Burrows

The Earl's Mistletoe Bride by Joanna Maitland

Available 5th November 2010

www.millsandboon.co.uk

M&B

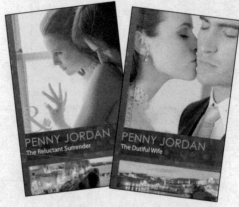

Spend Christmas with NORA ROBERTS

Daniel MacGregor is the clan patriarch. He's powerful, rich – and determined to see his three career-minded granddaughters married. So he chooses three unsuspecting men he considers worthy and sets his plans in motion!

As Christmas approaches, will his independent granddaughters escape his schemes? Or can the magic of the season melt their hearts – and allow Daniel's plans to succeed?

Available 1st October 2010

www.millsandboon.co.uk

2 FREE BOOKS
AND A SURPRISE GIFT

We would like to take this opportunity to thank you for reading this Mills & Boon® book by offering you the chance to take TWO more specially selected books from the Desire™ 2-in-1 series absolutely FREE! We're also making this offer to introduce you to the benefits of the Mills & Boon® Book Club™—

- **FREE home delivery**
- **FREE gifts and competitions**
- **FREE monthly Newsletter**
- **Exclusive Mills & Boon Book Club offers**
- **Books available before they're in the shops**

Accepting these FREE books and gift places you under no obligation to buy, you may cancel at any time, even after receiving your free books. Simply complete your details below and return the entire page to the address below. You don't even need a stamp!

YES Please send me 2 free Desire stories in a 2-in-1 volume and a surprise gift. I understand that unless you hear from me, I will receive 2 superb new 2-in-1 books every month for just £5.30 each, postage and packing free. I am under no obligation to purchase any books and may cancel my subscription at any time. The free books and gift will be mine to keep in any case.

Ms/Mrs/Miss/Mr _____ Initials _____

_____

Surname _____

Address _____

_____

_____ Postcode _____

E-mail _____

Send this whole page to: Mills & Boon Book Club, Free Book Offer, FREEPOST NAT 10298, Richmond, TW9 1BR